THE *DEVLIN*, SHIELDS RAISED, PUT ITSELF DIRECTLY IN THE *ENTERPRISE'S* PATH . . .

"Damn it, Kirk!" Captain Sherbourne shouted. *"I don't want to fire on you, but I will! Believe me, I will!"*

"I believe you, Captain," Kirk replied. "That's why we have our deflectors at maximum strength."

"Spock!" Sherbourne called. *"Certainly you can't be going along with this insanity! It just isn't logical to risk everything—"*

"But it is quite logical, Captain Sherbourne," Spock said. "Based on what we have experienced—what Captain Kirk has told and shown you—it would be illogical for us to do otherwise. We are the only chance the Federation has for survival."

The *Devlin's* helmsman spoke. *"All systems locked on, Captain. Ready to fire at your command."*

"I'm warning you, Kirk," Sherbourne said, shaking his head angrily. *"I'm warning everyone who can hear me on the* Enterprise—*"*

Suddenly, there was a scream from the *Devlin.*

"Full impulse power, now!" Spock ordered, and the *Enterprise* surged ahead.

Look for STAR TREK Fiction from Pocket Books

Star Trek: The Original Series

Star Trek: The Next Generation

STAR TREK

THE FINAL NEXUS

GENE DeWEESE

POCKET BOOKS

New York   London   Toronto   Sydney   Tokyo   Singapore

An *Original* Publication of POCKET BOOKS

POCKET BOOKS, a division of Simon & Schuster
1230 Avenue of the Americas, New York, NY 10020

This book is published by Pocket Books, a division of
Simon & Schuster, under exclusive license from
Paramount Pictures.

ISBN: 0-671-74148-9

First Pocket Books printing December 1988

10   9   8   7   6   5   4   3

POCKET and colophon are registered trademarks of
Simon & Schuster.

Printed in the U.S.A.

In appreciation of Esther Ansfield.

Like Commander Ansfield did when she popped
up unexpectedly on my computer
screen, she pretty much takes charge of whatever
situation she finds herself in—
despite any insecurities she may feel.

Chapter One

"CAPTAIN CHANDLER, to the bridge!"

Captain Jeremiah Chandler, already awakened by the shudder that had rippled through his cabin moments before, responded instantly, instinctively. Simultaneously he activated the bunkside comm unit and reached beyond it for his tunic, trousers, and boots.

"What is it, Mr. Ortiz?"

"Gravitational turbulence, sir."

"I felt it, Mr. Ortiz," Chandler snapped. "What's causing it?"

"The instruments show nothing, sir. That's why—"

"Hold our present position, and get as much data as possible. I'm on my way. I'll alert Commander Ansfield."

Without waiting for an acknowledgment, Chandler punched the commander's code into the comm unit. "Commander," he said briskly as he pulled on his tunic. "I need the science officer on the bridge."

"I thought you might when I felt that little shipquake," a low-pitched but feminine voice replied

a moment later. *"I was halfway to the door when you called."*

"Then don't let me delay you." Shutting off the comm unit, Chandler finished dressing and headed for the door. The cause of the turbulence would probably amount to nothing, but he welcomed the unexpected activity. After nearly three months of purely routine patrol along the Federation border in the vicinity of Starbase 1, virtually anything out of the ordinary—except possibly the appearance of a Klingon battle cruiser—was welcome.

As Chandler reached the turbolift, Commander Ansfield—short, wiry, and fiftyish—was waiting, holding the doors open for him. Her iron-gray hair, almost as short as Chandler's dark brown curls, showed no evidence of being rumpled from sleep, and he was sure she had once again been sitting up, leafing through the hundreds of antique nineteenth- and twentieth-century books that lined almost two full walls of her cabin.

"What kept you, Captain?" she asked as he slipped past her into the turbolift.

"Some of us spend the low watch sleeping instead of reading ancient literature," he said with a trace of a grin as the doors hissed shut. "What was it this time? Adventure? Mystery? Romance?"

"You don't want to know, sir."

"That bad, Commander?"

"No need to be judgmental, Micah," she said, using the nickname from his childhood. "Just say it's pure —or sometimes impure—escapism."

He nodded, remembering similar exchanges when she'd been a young teacher in the little midwestern town he'd grown up in. He'd been in high school at the time, and he'd often seen the carefully preserved volumes—hundreds, perhaps thousands—that had been passed down through the last half-dozen generations of her family. They had always fascinated him, though more as curiosities than as something he would want to actually sit down and read. He'd smiled when she'd first been assigned to his command and he'd realized she was planning to bring a dozen or more shelves of her favorites with her on the *Cochise*. She could have had the entire lot scanned into the ship's computer, but to her there was something special about having the books physically in her hands that—

Chandler's mind snapped back to the present as the turbolift doors slid open on the nearly empty bridge. Suddenly, inexplicably, the buoyancy brought about by the break in routine was replaced by a shiver, not of anticipation but of apprehension. He looked at the main viewscreen.

"Anything new, Mr. Ortiz?" he asked, realizing even as he spoke that his sudden uneasiness had made his words sharper than he had intended.

The slender blond lieutenant, one of three who made up the skeleton crew on low watch, bent over the science station instruments. He spoke without looking around.

"No further turbulence, sir, but the computer has analyzed the data recorded during the incident and calculated the probable location of the center of the disturbance."

By the time Ortiz had finished, Commander Ansfield was standing next to him, quickly studying the readouts. "A mass triple that of Sol less than a quarter AU almost directly ahead." She called up more readouts. "But there's nothing there now. The nearest detectable mass of even planetary size is more than a light-year away. Peculiar, to say the least."

Chandler, his eyes still fastened on the distant stars that dotted the viewscreen, blinked as, unbidden, an image of the *Cochise,* alone and vulnerable in the suddenly eerie darkness of space, darted through his mind. Involuntarily, he shivered, despite the purely rational realization that they were not in some distant, unexplored arm of the galaxy but safely within Federation boundaries, only a few parsecs from Starbase 1.

"Lieutenant Kronin," he said, turning abruptly toward the helmsman, "deflectors on automatic. And if you see anything out there, anything at all, put the deflectors up yourself, no matter what your instruments say. No delays."

Kronin, dark and thirtyish, acknowledged with a start. "Yes, sir."

Commander Ansfield glanced at Chandler curiously but said nothing.

"Any subspace activity, Lieutenant Grayson?" Chandler asked, turning to the communications officer, the final member of the low-watch bridge crew.

"Nothing local, sir."

Moving to look over the helmsman's shoulder, Chandler studied the controls a moment. The main viewscreen was already set for maximum magnification and centered on the area the computer had pinpointed as the center of the disturbance.

As both Ortiz and Ansfield had said, there was

nothing there, only the ever-present stellar background. And even that seemed sparse, Chandler thought, and once again he was struck with a sudden and inexplicable uneasiness, followed almost instantly by a flare of self-directed irritation. The reason for the sparse star field, after all, would be perfectly obvious to any first-year cadet! They were looking toward the zenith, almost directly out of the galactic plane. It was not as if they were looking in toward the Shapley center, where the star clouds made up such an intense background that their images had to be damped down. If the star field—

Abruptly, Chandler was positive that something had moved on the screen. It had been only a faint shimmer, as if something almost totally transparent had moved between the *Cochise* and the stars on the screen, but it had definitely been there, like something caught out of the corner of his eye. Thoughts of Klingon cloaking devices raced through his mind, despite the fact that there could be no Klingons within a thousand parsecs of the Federation.

"Any activity, Commander Ansfield?" he asked sharply, clamping down on his uneasiness but unable to totally suppress the tingle it had deposited on the skin of his back.

"Nothing," she said, turning toward him. "Did you see something?" Her eyes narrowed imperceptibly as she saw the intensity with which he was watching the screen.

"I don't know," he said. "It *seemed* that something moved out there."

"Stare hard enough, you could make the Rock of Gibraltar seem to move. What was it like?"

He shook his head, irritated at himself for imagining things and then being unable to describe accurately what he had imagined. "For about a second, the star field looked—different. That's all I can say. And if the sensors didn't pick up anything, it must have been my imagination."

"Possibly," Ansfield said. She was standing next to him now, looking up at the screen. "On the other hand, we discover new phenomena every day, phenomena to which sentient beings are sensitive but which no sensor can detect."

The tingle along his spine increased. "That is *not* what I want to hear from my science officer, thank you," he said.

"Becoming a science officer doesn't necessarily mean you have to close your mind to phenomena that science can't—yet—explain. Just the opposite, in fact. Besides," she added, leaning close so that only he could catch her almost whispered words, "if you'd been keeping up with Starfleet communications the way you should, you'd have a pretty good idea of what we've run into."

Frowning, he looked down at her. "Commander, I'm not in the mood for games. Now, if you think you know—"

"Another gate," she said, still half whispering.

And he remembered.

Mentally cursing himself for his inexcusable lapse, he tried to recall precisely what Starfleet had said. One of its heavy cruisers—the *Enterprise,* had it been?—had been investigating areas of gravitational turbulence in the Sagittarius arm. And at the center of at least some of those areas they had found dimensional gates, apparently part of some incredibly complex, millennia-old transportation system that reached, seemingly, into every corner of the universe.

And now, if the turbulence the *Cochise* had just encountered were also associated with a gate—

The deck shuddered soundlessly.

With only a darting glance at Chandler, Commander Ansfield was back at the science station. Chandler, standing next to the vacant command chair, activated the ship's comm system.

"Yellow alert," he snapped. "All personnel to their posts. All first-watch officers report to the bridge immediately. Lieutenant Grayson, inform Starfleet of our situation."

He didn't know what was happening, whether there was a gate out there or not. And even if there *was* a gate, he had no way of knowing where it led or what might be coming through. The *Enterprise* itself, he remembered now, had gone through one of the gates —inadvertently, the communication had implied but not stated—and had found itself millions, perhaps billions, of parsecs distant from the Federation. Nothing in the official Starfleet communication even hinted at what the *Enterprise* had found at its destination or how it had managed to find its way home.

Or how many casualties it had taken.

Angrily suppressing another shiver, Chandler focused on the forward screen. There was still nothing visible, nothing detectable by the sensors. The gate, if it existed, was totally invisible as far as the *Cochise* and its instruments were concerned. The *Enterprise*, the communication had said, had somehow modified its sensors to detect the gates directly, but that didn't help Chandler here and now.

The gate could be anywhere. It could be moving directly toward the *Cochise,* and he would never know—until it was too late. Nothing in the Starfleet communication had said the gates were fixed in space.

And—the thought kept returning, no matter how hard he tried to avoid it—there had been not even the slightest indication of what the gates might lead to, what they might let through into this part of the universe.

Abruptly, he mounted the steps to the command chair and dropped into it, pressing his body as deeply into it as he could, as if hoping the pressure against his back could muffle the increasingly intense and uncomfortable tingle that now had his spine firmly in its grip.

But it didn't help. His uneasiness only continued to grow. Relentlessly, it was being transformed into outright fear, a helpless fear he hadn't experienced for decades, not since that long-ago childhood night when, separated from his companions, he had spent more than a dozen hours waiting for rescue from the not-quite-silent darkness of the labyrinthine caves his overenthusiastic explorations had led him into.

A gate was out there. Of that he was now irrationally positive. And it wasn't simply waiting, motionless. It was bearing down on him, unseen, like a cloaked Klingon battle cruiser. He could literally feel it coming closer every second, could feel its alien menace as it closed in, preparing to engulf the *Cochise* in its invisible maw.

Engulf it and send it—where?

To what unknown corner of the universe?

He clamped his hands, vise-like, on the arms of the command chair, and he waited, straining to resist the impulse to cut and run at maximum warp.

But even as the impulse to flee grew steadily more powerful, more terrifying, a still-rational corner of Chandler's mind asked, again and again, *What is the matter with me? I've faced the Federation's enemies with hardly a tremor. I've beamed down to an unknown planet's surface feeling only anticipation and curiosity. So why, without the slightest concrete evidence of danger, am I now quaking in my boots? What is happening to me?*

But the only answer he received was yet another wave of sourceless, irrational terror.

Chapter Two

CAPTAIN JAMES T. KIRK watched the main viewscreen closely as Sulu brought the *Enterprise* out of warp drive a cautious five AU from the *Cochise* and held it motionless while Spock silently studied the sensor readouts. If there was a gate in the vicinity, Kirk wanted to know its precise location before he ordered so much as an attitude maneuver. The *Enterprise* had survived one unplanned jump across a billion or more parsecs. He had no intention of pressing his luck and taking a chance on a second.

"Well, Mr. Spock?" Kirk asked when the silence had stretched to nearly half a minute.

"Captain Chandler was correct in his assumptions, Captain," Spock finally replied. "A gate does exist, approximately forty million kilometers directly in front of the *Cochise.*"

"So, we know what area to avoid. What is its diameter at maximum expansion?"

"This gate does not appear to undergo a cycle of expansion and contraction, Captain. Its dimensions have thus far remained constant." Spock paused, his eyebrows angling upward almost imperceptibly. "However, its shape, while also essentially constant, is decidedly irregular."

"Not the usual circular disk?"

"Far from it, Captain. A highly elongated and extremely jagged ellipse is the least inaccurate description I would care to give. Its longest dimension is approximately twenty thousand kilometers, its shortest less than a quarter of that."

"Which is quite sufficient for avoiding it," Kirk said. "And the status of the *Cochise?*"

"The ship is undamaged as far as can be ascertained, Captain. Its deflectors, however, are fully energized."

Kirk frowned. "Any other ships nearby? Any obvious threat?"

"None, Captain. I can discern no matter of any kind beyond the usual assortment of particles to be expected in the interstellar medium."

"Take us in to a thousand kilometers, Mr. Sulu, but cautiously. Quarter impulse power."

"Aye-aye, sir."

"And Lieutenant Uhura, let's announce ourselves."

"Ready, sir. Hailing frequency open."

"Captain Chandler, this is Captain James T. Kirk of the U.S.S. *Enterprise.* We have been sent in response to your message to Starfleet. What is your situation?"

There was only silence in reply.

"No response, sir," Uhura said as she worked the controls. "They're not even transmitting a carrier frequency."

Kirk's frown deepened, and he turned toward the

main viewscreen. "Centered on the *Cochise*, Mr. Sulu, maximum magnification."

"Aye-aye, sir."

The stellar field expanded rapidly, the stars bleeding off the edge of the screen on all sides. Within seconds, a tiny image of the ship with its single warp-propulsion unit was visible in the center of the screen. The designation NCC-530 was clearly visible across the top of the saucer.

"Any activity, Mr. Spock?"

"Its sensors are fully extended, Captain, but their range is somewhat diminished by the power being drawn to maintain the deflectors at maximum. All other readings appear normal, all ship's systems in optimal operating condition."

"And the crew?"

"Sensors indicate approximately two hundred nominally humanoid life-forms, Captain, as one would expect on a fully crewed Saladin-class starship."

"And nothing else?"

"Nothing, Captain, either on board the *Cochise* or anywhere within sensor range."

"Lieutenant Uhura? Still no response?"

"Nothing on any standard Starfleet frequency or on any other known frequency."

"Very well. Keep trying. Put my greetings to Chandler on automatic, to repeat every sixty seconds."

"Done, sir."

"Mr. Sulu, continue the approach."

"Aye-aye, sir."

"Mr. Chekov, be ready to put up the deflectors on my order. Or at the first sign of any hostile action."

"Hostile action, sir?" Chekov turned to look at Kirk over his shoulder. "From the *Cochise?* But they are a Federation ship, Keptin—and ve are within Federation territory."

"A Federation ship that is acting very strangely, Mr. Chekov. And a Federation ship that is in close proximity to a gate that could lead literally anywhere in the universe. Just be ready."

Chekov's eyes widened as he turned back to face the controls. "You believe that something has come through, sir?"

"Anything's possible, Mr. Chekov."

"Aye, sir, I understand."

"How close, Mr. Sulu?"

"Four AU, Captain."

"Mr. Spock, I assume their sensors can detect us at this range."

"Undoubtedly, Captain. Whether they have received your subspace message or not, they know we are here."

"Any speculations on a reason for their silence, Mr. Spock?"

"None at this time, Captain, but—"

Without warning, a harsh voice burst from Uhura's receiver.

"Identify yourself!"

Frowning, Kirk complied. "As we have been broadcasting since shortly after our emergence from warp drive, I am Captain James T. Kirk, commanding the U.S.S. *Enterprise.* We are responding to—"

"I know who you say *you are,"* the voice interrupted. *"Show me!"*

"As you wish. Lieutenant Uhura, open a visual channel."

"Done, sir."

The forward viewscreen flickered, but nothing appeared. "They're receiving our transmission, sir," Uhura said, "but they're sending nothing visual in return."

"Captain Chandler," Kirk said. "A visual channel is open. Is something wrong with your transmission gear?"

"We have *been having some problems."* Chandler's voice came back abruptly.

"What kind of problems? Would you like to lower your deflectors so one of our technicians could beam over and—"

"No!" The word exploded from the speakers.

"Is there some trouble, Captain Chandler?" Kirk asked, purposely keeping his tone even and, he hoped, reassuring. It was obvious not only from Chandler's words and actions but from the brittle tension in his voice that something was very wrong. "Is there anything we can do to help?"

For a moment there was only silence, punctuated by the sound of Chandler's breathing and an almost inaudible murmuring in the background.

"You can maintain your present distance!" Chandler said.

"You heard the captain, Mr. Sulu," Kirk said smoothly.

"Aye-aye, sir. Three point four AU and holding."

"Now then, Captain Chandler, can you tell me what's going on? Less than two days ago, you told Starfleet you suspected you had discovered a gate similar to the one the *Enterprise* was recently involved with. What has happened since your message to Starfleet?"

"Nothing!" Chandler said sharply. *"Nothing has happened!"*

"Then why are your deflectors up? Has something come through the gate?"

"How would I know? According to Starfleet, the Enterprise *has the only sensors in the Federation capable of even detecting one of these gates, let alone anything that might come through!"*

"We've surveyed the area, Captain Chandler," Kirk said. "You were quite right; a gate does exist. It is approximately forty million kilometers directly in front of the *Cochise*. However, our sensors indicate nothing else within range."

"So you say." Instead of sounding reassured, Chandler sounded, if anything, even more tense, more suspicious.

Kirk was silent, trying to think what approach to take, trying to imagine what could have happened to Chandler and his ship. *Had* something come through the gate? Something undetectable even to the *Enterprise*'s modified sensors? Something that had taken over the *Cochise?* Was Chandler simply trying to warn them off? And if he was . . .

"Very well, Captain Chandler," Kirk said abruptly. "As long as you're experiencing no problems, we can place a space buoy to mark the location of the gate, and we can all be on our way back to Starbase. Mr. Sulu, prepare to launch—"

Suddenly, the sound of a struggle crackled across subspace from the bridge of the *Cochise*. A half-dozen voices—some shouting, some grunting, some gasping —could be heard. Something heavy, probably a body, thudded to the deck, followed by something metallic.

"Ortiz! The phaser controls!" A deep female voice punched through the chaos. *"Keep him away from the phaser controls!"*

Chekov's hands moved reflexively on the weapons console. Kirk motioned him to remain calm.

Then Chandler's voice, high-pitched and angry, drowned out everything else.

"Commander Ansfield! I demand you release me and obey my orders!" he almost screamed, and in the silence that followed, his breathing was harsh and ragged.

"I'm sorry, Captain," the woman's voice said. *"But I—"*

"The rest of you, help me! This is mutiny! Ortiz! Kronin! Nkrumah! I order you to help me!"

"We reached our decision together, Captain," the woman's voice said, softly this time, even sadly. *"You gave us no choice. In accordance with Starfleet regulations, with the full concurrence of Chief Medical Officer Nkrumah, I am herewith officially relieving you of command of the* Cochise *on the grounds of temporary emotional instability. I'm sorry."*

"You don't know what you're doing!" Chandler screamed. *"That's not the* Enterprise *out there! And even if it is, that creature that says he's Kirk is under the control of—"*

"Dr. Nkrumah," the woman said, and a moment later there was the distinctive hiss of a spray hypo, and Chandler abruptly fell silent.

"I'm sorry, Micah," the woman said softly. *"I'm sorry."*

For a moment, there was total silence on both ships. Then the main viewscreen on the *Enterprise* sprang suddenly to life.

"Full visual communication commencing, sir," Uhura said, and even as she spoke, the bridge of the *Cochise* rippled into sharp focus on the screen.

The captain—presumably Chandler—lay on the deck between the command chair and the helmsman's station. A commander in science blue kneeled next to him with a medical tricorder, beads of perspiration glistening on his ebony forehead.

"He'll be all right, Essie," the man said, and the small graying woman just behind him, also in science blue, let out her breath in an obvious sigh of relief and then, straightening, turned to face the viewscreen.

"Captain Kirk," she said, only a trace of a tremor in her deep voice. *"I'm Commander Esther Ansfield, chief science officer of the* Cochise. *I think we'd better have a talk. I'll drain the moat if you and your colleagues want to beam over."*

"Moat?" Kirk frowned, but before he could say more, Spock announced that the *Cochise*'s deflectors had been lowered.

Chapter Three

COMMANDER ANSFIELD WAS waiting in the *Cochise* transporter room as Kirk, Spock, McCoy, and a security detail of three, led by the imposing figure of Lieutenant Ingrit Tomson, materialized.

"Very pleased to meet you, Captain Kirk, Mr. Spock, Dr. McCoy," Ansfield said, offering a firm handshake to each as they stepped down from the platform, "although I can't say I'm overjoyed at the circumstances."

"I understand, Commander," Kirk said. "What you had to do couldn't have been easy."

"You have a gift for understatement, Kirk. No, it wouldn't have been easy under any circumstances, but I've known Micah—Captain Chandler—since he was a boy. But I had no choice." She paused, shaking her head. "I'm a science officer, not a starship captain, and I don't want to be one a minute longer than necessary."

"Understood, Commander," Kirk said, "although you appear to have things well in hand."

"I didn't say I *couldn't* be one, just that I don't *want*

18

to be. Now, the quicker we can get things wrapped up here, the quicker we can be on our way to Starbase 1. For a start, I assume you and your medical officer would like to have a look at the captain. And his log."

"Those would be good places to start," Kirk said as the group made its way into the corridor toward the turbolift. "On our way to sickbay, you can fill in a few details. Just what *has* been happening since Chandler's message to Starfleet?"

"I wish I knew. You saw—or heard, at least—what Captain Chandler was like. To some extent, he's been that way since we stumbled across this gate or whatever it is. I've never seen him in such a state. He's absolutely convinced that either the gate itself is ready to gobble us up or something that came *through* the gate is dead set on wiping us out."

"Was there any evidence to support him?"

She shook her head as they entered the turbolift. "Not a shred. Our sensors show nothing."

"And you? And the rest of the crew?"

"Did we go paranoid too, you mean? No, although we've all been on edge since this started. But that's probably largely because of the captain's behavior. Because we didn't see things his way, he's been acting as if he were afraid of *us,* too, not just that gate. He seemed to trust me a little more than the others—as I said, I've known him since he was a boy—so I was able, just barely, to talk him out of having most of the officers put in the brig or executed, particularly Commander Ortiz, who was in charge on low watch when the gate was found. You heard what he said about you, Captain. He was convinced you and your whole ship had been taken over by—by whatever you ran into when you went through that gate yourself a couple of months ago." She paused, her dark eyebrows arching inquisitively. "You weren't, were you?"

"Not that I know of," Kirk said with a faint smile. Then he added, "At least not by anything that two days of painfully thorough testing at Starfleet Headquarters could find."

The turbolift door opened, and they emerged into the corridor next to sickbay. "Right this way, gentlemen," Ansfield said, stepping out briskly.

Seconds later, they approached the bed on which Captain Chandler was restrained. On the diagnostic screen above the bed, his respiration and heart rate, already high, spurted even higher as his darting eyes fell on Kirk and the others from the *Enterprise*. A nurse stood next to the bed, and Dr. Nkrumah hurried from the nearby lab to meet them.

"Any progress, Doctor?" Ansfield asked.

"The paralytic agent has worn off, as you can see. All tests—"

"Paralytic agent?" McCoy asked, frowning.

Nkrumah nodded. "Commander Ansfield and I agreed. We knew the captain would realize what was happening the instant I used the hypo spray. We therefore wanted him to be immobilized as quickly as possible, before he had time to harm himself or us in a last-minute struggle. In his state of mind, even a few seconds of mobility could have been dangerous. Short of a phaser or a physical blow to the head, this was the quickest, most efficient method. This particular agent also has the advantage of wearing off more quickly than any sedative."

"And it leaves the victim conscious," McCoy said, still frowning. "Conscious but totally helpless."

"We felt that that, too, was an advantage, Doctor," Ansfield said. "That way, he could see what we were doing at all times. As paranoid as he was, if we'd knocked him out, who knows what he would've thought we did to him while he was unconscious?"

Grudgingly, McCoy had to admit that Ansfield was right. "And the tests you've run on him?" he asked.

"All results so far are perfectly normal," Nkrumah said. "Normal, that is, for someone in a constant state of uncontrollable fear. The brain activity, the blood pressure, brain and blood chemistry, hormonal levels, cellular activity, everything is consistent with a normal, healthy male human who just happens to be terrified."

"No foreign substance of any kind, Doctor?" McCoy asked, remembering uneasily the time he had accidentally been injected with an overdose of cordrazine. The state he had been in then—filled with terror, convinced with paranoid certainty that everyone around him, even his lifelong friend Jim Kirk, was his deadly enemy—was not unlike the state that Captain Chandler appeared to be in now. "No accidentally administered medication that could account for his agitation?"

Nkrumah shook his head, obviously taking no offense at the question. "The computer found nothing but small amounts of the mild tranquilizer I have been prescribing for him for the past eight months. And the remnants of the paralytic agent, of course. Nothing else."

"You wouldn't mind if I looked him over myself?" McCoy asked. He knew Nkrumah only by reputation, a good doctor but one who perhaps put too much trust in the infallibility of machines.

"Of course not, Doctor," Nkrumah said quickly. "I would be glad for any assistance you can render. I have to admit I'm totally stymied at this point."

McCoy stepped forward and looked down at Chandler. "Captain Chandler, I'm Dr. Leonard McCoy, chief medical officer of the *Enterprise.*" As he spoke, his southern drawl was a little more pronounced than usual, his crooked Georgia smile a little wider, a little friendlier. "Hope you don't mind a little more poking and prodding."

Chandler said nothing as McCoy took the scanner from his tricorder and brought it toward Chandler's body. Chandler twitched momentarily, then lay still, but his eyes, unnaturally wide, darted toward Kirk and then, even more rapidly, toward the others from the *Enterprise.*

Still holding the scanner a few inches from Chandler, McCoy turned to the others. "No offense, Jim, but you're frightening the patient. Why don't you and the rest of this mob go tend to other business? Dr. Nkrumah and I will tend to Captain Chandler."

Nkrumah looked momentarily discomfited by McCoy's directness, but Kirk nodded, smiling faintly.

"Good idea, Bones. See what your bedside manner can do." He turned to Commander Ansfield. "Why don't we adjourn to the bridge? I'm sure Mr. Spock would like to study the readings associated with the appearance of the gate. Wouldn't you, Mr. Spock?"

"Of course, Captain." The briefest of sideward

glances indicated, though only to Kirk, that Spock regarded the question, and accompanying answer, as one of those totally unnecessary exchanges that humans so often indulged in.

"And take your giant storm trooper with you," McCoy added, scowling as Lieutenant Tomson looked as if she were going to stay behind.

Outside in the corridor, Kirk nodded toward the door to sickbay. "Lieutenant," he said quietly. "I don't expect any trouble, but stick around, just in case. Stay out of Chandler's line of sight, but keep your eyes and ears open, and be ready for anything."

Tomson nodded her understanding and took up her post next to the door.

A minute later, the remainder of the group emerged onto the bridge. Spock went immediately to the science station and its links with the library computer. The computer's capacity was not quite as great as that of the *Enterprise* computer, but it would do.

The viewscreen, linked now to the bridge of the *Enterprise,* showed Engineering Officer Montgomery Scott seated uneasily in the command chair, watching the *Enterprise* viewscreen. When he saw Kirk and the others come onto the *Cochise* bridge, he breathed a sigh of relief.

"Ye made it, Captain. No problems?"

"None so far, Mr. Scott. Dr. McCoy stayed in sickbay to give Dr. Nkrumah a hand with Chandler. Spock is going to check through the *Cochise*'s records of the gravitational disturbances that led Chandler to suspect the presence of a gate. Are things still quiet at your end? No activity at the gate?"

"No' so much as a twitch, Captain."

23

"Good, Scotty. Carry on."

Turning from the screen, Kirk found himself the object of Commander Ansfield's pensive gaze.

"This 'gate' we seem to have stumbled across," she said. "Starfleet's communiqués weren't exactly brimming over with information."

"There isn't much information—reliable information, anyway—to be had."

"Possibly not, Kirk, but I'm not fussy. I'll settle for whatever unreliable guesswork you can give me. You've been through one of them, and, unless I miss my guess, you didn't come back either empty-handed or empty-headed."

Kirk couldn't resist a quick smile. "Not empty-handed by any means. Empty-headed is another matter. We brought back almost a thousand people, humanoids calling themselves the Aragos. They were originally from a planet a few parsecs from the gate in the Sagittarius arm. They'd gone through about fifteen thousand years ago and were—"

"Their ancestors, you mean."

Kirk shook his head. "No, not their ancestors. To make a long story short, when they went through the gate, they emerged into the middle of an interstellar war, and both sets of the combatants mistook them for the enemy. Luckily, they found a place to hide, a place already equipped with a hibernation system big enough for the lot of them. They were still there when we came through the gate. And the war was still going on."

"A fifteen-*thousand*-year war?" Ansfield shook her head disbelievingly. "Even the Klingons—"

"Strictly speaking, it wasn't the same war," Kirk

went on. "The whole affair was a chain reaction. World B destroys World A. Years later, World C comes out into space and is attacked by World B, who thinks they're only wiping out a group of survivors from World A. C fights back and destroys B, and pretty soon D comes along and is attacked by C, and so on. I know it may be hard to believe, but it had been going on for at least forty thousand years. We saw the results, hundreds of worlds, possibly thousands, melted down to radioactive bedrock, some a few thousand years ago, some tens of thousands."

Kirk paused, shaking his own head, as if to try to drive the images away. "It was that way for dozens of parsecs in all directions from the gate. We were lucky enough to get the current pair of combatants to start talking to each other, so *maybe* the chain has been broken. I sincerely hope so, at any rate."

Some of the color had drained from Ansfield's face. "But how in God's name did it get *started?*"

Kirk shrugged. "Maybe one truly insane, sadistic race, a race bent on wiping out everyone but themselves. Nobody knows, and at this late date I doubt that anyone ever will." He paused, glancing toward Spock, who was still absorbed in the records of the *Cochise*'s discovery of the new gate. "However, the ones who built the hibernation facilities left records indicating that they *suspected* that whoever or whatever had started the chain was somehow associated with the gate."

"Something came through the gate, you mean? But what could have—" Ansfield broke off, her eyes darting to the command chair normally occupied by Captain Chandler, then back to Kirk. "You can't possibly think that what happened to Micah has anything to do with something that happened—that *may* have happened—millions of parsecs away, hundreds of centuries ago!"

"You seem to have made the connection quickly enough yourself."

"Well, yes, but I'm *always* having crazy ideas! I mean, I was over forty with a guaranteed lifetime job in one of Earth's better, if stuffier, universities when I decided to enter Starfleet Academy and start a second career. *You're* a starship captain, which I always assumed meant you had to be more levelheaded than that."

"Levelheaded doesn't mean unimaginative, Commander. Once we saw how Chandler was acting, the thought of a possible connection between his actions and the appearance of the gate was only logical. Mr. Spock hasn't calculated the precise odds against its being a simple coincidence, but I'd say they're inordinately high. And you did say that Chandler would have fired on the *Enterprise* if you and the other officers hadn't stopped him. If this had happened near Romulan or Klingon space and he had been allowed to fire on another ship, whether Romulan or Klingon —or even another Federation vessel—anything could have happened."

"But if you thought we had some kind of plague on board, why did you beam over? Weren't you worried?"

Kirk shrugged. "We decided that if something had indeed come through the gate and reached the *Cochise* across forty million kilometers, it wouldn't have much trouble reaching the *Enterprise* whether we came over or not." He paused. "What we have to do now is find out if something did come through and, if so, what it was. And what we can do about it. Starfleet has been advised of the situation, and they've quarantined this entire sector of space."

Ansfield's eyes widened, letting some of her inner turmoil show through. "Which I assume means we're not allowed to leave the area." She sighed. "So what do we do?"

"It's already being done. We keep a close eye on Captain Chandler, we try to find out what happened to him, and we stay *very* alert to the possibility that, whatever it is, it may happen to someone else."

Even as he spoke, an odd uneasiness brushed him. Frowning, he turned toward Spock, who had just looked up from the instruments of the science station. For a moment, it was as if he were listening for something, his slanted eyebrows raised a fraction, his head cocked slightly to one side.

"Captain," he began, but before he could say more, McCoy's voice came from the bridge intercom.

"Jim, Commander Ansfield, you'd better get down to sickbay, fast! Something is happening to Captain Chandler!"

Chapter Four

RACING OUT OF the turbolift, Kirk saw that Lieutenant Tomson was no longer at her post in the corridor outside sickbay. Spock, Commander Ansfield, and the other two *Enterprise* security people followed on Kirk's heels as the door to sickbay hissed open for him.

Tomson, her phaser drawn, whirled to face them, her two-meter body lowered in a defensive crouch, and for just an instant Kirk saw the same terror in her eyes that he had seen in Chandler's. Holding up his hand in a gesture to halt those behind him, he came to a complete stop, but by then the look was gone. Beyond her, in the ward, McCoy and Nkrumah were both bent over Chandler.

"Sorry, Captain," Tomson said, lowering the phaser and rising to her full height but offering no explanation.

"Quite all right. I should know better than to rush up behind someone with a drawn phaser. Now, what's happened?"

"I don't know, sir. I heard someone scream, and—"

"That was Chandler, Jim." McCoy was standing back from the bed.

"Chandler? What happened to him?"

McCoy shook his head. "I wish I knew, Jim. No matter what Dr. Nkrumah and I did, he just kept getting more and more agitated. It was getting to the point where we were afraid he would injure himself despite the restraints. His heart rate and blood pressure were sky high and getting worse, so we finally decided our only choice was a strong sedative."

"Not a paralytic?" Ansfield asked sharply.

"No, Commander," Nkrumah said. "If we allowed him to remain conscious, if his agitation continued to grow, his blood pressure could have reached a point that would have brought on a stroke. It could have *killed* him. He had to be rendered unconscious, regardless of later consequences."

"So," Ansfield said, "you sedated him. Then what? Why did McCoy call us down here?"

McCoy grimaced. "It was crazy," he said. "Dr. Nkrumah gave him the shot, strong enough to knock out a horse. Should've started working in two or three seconds and had him dead to the world in ten seconds at the most. But the second the spray hit him, everything went the other way. His blood pressure and heart rate spiked even higher. It looked like he was simply going to explode, like a blowfish. Then he screamed. Like to deafened us. That's when I called the bridge."

"And since then?"

McCoy shook his head in puzzlement. "By the time I turned around from the intercom, he'd gone under. Just collapsed. His blood pressure took a nosedive, and he went limp, like someone had let the air out of a balloon."

"But he's all right?"

"As far as we can tell." McCoy glanced up at the monitors over the bed. "In fact, he looks better than he did before. The blood pressure's leveled off, and so has the heart rate. And the brain activity's quieted down a lot, too."

"Dr. Nkrumah?"

Everyone looked down at the bed, startled. Impossibly, Chandler was awake. He should have remained unconscious for at least another half-hour.

"Yes, Captain," Nkrumah said, trying to hide his astonishment. "I'm here. What is it?"

"Micah?" Before anyone else could do or say anything, Commander Ansfield had pushed past Kirk and the doctors and was at Chandler's side. "Just take it easy, Micah. We're taking care of everything."

"I'm sorry, Essie," he said. "I must've gone crazy. I—" He paused, looking at McCoy and Nkrumah and then lifting his head so he could see Kirk and the others. "Did it really happen? Did I actually try to fire on a Federation vessel?"

"You did, Micah," Ansfield said. "What happened? Are you over it now?"

He closed his eyes and laid his head back on the bed. He lay still, as if listening for something, or waiting.

Finally, he opened his eyes. "I *seem* to be all right.

30

But what the hell *was* it? What happened to me, Nkrumah?"

"We were hoping *you* could tell *us,* Captain," the doctor said.

Chandler shook his head. "All I know is, I was afraid of everything and everybody. That damned thing out there, that gate—" He broke off, the memory of the terror enough to send a shiver through his body. Pulling in a deep breath, he looked at Nkrumah. "Think it's safe to let me loose?"

"The fear is gone?" Nkrumah asked. "Totally gone?"

"Looks that way, but I can't guarantee it won't come back." He looked at Ansfield. "Essie, I think you'd better retain command until we get this sorted out. And keep someone close by to act as my keeper if I have a relapse." He paused, something half smile and half grimace pulling at his lips. "Someone with a phaser on heavy stun, who won't hesitate to use it on his captain. You have to get too close to use those hypo sprays. And they don't seem to last very long."

"As you wish, Micah. Let him up, Doctor." She glanced at Kirk, then stood watching Chandler as he sat up slowly, as if testing each muscle before actually using it.

"I think," she said when he was at last on his feet, "that as soon as the doctors give you another good checking over, you'd better hear what Captain Kirk has to say about the gates."

The checks revealed only that Chandler had, physically, returned almost to normal. The sedative, perhaps because of his extreme emotional state when it was administered, had been metabolized at several times the normal rate.

For nearly an hour after the checks were completed, Chandler was closeted in the briefing room with Ansfield, Ortiz, Nkrumah, and the officers of the *Enterprise*. A stony-faced lieutenant from *Cochise* security kept close watch on Chandler while McCoy kept a jaundiced eye on the guard. Kirk explained briefly what he had already told Ansfield, and Chandler in turn did his best to recount everything that had happened to him, everything he had thought or felt since the moment the gate had been discovered.

"I wasn't 'possessed,'" Chandler said at one point, a hint of defiance in his voice. "That's one thing I'm positive about. I may have been temporarily insane, but nothing *told* me to do any of the crazy things I did. I was just plain scared—of virtually everything and everyone."

"But *why* were you frightened?" Kirk persisted. "That's the whole point of this discussion, to see if we can find some hint of a reason."

"I don't know," Chandler said, grimacing as he tried to pull more details from his memory. "I remember thinking it was a lot like the time I was trapped in that cave back on Earth. I was just a kid at the time, and three of us were—" He paused, shaking his head and glancing at Commander Ansfield. "We were crazy is what we were. You know the cave I'm talking about, Essie."

She nodded, smiling faintly. "We had to send in search parties for at least one group every summer, Micah, so you weren't the only one a little crazy."

"Be that as it may," Chandler resumed, "three of us went in exploring, and we got separated. Or the other two purposely left me. They were fourteen or fifteen and hadn't really wanted a twelve-year-old like me along in the first place, so I've always wondered. But whatever happened, they disappeared. And then my light went out. It was supposed to be good for at least a year's continuous use, but it went out. And there I was in the dark, and I mean *total* darkness."

He shivered. The memory still had power over him. "They didn't find me until the next morning. It was the worst night of my life, ever, until now. But what I'm getting at is this. I knew there was nothing dangerous in that cave with me. I knew there was nothing that could hurt me—except myself, if I panicked. I *knew* it! But after a couple of hours, I was scared silly anyway. My heart must've been pounding away at over a hundred, and I could literally feel it all through my body. I hate to think what my blood pressure was. There were virtually no sounds, but I kept hearing things anyway, imagining spiders and snakes and God knows what else collecting all around me, watching me. It was all I could do to keep from trying to kick them or smashing at them with my useless light or with anything I could get my hands on. I even *saw* things, even though there wasn't a speck of light. It was mostly out of the corner of my eye, but sometimes there'd be something right in front of me. I know it was my imagination—I knew it *then*, even— but I was so keyed up, if a drop of water had fallen from the ceiling and hit me on the head, I think I would've either passed out or simply taken off running until I bashed into a wall or fell down a crevasse.

And the whole time, over and over, I kept telling myself how silly I was being. There was nothing there, nothing to hurt me or frighten me. All I had to do was sit down and wait and someone would be along to get me. But knowing, intellectually and logically, that I was perfectly safe didn't help. It didn't keep me from *feeling* the things I felt."

Chandler lowered his eyes, staring at his hands, clasped tightly on the table in front of him. "And that's as close as I can come to explaining how I felt these last two days. Only it was worse this time, a hundred times worse. I wasn't in the dark, so I could see perfectly well. I could look at the sensor readouts and see that they registered nothing. But no matter what I saw or didn't see, something deep inside me was still absolutely convinced that something *was* there, that it was all around me, literally all around me, like the darkness in that cave. And whatever it was, it was taking over all of *you!* I was the only one free of it. And I'd do anything, anything at all, even order another Federation ship fired on, to remain free of it, to keep it from taking *me* over."

He laughed nervously into the silence. "And if that isn't insanity, it will have to do until the real thing comes along."

"Not necessarily, Micah," Ansfield said. "As I've said before, there's no reason to say something doesn't exist just because our instruments can't detect it or our eyes see it."

"You're not making me feel any better, Essie. I think I prefer the insanity explanation, frankly."

"Nonetheless, Captain Chandler," Spock said, "it is

likely that Commander Ansfield is correct and that there is indeed an external cause for your state of mind."

All eyes turned toward the Vulcan science officer. "Explain, Mr. Spock," Kirk said.

"Yes, Spock, do explain," McCoy said, frowning. "I didn't think your logic would allow you to believe in anything you can't see or measure."

"Your concept of logic is far more confining than mine, Doctor. It is completely logical to look at the evidence as it exists and to follow where it leads."

"And where does it lead you this time, Mr. Spock?" Kirk prompted.

"You have already said, Captain, that the odds are overwhelmingly in favor of there being a connection between the newly discovered gate and Captain Chandler's behavior. You are, of course, correct. As you have pointed out, the type of behavior he has displayed could, under only slightly different circumstances, have led to open warfare."

"I know," Kirk said impatiently. "Something like this could have triggered that whole chain of wars in that other galaxy. I assume you have something new to add."

"Of course, Captain," Spock resumed, unperturbed by Kirk's interruption. "On the bridge, just moments before Dr. McCoy informed us of the change in Captain Chandler's condition, I experienced a sensation similar to but far less intense than that which Captain Chandler has described."

Kirk frowned, feeling a knot of tension forming suddenly in his own stomach. Having Spock, logically and matter-of-factly, verify Chandler's words made them more real, more immediately threatening. "And the source of this sensation, Mr. Spock?"

"Unknown, Captain, although it would appear to have originated within my own mind or body. That is to say, it was quite different from the emotions I have on occasion received through mental links with others. With those, I have always also received an impression, however faint, of the being transmitting the emotions. This time, there was no such impression, no sense of a link with another being. There was only the feeling itself, a feeling of being surrounded by, even immersed in, something inconceivably alien."

"But *something* had to cause it."

"Precisely, Captain. I am only saying that the sensation was, as far as I can determine, a firsthand sensation, not secondhand. It was as if my perceptions were being affected by a drug rather than by an external mental contact. At this time, I have no logical theory regarding its cause, other than the obvious observation that it, like Captain Chandler's more extreme sensations, is in some way related to the appearance of the gate."

"And you're positive, absolutely positive, that you weren't simply picking up Captain Chandler's own feelings?"

Spock shook his head tolerantly. "It is impossible to be one hundred percent positive of anything, Captain. However, even granting the possibility that the sensations I experienced did originate in the mind of another being, it was certainly not the mind of Captain Chandler. It would have to be the mind of a being far more alien than any I have ever encountered."

For a long moment, there was only silence around the table. Finally, Commander Ansfield spoke. "But you don't feel anything *now?*"

"No, Commander. The sensation lasted approximately thirty-four seconds and then ceased. It has not recurred."

Ansfield turned toward Spock with a frown. *"Approximately* thirty-four seconds?"

McCoy grunted. "To Spock, anything not measured in microseconds is a gross approximation. You'll get used to it." He turned to Spock. "And you say this happened when? Just *before* I called up to the bridge?"

"That is what I said, Doctor."

"How long before? A few seconds? A few minutes?"

"It began approximately eight seconds before your call, Doctor."

"Which would put the start at almost precisely the instant that Chandler screamed in my ear." McCoy turned to Kirk. "Jim, if something *did* come through the gate, something so alien none of our sensors can detect it, and if it did set up housekeeping in Chandler's head, and if it left when he screamed . . ."

Kirk nodded thoughtfully. "It was looking for someone else to act as host. It tried Spock but couldn't attach itself for some reason."

"Which means," Ansfield said abruptly, "it moved on to someone else! We have to find it! And the quickest way to start— Mr. Ortiz, take two security people to the bridge and keep watch on everyone there. Let me know the moment you arrive. I'll have everyone else—everyone, off duty and on—assemble on the recreation deck. If this thing has the same effect on its next host as it did on Micah, we'll be able to spot it. And if someone doesn't show up—"

"Commander Ansfield!" the comm unit barked. *"Lieutenant Aldrich, engineering. Ensign Stepanovich has gone crazy! He's killed Ensign Rinaldi and forced everyone else out of the control room with his phaser, and now he's locked himself in!"*

Chapter Five

"BRIDGE, THIS IS Commander Ansfield," she snapped. "Disable all controls in the engineering control room, now! Retain control on the bridge at all costs! Ensign Stepanovich has locked himself in the control room, and we have no idea what he may do. He is apparently being affected by the same thing that was affecting Captain Chandler the last two days. Try to establish communication with the ensign. Calm him down if you can. Locate someone he might consider a friend to talk to him. But disabling the controls has top priority. Lieutenant Aldrich, is there anything you can do from where you are?"

"Nothing, Commander. And I doubt that anyone on the bridge can, either. The control room is—"

"I know, Lieutenant! Whoever's in there can control virtually the entire ship. Can you cut into the control circuits directly? Through a wall? A floor? Anything?"

"Given enough time, possibly."

"Then get on it! Get everyone from engineering up there, and get them started!"

Pausing, she punched another code into the comm unit. "Security! Full detail to engineering deck. Report to Lieutenant Aldrich. Do whatever he says."

Shutting off the comm unit, she stood perfectly still for a second, then turned to the *Enterprise* officers. "Any suggestions, Kirk? Anyone? Anything helpful would be greatly appreciated."

"You might want to double-check your emergency battery power," Kirk said, "to be sure you're ready in case he cuts normal power."

"Understood," she said, snapping the comm unit back on and giving the necessary instructions.

"And disable the ship's phasers and photon torpedoes, in case he can figure out a way to start firing on the *Enterprise* from in there."

She hesitated, and for a moment Kirk thought he saw suspicion in her eyes.

"I'll consider it," she said, "once we find out just where we stand with Ensign Stepanovich. In the meantime, warn whoever you left in charge on the *Enterprise*. They can raise the deflectors or pull back out of range."

Kirk nodded, flipping his communicator open. He could hardly blame Ansfield for her suspicions under the circumstances. He had suggested, in effect, that she make the *Cochise* totally helpless.

"Kirk to *Enterprise*," he said as he followed the others into the corridor outside the briefing room.

"Scott here, Captain."

Quickly, talking as he and the others hurried toward the turbolift, Kirk explained the situation. "For now," he finished, "put up the deflectors. And see if

40

you can come up with any way of rooting our friend out of the control room."

"Aye, Captain. It can be done, but no' without time and tools. Ye remember Lieutenant Riley."

"I do, Mr. Scott," Kirk acknowledged with a grimace. Riley, temporarily demented by an alien infection, had similarly locked himself in the *Enterprise*'s engineering control room and had very nearly destroyed the ship before they had been able to dislodge him. "Contact me if you have any suggestions. Kirk out."

As on the *Enterprise,* the bridge was seven decks above sickbay and the briefing room. Halfway up, the lights faded into darkness, and the turbolift shuddered to a stop. A second later, the emergency lights, dim and red, pulsed into life. More slowly, the turbolift resumed its motion.

"I guess we'll see if our batteries are fully charged or not," Ansfield muttered.

A minute later, Ortiz manually opened the door, and the group emerged onto the bridge.

"What happened to the power?" Ansfield asked. "Did Stepanovich cut it off?"

"More than that, Commander," the tall Oriental woman at the science station said. "He's shut down the matter-antimatter engines."

"But why the devil— Have you been able to talk to him? Has he said anything?"

"The comm unit in the control room is on, but we haven't been able to get a word out of him," Lieutenant Richards at the communications station reported.

"He can hear you?"

"Affirmative, but he refuses to respond."

"Patch me in, Lieutenant."

"Right away, Commander."

"Ensign Stepanovich, this is Commander Ansfield. I'd like to talk to you." Her voice, Kirk noted, had suddenly lost its sharp edge. It wasn't soft, but, like McCoy when he was attempting a soothing bedside manner, she put more friendliness than command in it.

But there was no response. Stepanovich's breathing, loud and ragged, could be heard, but that was all.

"We know something's wrong, Ensign," Ansfield went on, talking into the silence. "We think that whatever has happened to you is the same thing that happened to Captain Chandler. We know that whatever you've done, it isn't your fault. Ensign? Do you understand what I'm saying?"

When there was still no response, Chandler stepped forward next to Ansfield. "This is Captain Chandler," he said, speaking almost as softly as Ansfield had. "I know what you're going through. I went through it myself for almost two days. I was afraid of everything and everyone, just like you are now, but I knew I didn't have any reason to be. You don't either. You have nothing to fear, especially from Commander Ansfield and myself."

"The captain's right, Ensign," Ansfield said. "He knows what he's talking about. He's been through it himself."

"Just stop and think, Ensign," Chandler took up when there was still no response. "Think about it rationally. I wasn't able to control the fear, but that was because I didn't know what was causing it. But now we know. It's being caused by something that came through the gate—and it doesn't mean any harm. Remember, whatever it is, it didn't harm *me* in the slightest. Now that it's left, I'm perfectly all right. And now that we know that, I'm sure *you* can control the fear you're feeling. You *have* to control it. Do you understand?"

Still, there was only the ragged breathing coming from the control room. Chandler and Ansfield exchanged glances.

"Think, Ensign," Chandler continued, his voice turning husky with the effort to keep his own remembered fear from showing through. "Look at the fear rationally. There's no basis for it. Something is making you feel that way, but it *can't hurt you.* It didn't hurt me, not in the slightest. And it left me. It left me and went to you, and now I'm perfectly all right. It will leave you, too, and you'll be fine. Unless you do something to hurt yourself. That's the only danger in the situation, Ensign. The only danger is that this fear you feel will make *you* do something to hurt *yourself.* Do you understand what I'm saying?"

When Chandler fell silent again, there was at first no sound at all from the control room, as if Stepanovich had begun holding his breath, but then, after nearly fifteen seconds, there was a shuddering moan.

"It's all right, Stepanovich," Chandler said quickly. "Just keep control of yourself, and everything will be all right. We'll help you. You don't have anything to worry about. All you have to do is stay in control."

The moan went higher in pitch, but still there were no words.

The turbolift door opened a moment later, and a young woman, an ensign in science blue, stepped through nervously.

"Commander Ansfield," she said, halting immediately in front of the turbolift doors. "I was told to report to the bridge. I'm Ensign Karen Laszlo. I'm a friend of Ensign Stepanovich."

Motioning the woman forward, Ansfield said, "Ensign Stepanovich, your friend Karen is here. She'd like to talk to you."

Hesitantly, as if intimidated by their rank, the woman came to stand next to Ansfield and Chandler.

"Andy, are you all right?" she began, but before she could say more, the moan from the control room turned to a scream and then cut off sharply.

"He shut off the comm unit, Commander," the communications officer said.

"Commander!" The voice of the lieutenant at the science station sliced through the half-dozen other voices on the bridge. "He's preparing to start the engines! Cold!"

"But he can't! It's impossible!" Chandler almost shouted, realizing as he did that all the comforting words he had spoken to the ensign had been lies. Whatever had possessed him had nearly killed him, and now it was going to kill his entire ship!

"Impossible or not, Captain," the lieutenant said sharply, "that's what he's trying to do!"

Ansfield's face drained of color. Like everyone on the bridge, she knew that, without the requisite warmup period of nearly thirty minutes, bringing the matter and antimatter together to start the engines was tantamount to suicide. They would become, literally, a small sun as the reaction between matter and antimatter, normally perfectly balanced, went out of control, annihilating itself and vaporizing the *Cochise.*

Chapter Six

"ALDRICH!" ANSFIELD SNAPPED into the comm unit. "Any progress on disabling the controls, especially those to the main engines?"

"To the main engines?" Aldrich's voice came back. *"It can't be done. There simply isn't any access except within the control room itself!"*

Ansfield swallowed once, her face still chalk pale. "Then we had better start abandoning ship. Captain Kirk—"

Kirk had already turned to the viewscreen, still linked to the *Enterprise*. Scott, anticipating Kirk's commands, was issuing his own. *"Take us back within transporter range, Mr. Sulu, fast. I'm on my way to the transporter room."*

"Scotty," Kirk said. "You'll have to use the cargo transporter as well. There are two hundred people—"

"Aye, Captain, I can count as well as any mon. And I'll need their communicators to lock onto."

Even before Scott finished, Commander Ansfield was on the shipwide intercom, instructing everyone to switch on communicators and ordering each deck to gather in a single spot to make pickup quicker and easier. "We have less than four minutes," she finished. "Good luck."

Then, for thirty seconds, there was silence.

"*Transporter range.*" Sulu's voice came from the *Enterprise* bridge, and almost simultaneously, Kirk's communicator came to life.

"*Transporter locking onto bridge personnel, Captain,*" Scott said.

"Wait, Mr. Scott." Spock, who had been studying the science station instruments since the station had been vacated a minute before, turned and strode to the engineering station on the opposite side of the bridge.

"Wait? *Are ye daft, Mr. Spock? We have less than—*"

"There is no longer any need to evacuate the *Cochise,* Mr. Scott." With swift precision, Spock's fingers darted across the engineering station control panel. A moment later, the *Cochise* shuddered and then was still.

"Cold-start procedure terminated, Mr. Scott."

"*Spock!*" Scotty's voice crackled over Kirk's communicator. "*How the devil did ye manage that?*"

"It was not my doing, Mr. Scott. Ensign Stepanovich halted the procedure himself. I merely reengaged the safety locks from the bridge. Unfortunately, the procedure was not stopped in time to avoid serious damage to the engines themselves. The balancing circuits in particular, in attempting to cope with the massive imbalance inherent in a cold start, were almost certainly burned out."

"Mr. Scott," Kirk said sharply. "Have any transfers been completed?"

"The cargo transporter beamed over nearly thirty from the engineering deck."

"Send them back, now!"

"Aye, Captain." Though his voice showed his puzzlement, he obeyed.

"Commander Ansfield," Kirk said, leaving his communicator on so Scotty could hear him as well. "Until we learn differently, we have to assume that whatever was affecting Captain Chandler and Ensign Stepanovich is still present. If it left Ensign Stepanovich, if that's why he was able to terminate the cold-start procedure, then we have to assume it has once again moved on to someone else. I would suggest that while we wait for Mr. Aldrich to force his way into the control room, you conduct the search you were planning to do earlier."

Ansfield nodded, the motion containing an odd mixture of briskness and sadness, and began issuing the orders.

But nothing was found. Everyone on the *Cochise*, except Ensign Stepanovich and the ensign he had killed, was accounted for. At the same time, a similar search was conducted on the *Enterprise*—with similar results.

Finally, after more than an hour, Lieutenant Aldrich's group gained access to the engineering control room.

Ensign Stepanovich was dead.

After halting the cold-start procedure, apparently by blasting the control panel with his phaser, he had turned the weapon, still set to maximum power, on himself. His body lay sprawled next to that of the ensign he had killed when forcing his way into the control room. The expression on his face, frozen in death, was one of sheer terror.

As far as anyone could tell, however, whatever had possessed him—if, despite Chandler's denials and Spock's convictions, *possession* was the right word—had died with him. A second search was conducted of both ships, and once again no hint of any alien presence was found.

Then they turned their attention to the gate itself.

One of the probes the *Enterprise* had used in its earlier study of the gates in the Sagittarius arm was modified so it would reverse course within less than a second of its passage through the gate. It was launched, but it didn't return or reappear anywhere within the five-thousand-parsec range of the probe's subspace beacon. Other probes, each modified differently, vanished as quickly and completely as the first. The sensors showed no alteration in the size or shape of the gate.

Then, after absorbing a half-dozen probes without a trace, the gate began to shrink. For more than two hours, it seemed to shrivel, as if a jagged wound in space itself had begun to heal. Finally, with a ripple of gravitational turbulence, it vanished completely, leaving not even a scar behind. Nor did it reappear, at least not anywhere within range of the *Enterprise*'s modified sensors.

With both the gate and whatever had come through it apparently gone, Starfleet Headquarters breathed a premature sigh of relief and lifted the quarantine. Within hours, all but a skeleton crew headed by Commander Ortiz were transported off the *Cochise*, and a tug was dispatched to collect the disabled ship, whose battery power was already running low and whose engines were beyond the repair capability of anything less than a full Starbase facility. The *Enterprise* was within minutes of engaging the warp drive for its return to Starbase 1 when two messages came in from Starfleet Headquarters almost simultaneously.

The first began by announcing that another gate had apparently been stumbled onto by a private scout ship on the opposite side of the Federation. A distress call had been received by the U.S.S. *Eddington,* but when it arrived on the scene, all ten aboard the scout ship were dead. Nine had been murdered. The tenth, like Ensign Stepanovich on the *Cochise,* had been a suicide. The scout's records showed a gravitational burst similar to that encountered by the *Cochise,* but the *Eddington*'s unmodified sensors could pick up no trace of the gate.

As a result of this new development, the message concluded, Starfleet Command "regretfully" reinstated the quarantine and ordered the *Enterprise* to evacuate the remainder of the *Cochise* crew and then proceed immediately to rendezvous with the *Eddington* and determine whether or not a gate did indeed exist in its vicinity.

The second message was received moments after the *Enterprise* entered warp drive. It contained the text of a preliminary report from Captain Sherbourne of the U.S.S. *Devlin,* the ship that had returned the Aragos—those who desired to be returned, at least—to their home world in the Sagittarius arm. Before he had more than glanced at the first few hundred words of the report, Kirk sent out a call to assemble the senior officers, including Chandler and Ansfield of the

Cochise, in the *Enterprise* briefing room. In the minutes before they all arrived, he completed skimming the report.

"As you all know," he said when the group was complete, "the Aragos had a technology almost equal to that of the Federation when the group we found in hibernation originally left their world and passed through the gate. Earlier this century, their planet was surveyed briefly by a Federation ship, and their civilization was found to be planetbound, essentially at a level equivalent to that of nineteenth-century Earth. Sometime in the last fifteen thousand years, their civilization had regressed to a pretechnological state, from which it is only now beginning to emerge."

He paused, indicating the report on the briefing table before him. "We now know when the regression occurred. And we can make a pretty good guess as to why. The *Devlin*'s sensors discovered a series of underground vaults, one of which contained records of that earlier civilization and of its destruction. The time can't be pinned down precisely, but it happened not long after they discovered the gate, probably shortly after the group we found went through. They hadn't had a war in more than four centuries, and within decades they had destroyed their entire civilization."

Ansfield shuddered. "You're saying one of the ships the Aragos were using in their study of the gate became . . . became 'infected' by these entities that hang around the gates? And it took the infection back home?"

"That's how it appears on the surface," Kirk agreed. "Luckily, enough people survived to keep the race going, and the planet itself was not totally destroyed. It was, however, a long road back."

"It would therefore seem, Captain," Spock said into the silence that followed Kirk's summary, "that the phenomenon presently associated with the gates has been associated with them at least as far back as fifteen thousand years. This information greatly enhances the probability that the chain of wars we encountered in that other galaxy was triggered by this same phenomenon at some still earlier time."

Kirk nodded. "My conclusion as well. The only possibly encouraging aspect of the situation is that the phenomenon—force or entity, or whatever it is—appears to be neither immortal nor capable of endless reproduction. The one on the *Cochise* seems to have disappeared when its 'host,' Ensign Stepanovich, killed himself. Since the *Eddington* reports no 'possessions' among its personnel, it would appear that whatever was responsible for the deaths on the scout ship whose distress call it was answering is gone as well. And whatever was brought to the Aragos planet fifteen thousand years ago may have been responsible for *starting* the wars that destroyed their civilization, but it, too, must have either died or dissipated at some point. The planet, after all, is peaceful enough today."

He paused, glancing toward McCoy before going on. "Even if that chain of destruction we encountered in that other galaxy was originally triggered by a similar force, it, too, must have long since vanished. The combatants we encountered were, under the circumstances, acting understandably, even rationally. If the force had still been active among them, we could never have gotten them to talk to each other or to us."

Kirk paused again, looking around the table. "Any arguments? Comments?"

"Just questions," Ansfield said, and she was echoed by a nod from Chandler. "Tons of questions."

"To which there are no answers—yet," Kirk said. He turned to Spock. "Mr. Spock, have you had any more 'feelings' like the one you described before, the one that occurred as Captain Chandler was being released?"

"None, Captain, and I have remained especially alert for any comparable manifestations. However, as you have pointed out, there is no way at this time to be certain that the source of Captain Chandler's and Ensign Stepanovich's irrational behavior is indeed no longer with us. That it departed—through death or some other form of dissipation—when its so-called host died is problematical at best. Similarly, the theories concerning the Aragos and that other chain of wars remain only speculation at the present time."

Kirk nodded. "Agreed, Mr. Spock. Until we know more about this—a great deal more—Starfleet's quarantine must be rigorously implemented. There's too much at stake to allow the *Enterprise* or the *Cochise*—or the *Eddington,* now—to approach any ship, any Starbase, or any populated planet."

He glanced quickly around the table. "Are we agreed?"

There were frowns, even grimaces, but no one disagreed.

Ten hours later, the *Enterprise* sensors verified the

presence of another of the misshapen gates roughly a billion kilometers from the *Eddington*. Immediately upon receiving the report, Starfleet Command, as Kirk had hoped it would, ordered the *Enterprise* to proceed to the vicinity of the original gate in the Sagittarius arm.

"Two more suspected gates were reported while you were in transit," Admiral Wellons explained, "one of them less than a parsec from Starbase 14. God knows how many more are out there that we haven't stumbled across yet. In any event, we feel our best chance of finding some way of understanding and coping with these things is to observe and investigate the gate you passed through and the cluster of smaller gates in the same area. See if you can find some link between them. What we are beginning to fear is that these lesser gates that have been appearing in and around Federation territory could be merely preliminary phenomena, leading up to another situation like the one in the Sagittarius arm."

"It's a possibility that we've considered, Admiral," Kirk said, "as well as the possibility that they are being intentionally created by the same life-form that we feel must have created the other gates."

"I assumed you had, Captain. However," Wellons went on, putting into words some of the same thoughts Kirk had been having since he had first been notified of the *Eddington*'s discovery, "whether these gates are being purposely created by some form of intelligence—hostile or otherwise—or are a natural phenomenon, our most immediate concern is that one of them may appear within range of a populated planet, or that whatever 'infection' they cause will be carried back to a populated planet, as it apparently was in the case of the Aragos planet. We *have* to learn more about these things, before it's too late. The Sagittarius arm is the only place where a large, stable group of them exists."

So far, Kirk added silently to himself as Wellons signed off.

Within minutes, the *Enterprise* was on its way.

Chapter Seven

FOR THE FIRST TIME since she had entered Starfleet Academy, Commander Esther Rebecca Ansfield was having trouble sleeping. Despite the comforting sight —and aroma—of the shelves of ancient books Kirk had allowed her to beam over from her cabin on the *Cochise*, despite the fact that there was very little physical difference between her old cabin and the one she now occupied, she hadn't gotten an uninterrupted eight hours of sleep since she had come aboard the *Enterprise*. Worse, when sleep wouldn't come, she hadn't been able to concentrate on her books, not even the romances or adventures. On the *Cochise*, no matter what the situation, she had always been able to lose herself in those perfectly preserved volumes with their always exaggerated, often idealized pictures of what nineteenth- and twentieth-century Earth had been like and their sometimes bizarre imaginings of what the future held.

But now . . .

Was it, she had wondered a dozen times in the last three days, some remnant of that thing that had invaded Micah's mind and then died—ostensibly—when Andros Stepanovich had killed himself? Were the suspicions Kirk and the others voiced right? Had some small part of it survived? And attached itself to *her?* Worse, had the creature survived intact? Had it learned of its limitations from its experiences with Micah and the ensign? Was it now simply biding its time, exercising more restraint, more cunning?

Could another creature have found its way onto the ship when the *Enterprise* had paused in the vicinity of the *Eddington?*

Or was her problem the result of something much more commonplace—a nervous reaction to the fact that she was on the legendary *Enterprise?* Perhaps Micah was right, she thought ruefully. Perhaps she *should* have beamed over to the *Eddington* with him and the rest of the *Cochise*'s crew, to wait—hope, really—for the quarantine to be lifted, instead of traipsing off on the *Enterprise,* halfway across the galaxy. She was not, as the cliché had it, getting any younger.

But that, she thought with a mental snort, was precisely the reason she had jumped at the chance when Kirk had requested that at least one officer of the *Cochise* accompany the *Enterprise* on its return to the gate three thousand parsecs away in the Sagittarius arm. She was well into her fifties, and a chance like this would not likely come again.

Or was her constant state of tension caused simply by the fact that she was now working with the man who had been responsible, albeit in a very indirect way, for her having switched careers in midlife? That situation was, depending on her mood, either icing on the cake or an embarrassment. So far, she had not mentioned it to him, although she'd had a dozen opportunities. Micah, in fact, was the only one she had ever told. There were times when she regretted telling even him.

Even during the hours between the evacuation of the *Cochise* and the transfer of all its personnel to the *Eddington*, she had been half afraid that, over a meal or during one of the captain-to-captain tête-à-têtes, Micah would casually remark, "You know, Kirk, you were Essie's inspiration for entering the Academy."

To Micah, it had always been "interesting," and he had never understood why she wanted it kept quiet. The trouble was, she had never been able to explain her reluctance rationally, even to herself. The closest she had ever come was the uncharacteristically fuzzy thought that making a decision of that magnitude based on what some, including her son, Paul, would consider a rebellious whim was "silly." The fact that the decision had been long in coming and had turned out to be the right decision, that her years in the Academy had been even better than her university days decades earlier, almost as good as her early years in teaching, her years of marriage to Vernon, didn't make any difference.

She could smile to herself when she thought about how it had come about, even about the disbelieving looks Paul, then twenty-four, had given her when she had first mentioned the possibility. However, the arguments between that first mention and her final decision had stretched over a dozen months and were difficult to smile about. And the prospect of talking about them, particularly to the man who, unknowingly, had figured in her final decision, still made her uncomfortable.

"Mother," Paul had protested a hundred times. "You've got a guaranteed lifetime job—a job that you've always loved. You can't seriously be thinking of throwing it over for something as insane as trying to get into Starfleet Academy at *your* age! If you want a little adventure, there are lots of easier, safer ways to get it."

He had almost convinced her—despite her growing conviction that, since Vernon's death, teaching had somehow lost its magic. Before, each new day in class had been fresh, a new challenge. But after his death, the faces in her classes started looking the same, the problems the same, the courses and the theses to be graded the same.

Still, Paul's constant objections, his overwhelming appeals to practicality, kept her from acting, kept her from, as he said repeatedly, "making a fool of yourself."

Until one day.

Her classes had seemed particularly repetitious—even pointless—that day, and during her weekly evening out with Paul and his new wife, Claudette, she had said so.

"Oh, Mother," he had said after an eye-rolling sideways look at Claudette. "Don't tell me you're going to start up that Starfleet Academy nonsense again!"

From there it had only gotten worse, until Paul, shaking his head condescendingly, said, "Mother, you're fifty years old! What do you want to do, go into the record books as the oldest Starfleet ensign in the history of the Academy?"

And that was when she remembered the story she had seen a half-dozen times in the last week, the story about how one James T. Kirk was about to become "the youngest starship captain in Starfleet history." And she remembered thinking, the first time she had seen it, *Why are they making such a big deal out of it? Someone has to be the youngest.*

Suddenly, she had grinned, earning an uncertain smile from Claudette and a puzzled frown from Paul. *"Someone* has to be the oldest," she said, wondering why it had taken her so long to realize it. "So why shouldn't it be me?"

From that point on, she had never looked back. With Micah, already a commander, as her sponsor, she was accepted into the Academy. She had graduated near the top of her class and managed, with a little help from her near-eidetic memory, to do it in a year less than standard. And once in space, her years of teaching, her ability to work with people, and her no-nonsense way of almost instantly cutting to the heart of any matter enabled her to move up so rapidly that, had she graduated at a "normal" age, she might have been in the running for "youngest commander in Starfleet history."

And now the "oldest ensign" and the "youngest captain"—neither record had been surpassed in the intervening years—were on the same ship.

And the oldest ensign, unfortunately, really *was* acting like a fool this time. She could imagine what Paul would say if he—

And then, in an instant, she realized what her problem was. Indecision. Plain and simple indecision!

And why the devil had that realization been so ridiculously long in coming? The last time she had had similar symptoms had been during the year she was struggling with her decision to enter the Academy—a decision she had delayed again and again simply because of Paul and his patronizing objections. The instant she had made the decision, the symptoms had gone away, and her sleeping habits had returned to normal.

She would tell Kirk. From what she had seen, he was a nice enough young man. And, as she had repeatedly told Paul, there was no big deal about being the oldest or the youngest. So they were now both on the same ship. So what? Everybody had to be *somewhere*.

Laughing, she felt the knot of tension begin to unravel.

Within minutes, she was sound asleep.

The stars of the Sagittarius arm lay spread out before the *Enterprise*. Beyond them hovered the deadly, shrouded mass of the Shapley center. In the center of the viewscreen, driven by the Aragos-modified sensors and a specially designed computer link, the gate flickered in and out of existence, expanding and contracting in milliseconds, like a mammoth, spaceborne ghost of the neon signs that had once lured travelers into twentieth-century gambling casinos.

Which, Kirk couldn't help but think, was not an inappropriate image. To even approach this or any other gate was purely a gamble, even more now than it had been before, when all one had had to worry about was where, if anywhere, the gate would transport you once you entered it. Even Spock had been unwilling to quote odds on what might happen this time.

The *Enterprise* had passed through this particular gate twice before. The first time, it had deposited them in a corner of the universe so remote that no one had been able to even guess at its distance from the Milky Way galaxy. The second time, it had returned them to the spot in the Sagittarius arm from which it had snatched them in the first place. But neither time had there been any evidence of the sort of "entity" that had taken over Chandler and Ensign Stepanovich and, in all likelihood, countless others down through the millennia.

But what would they find when they approached it this time? Would such an entity be waiting for them? In the days since they had verified the existence of the *Eddington*'s gate and then sped out of the Federation toward the Sagittarius arm at warp seven, they had received a half-dozen messages from Starfleet Headquarters, each one bringing the unwelcome news that another suspected gate had appeared somewhere in the Federation or the surrounding Treaty Exploration Territory. Because of the warnings Starfleet had issued repeatedly, only one ship, another private scout, had approached a gate once the gravitational bursts that seemed to announce their birth had been noted. All other ships had maintained their distance or backed away. None had approached more closely than a billion kilometers, the same distance the *Enterprise* now maintained from the Sagittarius arm gate.

As a result of this caution—or perhaps as a result of

sheer luck—only the one scout had been "infected," and it had destroyed itself in a successful version of the cold-start suicide that Ensign Stepanovich had tried to perform on the *Cochise*.

A program to modify the sensors on all Starfleet vessels to match those of the *Enterprise* was under way and being accelerated daily. Once every ship was modified, the gates could be detected with or without the trademark gravitational burst. This would at least prevent more ships from blundering into a quiescent gate, one whose gravitational birth throes had gone unobserved. It would not, however, do anything at all to allay Starfleet Command's most immediate fear— that a gate would appear within range of a populated planet.

"Computer analysis indicates the cyclic pattern of expansions and contractions has been altered, Captain," Spock said, not looking up from the science station readouts he had been observing almost continuously since the *Enterprise* had emerged from warp drive more than ten hours earlier. Already he had determined that every one of the smaller gates—the "gravitational anomalies" the *Enterprise* had originally come to the Sagittarius arm to investigate—was similar to the gates that had appeared in Federation territory: small, constant in size, and jaggedly irregular. And three of the original group had vanished.

"Altered?" Kirk turned from the viewscreen and moved toward Spock and the science station. "In what way?"

"Each cycle is still eight point six nine three hours in duration, but now there are periods of up to ten point two one minutes during which the gate remains at what appears to be its maximum diameter of nearly one million kilometers."

Kirk frowned. Based on what they had learned—guessed—earlier, the distance the gate transmitted an object appeared to be inversely proportional to the gate's size at the moment of transmission. When the *Enterprise* had passed through, it had been at its smallest, less than a kilometer in diameter. Its energy density had been incredibly high, and it had thrown them millions, possibly billions, of parsecs.

"At that diameter," Kirk said, "its destination must be very nearby."

"Perhaps, Captain. However, because it previously reached that maximum diameter only once each cycle and remained so for approximately forty-four seconds, six times longer than it remained at any other size, I surmise that this maximum expansion may represent its quiescent state, during which it is not capable of transmitting an object anywhere. The forty-four-second interval could have simply marked the beginning of each new cycle."

"A dead spot between cycles, Mr. Spock? Or a malfunction? Like a tooth missing from a cogwheel? The beginning of the larger dead spots—malfunctions—that exist now?"

"Both are of course possible, Captain."

"And the smaller, irregular gates, both here and elsewhere—could they be some kind of . . . malfunction of the gate system?"

"There is no way to accurately assess the odds, Captain, but I would consider it quite within the realm of possibility. Even the Federation's fear that the lesser gates are precursors of a larger one is not totally without merit. If, that is, we assume that all these gates are indeed part of a single, seemingly universe-wide system. However, there is as yet no firm evidence to indicate either the validity or the invalidity of such an assumption. We have not, in fact, even established beyond doubt that the phenomena that have begun appearing in Federation space are truly gates."

Kirk thought a moment. "They showed up as gates on the sensors. Badly misshapen gates, but gates nonetheless, and no more misshapen than the cluster of gates here in the Sagittarius arm. In any event, the probes we sent through went *somewhere.*"

"True, Captain, but the fact that the probes disappeared does not prove that they reappeared—anywhere. During our previous investigation here in the Sagittarius arm, the probes did, with some exceptions, reappear at varying distances, thereby proving that the phenomena were indeed some form of gate."

"But some did disappear altogether," Kirk said, nodding. "What about those? Were they destroyed? Transmitted beyond the range of our sensors?"

"Those are, of course, two possibilities, Captain. There are, however, far too many unknowns to allow even preliminary conclusions at this point."

Kirk stood silently behind Spock for a long moment. Then he turned and walked thoughtfully back to the command chair, his eyes on the viewscreen and the gate that flickered there.

"It's about time," he said, "that we started narrowing things down, one way or another. Ahead, Mr. Sulu, quarter impulse power. Mr. Chekov, deflectors up."

Both men acknowledged, and the *Enterprise* crept ahead, sublight.

Commander Ansfield emerged onto the bridge a few minutes later. For several seconds, she stood just to one side of the turbolift doors, watching the flickering gate. Of late, she had spent much of her time on the bridge, figuratively looking over Spock's shoulder, even taking the station on occasion when Spock was called away. Though she was not as quick or precise as Spock, her memory and analytical instincts made Kirk realize that Chandler had been lucky to have her as his science officer. There were times when her human "intuition" made her more than an overall match for Spock.

"You're taking us in for a closer look," she said finally. "I wondered how long it would take you to get around to it."

Kirk smiled faintly. In more and more ways, especially since she had revealed her "secret" to him, Ansfield reminded him of Dr. McCoy. Their directness and occasional sarcasm were similar, as was the inner vulnerability they both tried to hide under a sometimes bristly exterior. She even seemed to share some of McCoy's reservations concerning dependency on machines. Her library of ancient books, transported with her from the *Cochise,* was of continuous fascination to the doctor, although the fact that they were mostly fiction rather than nonfiction dampened his enthusiasm at times, particularly when she would laughingly point out some character—usually a courtly or straitlaced minor character in the romances—that reminded her of him.

"Five hundred million kilometers, sir," Sulu called out.

"Hold at that distance," Kirk said. Then, punching the button that would send his voice throughout the ship, he continued, "We are now a half-billion kilometers from the Sagittarius gate and holding. We will resume our sublight approach in another minute."

Kirk paused, his eyes once again darting briefly toward the viewscreen and the flickering gate. "Everyone," he resumed, "remember the drill. From this point on, no one, absolutely no one, is to be left alone at any time. Groups of three or more are to be maintained whenever feasible. All personnel must—repeat, must—carry phasers, set and locked on medium stun. If anyone—and that emphatically includes myself and all senior officers—displays any of the symptoms previously displayed by Captain Chandler or Ensign Stepanovich and appears to be losing control, whoever notes those symptoms is to act immediately."

Turning back to the viewscreen, he watched it another long moment and then said, "Resume approach, Mr. Sulu."

Even more slowly, the *Enterprise* began again to inch forward. McCoy, looking annoyed at the orderly who had insisted on accompanying him, stepped onto the bridge as Sulu announced the three-hundred-million-kilometer mark.

At approximately two hundred fifty million kilometers, Spock looked up sharply from the science station instruments. For a moment, he stood perfectly motionless, expressionless. Then he turned to face Kirk.

"Captain, the manifestation I experienced upon the release of Captain Chandler has returned."

All eyes focused abruptly on Spock. "All stop, Mr. Sulu," Kirk snapped. "Ready to reverse power on my command."

"Aye-aye, sir. Ready."

"Mr. Spock. Evaluation. Is it the same as before?"

For another five seconds, Spock stood motionless, his head cocked slightly, as if trying to listen to something only he could hear. Kirk could not keep a chill from settling on his spine, and he noticed that the others were as motionless as Spock.

"It is similar, Captain," Spock said finally, "but not identical in a number of ways. For one, this manifestation is more powerful. For another, although the sensations that I am experiencing arise from within myself, and within myself alone, there is a sense of another being, totally alien, somehow touching me."

A barely perceptible shiver ran through the Vulcan's body, the first time Kirk could remember seeing such a thing.

"I feel it, too, sir." Uhura spoke from the communications station, and as she did, Kirk realized that he, too, was experiencing something similar.

A mild, very mild, version of Chandler's description fit the feeling to some extent. Kirk had a strong and very distinct feeling that something was hovering in the air around him, something elusive and, as Spock had said, alien. He had the uneasy feeling that if he could turn his head quickly enough, he could catch a glimpse of it out of the corner of his eye.

"Reverse power, Mr. Sulu, slowly. Let's see if this thing has a limit to its range."

For a moment, Sulu didn't move, but then, as if suddenly released from invisible restraints, his hands darted to the control board. "Reverse power, sir," he said, his voice loud in what was now an almost breathless silence.

Once again, Kirk spoke on the shipwide intercom. "Contact has apparently been made," he said. "We have experienced sensations indicating the phenomenon associated with the gates is present. Impulse power has been reversed. We are pulling away from the gate and will continue to—"

Abruptly, Kirk stopped, his mind and body almost literally frozen by a sudden, irresistible wave of sheer terror. In the fraction of a second between one word and the next, unreasoning fear swept out of the darkness of space and closed over him like the icy waters of a lightless, bottomless sea.

Chapter Eight

EVERY MUSCLE IN Kirk's body was piano-wire taut, every nerve raw with a hypersensitivity he had never before experienced. His lungs spasmed, pulling in a chestful of air. His fists clenched, his fingernails digging into his palms, threatening to draw blood.

All eyes on the bridge darted toward him. The two security guards who stood on either side of the turbolift doors, as well as the orderly who had accompanied McCoy, had their phasers in hand, waiting tensely, silently.

Spock, one eyebrow angling slightly upward, was the first to speak. "Captain, from the sudden alteration in your own demeanor, I assume that the phenomenon has attached itself directly to you."

"Jim!" McCoy, suddenly coming unfrozen, started to rush forward, but Spock gripped the doctor's arm.

"It would be better, Doctor," Spock said dispassionately, "if you were to maintain your distance and your objectivity."

"Blast you, Spock!" McCoy snapped, trying to

wrench free but finding the Vulcan's grip unbreakable. "Can't you see—"

"I see precisely what has happened, Doctor. I also see that if the captain is to successfully combat this phenomenon, he will have need of all the logic and rationality he can muster. The last thing he needs at this precise moment is to witness another person displaying an unwarranted emotional reaction to his own situation. Total rationality and logic are imperative." Spock turned to the helm. "Mr. Sulu, increase reverse power and—"

"No!"

The single word erupted from Kirk's lips like a bullet. Sweat beaded his face and stained his tunic. He clamped his eyes shut but snapped them open almost instantly, as if the darkness behind them was more terrifying than the bridge and the officers around him.

He pulled in a breath, the air rasping through his constricted throat. The cords in his neck stood out like flesh-covered steel rods.

"Spock is right." Kirk's voice was a harsh whisper, each word an almost superhuman effort. "We have to be logical. This phenomenon, this *thing*—whatever it is—is here, in me. Where it can be observed."

He stopped, and for a moment his mouth worked silently, as if he were suppressing a scream. "For the moment," he went on, his voice still little above a grating whisper, "I am still in control of my actions. Mr. Sulu, keep on the present course at the present speed. I will . . . describe my impressions as the distance between ourselves and the gate increases."

He turned toward McCoy, the movement stiff,

almost spastic. "Bones, get your tricorder operating. Compare your readings with those you got from Captain Chandler."

"Jim, a sedative—"

"No!" Again, the word was like a bullet. "You saw what happened when you and Nkrumah gave Chandler a sedative. The thing left. It ended up in Ensign Stepanovich."

"A milder one, then, something that—"

"No! Even if you were sure it would work, I want to stay alert. I'm not—I don't *think* I'm about to go berserk, so let's leave things as they are. Just see what you can learn from the outside with the tricorder. I'll see what I can learn from the inside."

Swallowing audibly, McCoy stepped forward, unsheathing the tricorder scanner.

"It's very much like what Captain Chandler said," Kirk continued, struggling with each word. "Logic—which is what I *must* listen to!—tells me I have nothing to fear. Yet I fear everything! And nothing! I'm not afraid you're going to stab me with a hypo, Bones, or that you're going to break me in two, Mr. Spock. It's just that—that . . ."

When Kirk fell silent, breathing heavily, McCoy shook his head at the tricorder readings. "Your heart rate is over a hundred and fifty, Jim! And your blood pressure and adrenaline level—it's the same as with Chandler, only worse. Let me give you something to at least *try* to bring you down off the ceiling before you—"

"No, Bones! As long as it's in me, we know where it is!" Kirk clenched his teeth, then looked toward the viewscreen. "What's our distance, Mr. Sulu?"

"Seven hundred million kilometers, sir."

Kirk was silent for a long moment. Stiffly, he lifted one clenched fist from the arm of the command chair and watched as, one finger at a time, he forced the hand to open.

"Seven hundred ten million, sir."

"If anything," Kirk grated, "it's getting worse." He grimaced, then swallowed audibly. "All stop, Mr. Sulu. Hold at present distance."

"Aye-aye, sir."

As Sulu's fingers tapped in the orders, Kirk's terror decreased. His heart still pounded, sweat still oozed from his pores, but the effort required not to scream, not to lash out with deadly violence at everyone and everything on the bridge, was not quite as great as it had been a moment before.

"Mr. Spock, I think that's what it wanted," he said. "It's eased off, just a little."

"If it did, I sure as blazes can't tell it from any of your readings!" McCoy snapped, still scowling at the tricorder screen.

Then, as abruptly as it had appeared, the terror was gone. One instant, it seemed that every muscle in Kirk's body was fighting every other muscle. The next instant, all resistance vanished. His body twitched and was suddenly limp, as if every ounce of strength had been drained out of him, leaving him a flaccid shell.

He slumped, his breath whooshing out as if from a punctured balloon, his limbs like those of a marionette whose strings had just been slashed.

McCoy's tricorder readings swooped toward levels indicating near-unconsciousness.

Spock elbowed McCoy aside, punching a button on the arm of the command chair. "This is Commander Spock," he said, his voice unchanged. "The phenomenon has apparently left the captain. Be on the alert for its reappearance elsewhere."

He stepped back, looking down at Kirk and McCoy. "Doctor?"

McCoy studied the tricorder another second. "Almost the same as Chandler when it let *him* go. Readings normal except for residual effects, which will probably take a while to wear off." He paused, looking more closely at the still-slumping captain. Turning, he motioned to the orderly who had accompanied him to the bridge.

"Give me a hand, Davenport. Jim, you'll be better off in sickbay, in bed, at least for an hour or two."

"Never mind, Bones," Kirk said, forcing his rubbery muscles to obey as he straightened himself in the command chair. "Chandler was fine in five or ten minutes, and so will I be. The question right now is, where did whatever it was go? Spock, I think I heard you putting out an alert."

"Affirmative, Captain. However, I do not believe that another crew member has yet been targeted. I am once again experiencing the same manifestation as before." He looked toward Uhura. "And you, Lieutenant? I believe you experienced the earlier sensation the same as I."

"I experienced *something*, yes, but now—" She shook her head. "I don't know. I'm frightened, but under the circumstances fear would seem normal." A nervous smile flickered across her lips, touching her eyes. "Even logical."

"Perhaps so, Lieutenant," Spock observed. "For humans."

"For *anyone* with enough brains not to turn his back on a Klingon, Mr. Spock!" McCoy snapped. "Anyone who *isn't* afraid just doesn't have the sense to—"

"Bones, Spock, enough," Kirk interrupted. "Let's just say for now that if I *hadn't* hung on to logic for dear life these last few minutes, someone would've had to turn a phaser on me to keep me from killing someone, maybe even myself."

He paused, pulling in a still-ragged breath, and punched the button that would hook him into the shipwide intercom.

"We will be starting toward the gate again in a moment," he said. "The phenomenon, entity, whatever, is no longer attached to me but appears still to be in the vicinity. All my earlier orders still apply."

Turning off the intercom, he looked up at the viewscreen and the still-flickering gate. "Ahead, Mr. Sulu, minimum impulse power. We'll see what we run into *this* time."

They crept forward for nearly half a day but ran into nothing. Nothing new, at any rate. The sensors continued to show only the gate, flickering in space before them. Spock indicated that according to his own internal barometer, the phenomenon's strength remained constant, the sensations he felt neither increasing nor decreasing as the *Enterprise* approached the gate.

Several human crew members reported similar sensations, and dozens who were off-watch were awakened by unusually intense nightmares, usually involving childhood phobias they thought they had long since outgrown. With one, it was spiders and snakes. With another, like Chandler, it was simply darkness. Even McCoy reported a "bad dream," involving his own medical equipment.

"All those blasted machines I have to depend on," he said, "just developed lives of their own." He had awakened when a cluster of medical tricorders led by a laser surgery unit cornered him in what looked like a nightmarish version of the engineering deck.

Finally, the *Enterprise* hovered barely a thousand kilometers from the gate. On the viewscreen, its constantly shifting colors had become as spectacular as a randomized version of the relativistic starbow of warp drive. At this distance, the Aragos-modified sensors were picking up not just the outlines of the ever-changing gate but what looked like details of structure, also continually changing. Whether they were seeing the energies that made up the gate or were glimpsing what lay beyond it, no one could tell.

To many, Kirk included, the display was almost hypnotic. Dozens of secondary screens all over the *Enterprise* were continually carrying the images to fascinated crew members.

Virtually everyone aboard had a theory, of course, some as nightmarish as the fear itself. Others ranged from misperceived natural phenomena to well-meaning but "careless" higher life-forms. Regardless of their fears and nightmares, however, Kirk knew he had no choice but to go ahead with the investigation, and quickly. Already they had received word from

Starfleet Headquarters that two more gates had appeared in Federation space, including one within a half-parsec of Starbase 2.

Spock attempted to establish mental contact, with no apparent results.

"I still have the sense of another being of some kind hovering about me," he said after abandoning the attempt. "But that is all. There are no images, no thoughts that I can detect."

Kirk then ordered a probe, modified to reverse course instantly and return through the gates, launched during one of the gate's so-called quiescent periods. It failed to return.

Spock suggested that the experiment be repeated, this time using a shuttlecraft equipped with remote controls and full sensors.

"Explain," Kirk said. "I assume you have a logical reason for suggesting a shuttle rather than another probe."

"I have a theory that I wish to test, Captain."

"And that theory is?" Kirk prompted when Spock fell silent.

"I would prefer not to go into detail at this time, Captain."

Kirk frowned. "Can I assume, therefore, that you have no logical underpinnings for this theory? That it is simply a 'hunch'?"

"It is a possibility to which certain information points, but it is impossible to determine whether I have interpreted that information correctly."

"You can certainly tell me *something*." Kirk rose from his chair and stood by the railing next to Spock's science station. "I would like to at least keep up a pretext of commanding my ship and making informed decisions."

"There has never been any doubt, Captain, that you—"

Kirk threw up his hands. "Then talk to me, Mr. Spock, talk to me."

"As you wish, Captain. At this time I can only say that, in reanalyzing the computer records made at the times we passed through the gate, I have been led to believe that the gate consists of more than a simple 'opening' between two widely separated points in the universe. It appears at least possible that its entry and exit points are separated internally by a physical space of some kind, a space of considerable dimension and quite unknown properties. This space may be the source of the phenomenon we are attempting to deal with."

Chapter Nine

KIRK FROWNED. "You're saying we have to pass through some kind of—of connecting tunnel to get through the gate? That it has, in effect, a front door and a back door?"

"I have no knowledge of its shape or nature, Captain. I only know that *something*—possibly a physical space, possibly something else—appears to separate the entry and exit points of the gate."

"And what led you to this conclusion, Mr. Spock? If it's not violating your ethics to reveal this information," Kirk added, a touch of sarcasm edging his words.

"It has nothing to do with ethics, Captain, only with a reluctance to advance theories that are not logically supportable."

"Then explain the basis for your hunch, Mr. Spock. I won't hold it against you if you make an occasional intuitive leap." Kirk sat down again.

"As you wish, Captain. As you will recall, for the brief periods of our passage through the gate, the sensors registered nothing. It was as if not only the external universe but the *Enterprise* itself ceased to exist for those moments. Time, however, apparently continued for us at its normal rate. Our chronometers registered the time we entered the gate and the time we left it. The transit time determined from these readings was markedly different for our two passages. In the first instance, it was on the order of microseconds, whereas during our return, it was well over a millisecond. It was only when I thought to compare the speeds we were traveling during the transits that I discovered that they bore an inverse linear relationship to the transit times. One reason for this relationship could be the presence of a physical space through which the *Enterprise* passed during those transits. If that is indeed the case, my calculations indicate that the distance traveled during each transit would be approximately one hundred thirty-seven kilometers. With the shuttlecraft, I hope to confirm—or disprove —the existence of that space."

"Why not with another probe?"

"As I'm sure you're aware, Captain, the speed of a probe, once launched, is fixed, and its maneuverability is severely limited. During the ninety-seven milliseconds it would take for a probe to execute a hundred-and-eighty-degree course change, it would exit the far side of the gate. A shuttlecraft, on the other hand, can travel at virtually any speed. It can be guided to the gate and be sent through it as slowly as if it were coming in for a landing on the hangar deck. The advantages for our purposes are obvious. Ideally, of course, I would prefer to pilot the shuttlecraft and observe the phenomenon directly myself, but at this point, such action could be considered premature."

Kirk nodded. "Very well, Mr. Spock. Make the necessary preparations."

It took Spock, Commander Scott, and a half-dozen Engineering personnel two hours to install one of the Aragos-modified sensors in the shuttlecraft and to jury-rig a link that allowed Spock to control the shuttlecraft through the *Enterprise* helm. During that time, whatever it was that hovered invisibly over everyone in the *Enterprise* grew weaker, despite their proximity to the gate, and by the time the shuttlecraft was ready for launch, there was little more than what could be considered "normal" tension anywhere among the crew. Only Spock insisted that he could still sense the to-him-unmistakable signature of its alien presence, but it had no discernible effect on him as he maneuvered the shuttlecraft out of the hangar deck and brought it to a stop less than a kilometer from the gate.

At that distance, the view of the gate through the shuttlecraft sensors was even more spectacular than it was from the thousand-kilometer-distant *Enterprise*. Kirk and dozens of others were reminded of the tapes of the first ship to not just orbit Jupiter but to descend directly into the center of that massive, millennia-spanning storm still known as the Great Red Spot. The vibrant colors shifted wildly and continuously, sometimes vanishing into momentary blackness or a blinding flash of white. Shapes like kaleidoscopic Rorschach tests appeared and disappeared seemingly at random, sometimes bursting out from a single point, sometimes snapping into view, appearing fully formed in an instant, sometimes emerging slowly, like an approaching dawn.

"Quiescent phase due to begin in three minutes," Spock announced as he slowly and meticulously began to move the modified shuttlecraft forward. Chekov, at the navigator's station next to him, alternately watched the viewscreen and his own controls, while at the science station, Sulu's intensity as he watched its readouts almost matched Spock's.

On the main screen, the ever-shifting fabric of the gate continued to expand until, only yards short of its goal, the shuttlecraft halted. For a moment, then, Spock switched to the visible image being transmitted from a camera mounted near the rear of the shuttle. Instantly, the pyrotechnics of the gate vanished, leaving only the stars and the distant Shapley center and, in the foreground, the forward ninety percent of the exterior of the shuttlecraft. Satisfied, he switched back to the view from the sensors and waited.

Abruptly, the image on the viewscreen changed as the gate entered its supposedly quiescent state. The vibrant, computer-generated colors, representing whatever unknown energies the Aragos-modified sensors detected, vanished in an instant, replaced by a uniform gray. Even at this distance, no more than a dozen yards, no detail was visible. Through the eyes of the sensors and the computer, the gate looked like nothing more than an impossibly massive fogbank.

"Moving forward to contact," Spock announced impassively.

On the screen, nothing seemed to change. The only motion was the clock display in one corner of the screen, flickering as it counted down the seconds that remained in the quiescent cycle.

"One meter to contact," Spock said, observing not

the screen but one of the jury-rigged readouts. Chekov only nodded. His readings indicated that the *Enterprise* remained motionless with respect to the gate.

"Contact . . . now," Spock said.

The clock display brightened as it passed the nine-minute mark, but that was all that happened. The "fog" on the viewscreen remained unchanged.

"According to the instruments," Spock said, "the forward one point five meters of the shuttlecraft are within the gate. I am holding at that point."

For a good fifteen seconds, there was only silence and motionlessness, both on the screen and on the bridge, as Spock waited and watched.

Finally, he tapped a switch, once more bringing up the camera image from the rear of the shuttlecraft. As before, the bulk of the craft itself filled the bottom of the screen, while the rest of the screen held only the star field and the distant, deadly glow of the Shapley center. To visible light, even at this distance, the gate did not exist. The forward meter and a half of the shuttlecraft, supposedly within the boundary of the gate, appeared unaffected.

Glancing at the clock display, Spock nudged the shuttlecraft forward another meter, then two.

Still there was no change, either in the visible image or in the one provided by the sensors, although the sensors, mounted in the front bulkhead of the shuttlecraft, were theoretically within the gate.

"Fascinating," Spock murmured, and he nudged the shuttlecraft forward again.

Abruptly, approximately as the midpoint of the shuttlecraft crossed the theoretical boundary, every-thing changed.

The shuttlecraft vanished instantaneously from the *Enterprise* sensors, including the Aragos-modified ones.

Simultaneously, all signals from the shuttlecraft were cut off, as if the shuttlecraft itself had ceased to exist.

The gate itself, still visible through the *Enterprise* sensors, shimmered for a fraction of a second.

Then, without warning, the signals from the shuttlecraft returned. The visible image the signals brought, however, showed nothing, only total blackness without even the faintest star in the background. The sensors showed little more, only a dull, all-enveloping grayness, not unlike what they had shown from just outside the gate.

Suddenly, the gate shrank. Still visible on an auxiliary screen through the *Enterprise* sensors, the chaos of colors and shapes resumed their mad dance. Despite the clock display's insistence that there were another seven point eight minutes left in the quiescent state, the gate had resumed its cycle.

From the shuttlecraft signals, however, there was no indication of any change. It still hung in a featureless limbo.

Experimentally, Spock operated the control that would turn the shuttlecraft and bring it back out.

On his instruments, there was no feedback, no indication whether the shuttlecraft had responded or not.

And the shuttlecraft did not emerge from the gate.

"It appears," Spock said slowly, "that it would have been advantageous for me to have piloted the shuttlecraft personally after all."

Kirk shook his head. "I'd sooner lose a dozen shuttlecraft than one first officer, Mr. Spock. Besides, it could still—"

Suddenly, without warning, the *Enterprise* shuddered violently, as if caught in the grip of a massive tractor beam, and, an instant later, began to plunge helplessly forward toward the heart of the gate.

Chapter Ten

"REVERSE POWER, Mr. Spock!" Kirk snapped.

"It has already been done by the computer, Captain," Spock said, but even as he spoke, his fingers were stabbing at the controls, overriding the computer. As he had assumed, it did no good. Maximum impulse power was already being applied.

"Mr. Spock! What's happening?"

"Unknown, Captain. It appears that we are being drawn toward the gate by gravitational turbulence of unprecedented magnitude. Only a neutron star or a black hole—"

Abruptly, Spock stopped speaking, his eyes on the visible image on the auxiliary viewscreen. Directly in the path of their headlong flight, the shuttlecraft had reappeared, emerging from the gate. His attempt to reverse its course had apparently been effective after all.

Silently, his fingers darted across the controls, and two things happened virtually simultaneously. The shuttlecraft vanished, once again swallowed up by the gate, presumably drawn back in by the same wave of gravitational turbulence that gripped the *Enterprise*. A split second later, the impulse engines shifted out of full reverse and instead directed all their power at ninety degrees to the ship's path in a desperate attempt to change that path, to steer the *Enterprise* not directly away from the gate but away from that point in the gate where, in all likelihood, the shuttlecraft lay waiting for collision.

Kirk and Chekov and the others on the bridge, realizing what Spock was attempting, could only brace themselves.

For a moment, the visible image of the star field on the auxiliary screen shifted, telling Spock that some minuscule course change had been accomplished. But was it enough?

Even as the question formed in the Vulcan's mind, the *Enterprise* slewed into the gate.

And the universe vanished.

The *Enterprise* bridge was gone.

The stars beyond it were gone.

Spock's own body and all the associated physical sensations were gone.

Only his mind, fully functional and fully rational, remained.

This was the "nothingness" that the *Enterprise* sensors had registered—or, more accurately, had been unable to register—during its two previous passages through the gate. There had been no time—less than a millisecond—for this limbo to register on human or Vulcan senses.

But now—

How fast had the gravitational turbulence been dragging them? How much had the impulse engines been able to slow them? Were the impulse engines still operating, as the shuttlecraft engines apparently had continued to operate? Were they having any effect if they were? Did this "space" inside the gate have the same dimensions at all times, or did it vary as the gate went through its cycle?

Spock had no way of knowing the answers to any of these questions. He could not even be positive that, here, anything physical existed.

He thought.

Obviously, *he* still existed. He could not feel his body, nor could he see anything around him, but he—the thinking, reasoning entity that was Spock—obviously still existed.

Twice before, he, and everyone else on the *Enterprise*, had passed through this gate and returned to normal space, physically whole and mentally unimpaired. Admittedly, those previous exposures to this environment had been much briefer, but there was no reason to believe they would not be whole when they returned from this longer stay.

If they returned.

If they were not trapped here forever.

But even if they *were* trapped here—

Suddenly, an eagerness gripped Spock, an anticipation he could not remember having felt—could not remember having *allowed* himself to feel—in the whole of his rigidly controlled adult life. He was, literally, in a whole new world, a whole new universe perhaps, all aspects of which were unknown to him.

He had a whole new universe to learn about. He had only to determine how that learning could be accomplished.

Perhaps he would someday return to normal space, to the body whose sometimes illogical requirements had made it a burden far more often than it had been a help. Perhaps he would bring with him the knowledge he had gained here. That, he suspected, would be preferable, but it was far from essential.

To gain knowledge, *that* was the one essential. And now, with no body to weigh him down, with no external responsibilities to fulfill, he could devote himself to that purpose and that purpose alone.

For what could have been a minute, or an hour, or an eternity, he simply existed, anticipating the beginning of that leisurely pursuit, reveling in the pleasures he knew it would bring, pleasures he had until now denied himself.

Finally, he stirred.

He reached out with his mind and found—nothing.

The first stirrings of uneasiness brushed at the edges of his thoughts.

He reached out again.

Still there was nothing, and the uneasiness edged higher.

Surely—

Abruptly, Spock's thoughts turned inside out. The anticipation he had allowed himself to feel turned to a dread he could not control. To have an eternity of time before him, to have nothing to fill that time, to have nothing to *learn*—

Desperately, he reached out yet again, bringing to bear all the mental discipline at his command. Surely there must be *something* besides himself in this limbo. The others aboard the *Enterprise*—their minds must certainly have survived the same as his.

And as their remembered images formed in his mind, he felt their presence.

Somewhere in this seeming nothingness around him, they still existed, each as alone as he himself.

More alone, for they did not have the mental training and discipline he had been subjected to. Nor did they have the inherent ability to voluntarily touch the mind of another directly, without the need for physical contact.

And with that thought came another: he *did* have responsibilities here.

He had allowed himself to forget, but his responsibilities were, in fact, even greater than they had been in that other, physical universe. In this seemingly nonphysical environment, he was better suited to survive with his sanity intact than were any of the others; therefore, it was his responsibility to help them if he could. His first thoughts—illusions, really —of total freedom from all things physical had been mere rationalizations, reactions to a lifetime of discipline and responsibility. Somewhere deep within him, no matter how sternly repressed, no matter how illogical, a desire for release—for escape from reality —existed, must have always existed. That had been the source of those feelings.

But now that he was consciously aware of its existence, this desire could be dealt with, as had all the other, shallower emotions that his human half had threatened him with over the decades.

Once again, he reached out, searching for the minds of the captain, Dr. McCoy, and the others.

But even as he did, even as he felt the first glimmerings of contact, he felt something else.

Fear. The same fear he had observed so dispassionately on the bridge of the *Enterprise.*

But here there was more.

There was another being hovering about him.

A sapient being, as capable of thought as Spock himself.

It was not attacking or even threatening him, but it was, without doubt, associated with the fear.

He did not know *how* he knew, yet he accepted this illogical knowledge and treated it as real.

Whatever had touched his mind on the bridge of the *Enterprise,* in normal space, was here, in this limbo within the gate.

But there was a difference. Though the fear was present, it was a fine, chilling mist, not the heavy, waterlogged dread it had been in that other, now-distant world.

And the contact that Spock sensed was unlike any he had ever experienced. Paradoxically, fascinatingly, it was both delicate and powerful, like a moonlit spider web held rigidly in place by an invisible force field.

Did it somehow reflect the mind behind it? he found himself wondering. A powerful mind capable of the most intricate patterns of thought? Or was it simply the effect of this place that he found himself in?

Before he could attempt to speculate further, a new thought appeared in his mind. The being, whatever it was, wanted something.

There were no words, no images, only an impression so strong that it amounted to a firm conviction.

It wanted something.

And it was not leaving—*could* not leave—until it obtained that something.

Suddenly, with shocking unexpectedness, a sense of motion gripped Spock, a swirling, dizzying motion.

Still there was no sense of his own physical body, and yet there was an overwhelming sensation of spinning wildly, as if his very mind were being drawn into a deadly, silent whirlpool.

For an instant, he tried to resist, but his efforts were as useless as the raging outputs of the impulse engines had been against the impossible spurt of gravity that had dragged the *Enterprise* here.

Then, as quickly as it had vanished, the universe returned.

As if a light had suddenly been turned on, Spock found himself once again on the bridge of the *Enterprise.*

His fingers still hovered over the controls he had pressed to divert the *Enterprise* from the path that would have sent it smashing into the shuttlecraft, though it surely must have been hours since that action. In an act that was as much instinct as logic, he killed the impulse engines.

According to the chronometer, less than five seconds had passed.

Chekov, his hands reaching for the same controls they had been reaching for before, was still next to him at the navigator's station. The captain, still seated in the command chair, was still turning toward Sulu at the science station.

Chekov's hands faltered and stopped. His eyes were wide with surprise. The captain brought the chair to a lurching stop and swung it back to face the viewscreen.

"Spock, what the devil have you—" McCoy began angrily.

Kirk cut him off with a terse, "Later, Bones!"

All eyes were on the viewscreen. The universe, Spock and the others saw instantly, had not fully returned after all. There were no stars, no blackness of space. There was only an indistinct grayness, like the surface of the gate during its supposedly quiescent period.

And, in the foreground, the shuttlecraft.

"Can I assume, Mr. Spock," Kirk said quietly, "that this is the space you wanted to explore?"

"At least a portion of it, Captain." He nodded.

"And the reason for the gravity wave that dragged us in?"

"I can only speculate, Captain, but it is logical to assume that it was triggered in some way by the shuttlecraft's activities, perhaps its reemergence, which was virtually simultaneous with the start of the gravity wave."

"But the complete *Enterprise* emerged from it before, and nothing similar happened."

"Possibly the effect is related to the velocity with which the entrance or exit is made, Captain. Doubtless, the gate was designed for ships to pass through rapidly. The extreme slowness with which the shuttlecraft entered and exited may have strained the system in some way or caused a malfunction. Remember that massive gravitational turbulence has been associated with most of the other gates we have encountered."

"All of which is academic," Kirk said abruptly, "if we can't find our way back out of here. For a start, let's see if we still have any control over the shuttlecraft."

Experimentally, Spock sent a command.

The shuttlecraft obeyed, turning its bow toward the *Enterprise.*

In quick succession, then, he put the views from the shuttlecraft on the screen. The one provided by the Aragos-modified sensors showed only chaos, as if they were being overloaded or were receiving only static. The image from the shuttlecraft camera showed essentially the same scene that the *Enterprise* viewscreen had shown, except that the *Enterprise* itself, not the shuttlecraft, floated in the midst of the diffuse grayness that obscured everything else—if, indeed, there was anything out there to obscure.

Kirk punched the button for the engineering deck. "Status report, Mr. Scott."

"All systems fully operational, Captain," Scott replied, a touch of pride mixed even then with the tense uneasiness in his voice. *"If no' for what I see on the screen, there'd be no way o' telling we'd been taken on this wee detour."*

"It's nice to know that *something* is working the way it's supposed to. Thank you, Mr. Scott."

Switching off, Kirk glanced around the bridge. The two security guards still stood flanking the turbolift door. McCoy and the orderly were near the unoccupied engineering station. Commander Ansfield was watching Chekov at the science station. Lieutenant Uhura flicked a final switch and turned to Kirk.

"No activity on any frequency, Captain, subspace or otherwise."

"I can't say that I expected any in here. Wherever 'in here' is. Mr. Sulu? Do our sensors show anything?"

"Only the shuttlecraft, sir."

"Mr. Spock? You're the one who suggested the existence of this space. You also suggested it might be the home of whatever it is we've been dealing with."

"I cannot, of course, be positive, Captain, but I have reason to believe that is true."

Almost everyone on the bridge glanced around uneasily. "What reason, Mr. Spock?" Kirk asked.

"It is difficult to explain logically, Captain."

"Then do it *il*logically," Kirk said, a touch of irritation edging his voice. "But do explain it."

"As you wish, Captain." His voice as impassive as ever, Spock recounted his experience between the moment the ship had entered the gate and the moment "reality" had returned. Except for uneasy glances toward the viewscreen and the featureless fog it displayed, there were no reactions. Even McCoy only grimaced, saying nothing.

For several seconds after Spock finished, there was only silence.

Finally, Kirk glanced at the others. "My own impression of the time we spent in—in limbo was more on the order of minutes. Dr. McCoy? Sulu?"

"Only seconds, Jim," McCoy said.

"A minute, possibly two," Sulu added, and the others chimed in with other estimates. No estimate approached that of Spock himself.

"As you would say, Mr. Spock, fascinating," Kirk said. "Analysis? Comments?"

"Fascinating indeed, Captain. It has often been

proven that, without external physical cues, one's perception of time is extremely subjective. It would seem logical that if even those cues provided by one's physical body—heartbeat and respiration, for example—are removed as well, the degree of subjectivity would increase even more. Our experiences would appear to bear that out."

Kirk nodded. "And this 'entity' you encountered—"

"I could not say that I encountered it, Captain, only that I was aware of its existence, as, to a much lesser degree, I am still aware of its existence. I did not encounter it in the sense that you and Captain Chandler encountered it."

"But you said it wanted something? But you had no idea what?"

"Correct, Captain."

"And there was no evidence, no feeling, of hostility?"

"None, Captain, nor of friendship. There was only a feeling of—perhaps *need* would be an appropriate description."

McCoy, listening silently until now, snorted. "What it probably 'needs' is another meal, the kind it got from Ensign Stepanovich!"

"Meal, Dr. McCoy?" One eyebrow angling slightly upward, Spock turned to the doctor.

"It's plain as the points on your ears, Spock. This thing, whatever the blazes it is, gets its jollies by scaring people to death. You must remember that—that obscenity on Argelius 2!"

"Of course, Doctor. That entity, similarly incorporeal, obtained its sustenance from the emotional emanations of humans that it frightened and killed, as it had done previously, while inhabiting a human body on your nineteenth-century Earth."

"The body of a bloodthirsty killer named Jack the Ripper!" McCoy snapped.

"Who was also, if I'm not mistaken, a physician," Spock pointed out.

"Before that thing took him over, yes!" McCoy sputtered. "After that, he was nothing but a butcher!"

"I was merely stating a fact, Doctor. I did not mean it to be taken personally."

"Bones," Kirk said warningly, cutting off another retort. "Spock."

McCoy scowled silently for a moment, then shook his head. "Sorry, Jim."

"Any opinion on Dr. McCoy's suggestion, Mr. Spock?"

"Only that it would appear to be invalid, Captain."

"Why, Mr. Spock?"

"There are too many dissimilarities, Captain. The being we encountered on Argelius 2 took over a body and then used that body to commit atrocities against other people. It absorbed the emotional emanations from its victims, not from its host. The present being appears to induce terror in its host simply by its presence."

"Terror that results in suicide or in attack on others," Kirk said. "I see your point. However, just because this being operates differently from the one on Argelius 2 doesn't mean that they can't be similar. Perhaps this one employs mental rather than physical means to induce the emotions it feeds on."

"I cannot logically deny that possibility, Captain. I

can only say that, based on my own experience, there is no evidence that it feeds on these emotions."

"All right, then . . ." Kirk thought for a moment. "Do you find any of the other theories more acceptable? What about the suggestion that the gates are the cosmic equivalent of a rat warren, and the entities are the equivalent of rat poison, something to keep us lower life-forms under control?"

"That could be a more tenable theory, Captain. The entity or entities, with their ability to inspire fear and trigger suicidal wars, would appear to be a rather effective poison to virtually anyone using or even approaching the gates. That theory, however, would still not account for my distinct impression that the entity needs something from us."

"And since when have you Vulcans begun to believe in anything as illogical as impressions?" McCoy asked with a snort.

"Impressions are neither logical nor illogical, Doctor. They simply exist. It is only what one does in response to impressions that could be considered in those terms. If I were to—"

"And you have no theory of your own," Kirk broke in, "to account for this supposed need?"

"I do not have enough facts to justify the formulation of a theory, Captain. I can only state that, though the sensation I experienced could be described as fear, I experienced no accompanying sense of either malice or menace."

McCoy snorted again. "You're not saying this thing is *harmless,* are you, Spock?"

"Of course not, Doctor. I am merely saying that I sensed no *intention* to harm."

"Then I'm sure we can all die happy, knowing our killer didn't *intend* to kill us!" Turning, McCoy stalked off the bridge. The orderly who had accompanied him had barely enough time to dart into the turbolift before the doors hissed shut.

For a moment, Kirk frowned after the doctor, wondering uneasily if McCoy's sharp reactions were solely the result of his own rough-edged personality and the natural tension of the situation they found themselves in or if he had been influenced by the entity that Spock indicated was still nearby. For another moment, he searched his own feelings, looking for some trace of the terror he had felt and fought before.

But if it was there, it was too weak to be discovered by such a purely intellectual search through the welter of other emotions—tensions—that, though under control, were nevertheless a constant pressure. Whether his uneasiness over their present situation was any more intense than it would normally be, he couldn't tell.

"Mr. Spock," he said. "Bring the shuttlecraft in. I think it's about time we started looking into the possibility of getting out of here. It is possible, isn't it?"

"I have no way of being positive, Captain," Spock said as he began maneuvering the shuttlecraft toward the rear of the *Enterprise* and the hangar deck doors. "But we have no reason to assume it is not. As you know, we have apparently passed through this space twice before, only at a much more rapid pace. The obvious difficulty lies in determining the direction in which the entrance to the gate lies."

"And the difficulty of determining just when to go back through, assuming we can find it in the first place?"

"That may not be a problem, Captain, if what I suspect is true."

"And that is?"

Spock paused a moment, devoting his full attention to bringing the shuttlecraft in for a landing on the hangar deck. As the massive doors clamshelled shut behind it, he resumed.

"I suspect, Captain, that this particular space is permanently linked to the entrance we were drawn through. Do not forget that the gate had already begun its cycling when we entered. The shuttlecraft had entered during the so-called quiescent phase, whereas we entered approximately forty-seven seconds later, during an active part of its cycle. Even so, both the *Enterprise* and the shuttlecraft are here, together."

Kirk was silent a moment, glancing at the screen. "Very well, Mr. Spock," he said. "That's one difficulty we may not have to deal with. However—"

"Captain!" Uhura cut in sharply. "Something's out there! Something is trying to communicate with us!"

Chapter Eleven

"PUT IT ON the screen, Lieutenant," Kirk said instantly.

"It's not a visual signal, Captain. Or voice."

"That doesn't leave a lot, Lieutenant. What *is* it?"

"Apparently some kind of code, sir. And it's a—a standard radio frequency, not subspace."

"Standard radio?"

"Yes, sir, an old-style electromagnetic signal, of the kind normally limited to use in the immediate vicinity of a planetary surface."

"And the code?"

"Our communications equipment can receive it, but the computer will have to decipher it."

Spock moved quickly to the science station, while Sulu stepped aside and returned to the helm.

Spock inspected the readouts briefly and then called up another series. "The code appears to be a comparatively crude construct designed for direct communication between certain old-style computers, Captain," he said, one eyebrow angling minutely upward. "Federation computers have required nothing like it for at least a century."

"And the source? Another ship? A planetary body somewhere in here?"

"Unknown, Captain. Nothing physical registers on the sensors. The radiation is simply there, totally nondirectional. It is, literally, coming at us with equal strength from all directions, not unlike the background microwave radiation that permeates our universe."

"Can the ship's computer decipher it?"

"Also unknown, Captain. However, the computer can, of course, absorb the raw data into its memory banks and then attempt to analyze them for intelligible content."

"Very well, Mr. Spock, feed it into the computer. But monitor everything that passes through that link. And set the link to shut down automatically if information should start to flow the other way."

"As you wish, Captain." He worked the controls and then watched. "The data transfer rate is unusually slow," he observed after a few seconds.

For nearly an hour, the data continued. All efforts to locate the source failed. Their entry into the gate—into this bubble of seemingly real space in the midst of the nothingness—must have somehow triggered the transmission.

Finally, it stopped. For another few seconds, the electromagnetic signal—now an empty carrier—remained, like the blank leader tape at the end of an old-fashioned video or audio tape. Then it, like the code, simply vanished.

Spock watched the readouts as the computer began its analysis.

After less than a minute, one eyebrow again angled upward slightly.

"Yes, Mr. Spock?" Kirk prompted when Spock continued to watch the readouts silently.

Spock remained silent another few seconds, then straightened and turned. "It appears, Captain, that we have been given a map."

"A map?" Kirk frowned. "Of what?"

"I can only assume, Captain, that it is a map of at least some portion of the system of gates."

"Of more immediate interest, can it get us out of here—and back to the Sagittarius arm rather than a battle zone halfway across the universe?"

"If the computer analysis is reliable, Captain, yes. There is what appears to be a short series of navigational commands highlighted."

"Then let's do it, Mr. Spock."

"Of course, Captain."

Two minutes later, with the ship's computer using the highlighted navigational commands to control the helm, the *Enterprise* oriented itself. Or so the instruments said. Visually, there was no way of telling that it was doing anything at all.

Then, with quarter impulse power applied, the *Enterprise* surged ahead.

Everyone, particularly Spock, braced for another protracted bodiless passage through limbo.

It didn't come.

Instead, the trip was, as far as anyone, including Spock, could tell, as rapid as either of the two previous trips through the gate. One instant, they were surrounded by gray nothingness. The next instant, the stars of the Sagittarius arm surrounded them.

The chronometer showed that only milliseconds had been absorbed by the emergence.

Behind them, the gate put on the same spectacularly chaotic show for the sensors that it had before, while appearing to be totally nonexistent in visible light.

"Lieutenant Uhura," Kirk said when they were safely away, a billion kilometers from the gate. "Open a channel to Starfleet Headquarters."

"Right away, sir."

"Mr. Scott."

"Aye, Captain." Scotty's voice came from the intercom.

"Now that we're back in normal space, Mr. Scott, run a complete check—and I mean *complete*—of all ship's systems. I want to know if anything, anything at all, was affected in even the slightest way by our stay in that limbo inside the gate."

"Aye, Captain, but I dinna think—"

"Just do it, Mr. Scott," Kirk snapped, and then, his voice softening, he went on. "Between the stress of the gravitational turbulence that pulled us in and prolonged exposure to totally unknown conditions, anything could have happened. And if we're going to make use of this map we've been given, we'll be spending a lot more time in there. Before we go back in, I want to know if anything has changed, not just for the worse but if anything works better than before, or differently—in *any* way. I want all the information you can give me about the effect of our exposure so I can at least make an educated guess about what, if anything, even more exposure will cause."

There was a brief pause, and then, *"Aye, Captain, I see what ye mean, but it'll take time."*

"We're not going anywhere until you finish, Scotty."

"Aye, Captain. I'll let ye know."

Glancing toward Uhura as he punched the buttons to connect him to sickbay, Kirk saw that she was still waiting for a response from Starfleet.

"What is it, Captain?" McCoy's gravelly voice responded.

"Bones, Scotty is giving the ship a thorough physical. I'd like you to do the same for a few crew members."

"Did you have anyone particular in mind, or do I have them draw straws for the honor?"

"Pick some at random," Kirk said, ignoring the sarcasm in McCoy's voice. "Say, those due for their physicals in the next week anyway. But for the others, talk to as many as you can, find out how much subjective time each of them experienced during that period after we were pulled into the gate. Select your subjects to get a good sample from several points in the range, from those, like Spock, who thought hours may have passed, to the ones who felt only seconds passed."

"No one I've talked to so far thinks anything more than a few minutes could have gone by, so if you want someone who thought he was in there for hours, you'd better send Spock down."

"If it comes to that, I will." He glanced at Spock. "Meanwhile, get the checks started. And make them thorough, everything your machines down there can do—and more, if you can think of a way."

"Aye-aye, sir," McCoy said, both the words and the stiff tone uncharacteristic of the doctor.

"If I might suggest it, Captain," Spock said when McCoy had signed off, "a check of Dr. McCoy himself would not be amiss."

Kirk nodded. "I know, Mr. Spock. I assume the changes are, if anything, the effect of this entity you tell me is still lurking in the wings."

"Or a residual effect of the disembodied state we experienced after entering the gate, Captain. I noted unexpected changes in my own outlook during that period, but I believe I have been able to compensate for them. Dr. McCoy, who can sometimes be exceedingly human, may not have been as successful."

"Captain," Uhura broke in. "I have a channel to Starfleet Headquarters."

"Thank you, Lieutenant," he said, turning sharply in the command chair. "This is Captain James T. Kirk of—"

"I know who you are, Jim," the familiar voice of Admiral Noguchi interrupted with uncharacteristic brusqueness. *"Where have you been? We have been trying to contact you for the last three hours."*

"We were inside the gate, Admiral, until—"

"Inside? You did not request permission for such a maneuver, Captain!"

Kirk frowned. "I didn't realize it was required, Admiral. The *Enterprise* was sent here to do a job. I assumed we were authorized to do whatever was necessary."

There was a long pause, longer than could be

accounted for by subspace delay alone. When Noguchi spoke again, his voice was less harsh, still that of an admiral to a captain but with a touch of family friend and, to a lesser extent, mentor.

"You were, Captain, of course," he said. *"Tell me, what did you find?"*

"Most importantly, Admiral, we have what Mr. Spock tells me is a map of the gate system."

"A map? But how—? Never mind, Jim. I have the feeling you had better start from the beginning. What happened?"

Quickly, Kirk summarized everything that had happened since their decision to send a shuttlecraft into the gate.

"Remarkable," Noguchi said when he had finished. Kirk could almost hear the admiral shaking his head. *"You do have a knack for stumbling into the jackpot, Jim."*

"Thank you, sir," Kirk said, smiling. Though their face-to-face contacts had been few since Noguchi had given him the *Enterprise* and its first assignment, their relationship had grown over the years, one aspect of which was the admiral's seeming bemusement at the number of startling discoveries Kirk and his ship had figured in.

"However," Noguchi said, sobering, *"you are not to use that map, and you are not to reenter that gate or any other until further notice."*

Kirk's smile vanished into a frown. "Not *use* it, sir? I don't understand."

"Three hours ago, at approximately the time you were being dragged into that gate in the Sagittarius arm, a new gate appeared less than a parsec from

Starfleet Headquarters. The gravitational turbulence that marked its appearance was such that, had it been in the vicinity of a planetary system, the planets' orbits would have been seriously disturbed. Had it appeared within a system, it would have virtually destroyed any planet within a billion kilometers."

"You certainly don't think there's a connection, Admiral?"

"I don't know. Mr. Spock can calculate odds better than I. For the moment, however, you are not to reenter that gate under any circumstances." Noguchi paused. *"You will return to Starfleet Headquarters. We will use our own computers to perform the analysis."*

"But the entity that Spock encountered will in all likelihood still be with us. If it attaches itself to someone in Starfleet Headquarters—"

"I am confident that we will be able to cope, Captain."

"With all due respect, Admiral, you have not experienced it directly. I have. I have felt its power, and I have seen what it can do to others. Ensign Stepanovich of the *Cochise* was—"

"Ensign Stepanovich had little experience dealing with alien life-forms. Rest assured, we will take every precaution."

"The gate here needs to at least be monitored, Admiral," Kirk pointed out.

"The Devlin *is not more than a dozen parsecs from your present position. They will monitor the gate. Now, Captain Kirk, if you're finished debating, you will return to Starfleet Headquarters!"*

Kirk frowned but said, "Very well, Admiral. We'll get under way as soon as the *Devlin* arrives."

"Now, *Captain Kirk! Leaving the gate unmonitored for the few hours it will take the* Devlin *to reach it is of less importance than getting this map of yours into our computers for a full analysis. Understood, Captain?*"

"Understood," Kirk said stiffly, knowing it would be pointless to suggest transmitting the map via subspace link. Despite Noguchi's words, the admiral's prime concern was obviously not the delivery of the map to Starfleet Headquarters. It was to keep the *Enterprise* from reentering the gate.

"Good," Admiral Noguchi said, and the connection to Starfleet was broken.

Kirk glanced around the bridge. "We have our orders. Mr. Sulu, lay in a course for Starfleet Headquarters."

"Aye-aye, sir, but the helm is still rigged as a remote control for the shuttlecraft."

"Will the extra connections interfere with normal operation?"

"No, sir. As long as the shuttlecraft is deactivated—"

"Then keep it deactivated. According to the admiral, we can't afford the time to disconnect the special circuits until we're under way. Lay in the course, Mr. Sulu, and get us moving, warp factor six."

"Aye-aye, Captain," Sulu responded, with only the briefest of sideways glances in Spock's direction.

"Mr. Scott," Kirk said, activating the intercom to engineering. "Pending your approval at the completion of your check of all systems, we will be increasing to warp factor eight. Meanwhile, I'd like a progress report."

"Captain, I would no' recommend—"

"Nor would I, under normal circumstances," Kirk said sharply. "Starfleet, however, considers time to be of the essence. Now, that progress report, please."

"Aye, Captain," Scott said, the reluctance obvious in his sighing tone. *"I would estimate another hour till completion o' the checks you requested."*

"And the results so far, Mr. Scott?"

"All systems are fully operational, Captain, and no irregularities have been detected anywhere."

"Thank you, Mr. Scott. Inform me the moment your checks are complete."

"Aye, Captain," Scott said, in much the same tone that Kirk had used in his final words with Admiral Noguchi. *"But ye do realize what would happen if a problem* did *develop at warp eight?"*

"I realize the dangers, Mr. Scott," Kirk said, but as he spoke, he felt a shiver ripple up his spine. No one knew precisely what would happen if the warp drive failed at such speeds. There were several theories, each worse than the last, but reality, Kirk suspected, could be the worst of all. "Just make sure a problem *doesn't* develop."

"Aye, Captain," Scott said, breaking the connection abruptly.

"Mr. Sulu?"

"Course laid in, Captain."

"Ahead warp factor six, then, Mr. Sulu."

"Aye-aye, sir."

With another brief glance toward Spock, Sulu executed the command, and the *Enterprise* surged forward. The brilliance of the relativistic starbow filled the screen for a second before it was replaced by the computer-generated image of the star field ahead.

"Now, Mr. Spock, what can you and the computer tell us about this map we seem to have been given?"

"As much, I suspect, as the computers at Starfleet Headquarters."

Kirk smiled faintly, briefly. "I suspect as much myself. Proceed."

"Very well, Captain. First, calling it a map is perhaps misleading in that the points—the destinations—it identifies are not laid out as, for example, a star chart of the Federation is laid out. A more accurate term would be *descriptive list,* primarily of the destinations that can be reached from the Sagittarius arm gate."

"And it tells you—or the computer—how to reach each of these destinations?"

"It does, Captain, in terms of the time during the cycle at which the gate must be entered. The starting point of each cycle was, as I suspected, the forty-four-second 'quiescent state.' All times are measured from the end of that forty-four-second period. Based on a preliminary analysis, the destination we reached during our first, accidental entry can be reached only once during each cycle, fifty-three minutes and ten seconds into the cycle. All other destinations can be reached at least twice during each cycle. Many can be reached dozens of times."

"Could it be unique in that respect," Kirk asked, "because it is so distant?"

"That is possible, Captain. However, that destination is unusual, though not unique, in another respect. It is one of only a dozen for which secondary destinations are shown."

"Secondary destinations?"

"Destinations that can be reached through the gate that exists at those destinations but cannot be reached directly through the Sagittarius arm gate, Captain. Though I cannot be positive from the existing data, it would appear that this gate serves, in effect, as a hub for thousands of destinations, and those other gates serve, in turn, as hubs for a similar number of other destinations, although only a small number of these secondary destinations are actually shown."

Kirk was silent for several seconds, aware once more of the shiver that crept along his spine but unsure whether it signaled the return of the entity that had previously descended on Chandler and himself or was simply his own visceral reaction to the magnitude of what Spock had said.

"That would mean millions of destinations, Spock," he said finally, "just in the first two stages."

"Precisely, Captain."

For a moment, Kirk seemed lost in the immensity of this thing they had stumbled onto, but then he pulled himself back to practical reality. "How does it identify the destinations? Does it indicate anything at all about their locations? Their distances?"

"Nothing, Captain. There is a code number for each, originally in a base-twelve numbering system. For the hub gates and a small number of others, there are also what appear to be three-dimensional star charts for the areas immediately surrounding the gates. For the Sagittarius arm gate itself, there is a quite extensive chart, showing all major stars within thirty parsecs."

"Put it on the screen."

"As you wish, Captain."

A moment later, the auxiliary screen over the science station was alive with hundreds of stars.

Commander Ansfield, who had been watching silently the whole time, frowned. "That doesn't look right, Spock. The pattern doesn't look right."

Kirk frowned as he glanced at her. "You remember the star patterns that well, Commander?"

"I may be dense in some areas, Kirk, but my memory is close enough to photographic to have gotten me through the Academy a year ahead of schedule. Those are not the patterns I saw. Spock, are you sure this is the right chart?"

"One-hundred-percent certainty is impossible, Commander." He paused, studying the display as it slowly rotated. "But you are right. This is not the pattern we observed. However, I believe it is indeed the correct chart."

Quickly, precisely, Spock tapped a code into the computer. As he finished, a second star pattern, the stars in this one tinted green, was superimposed on the screen.

"That's the pattern," Ansfield said. "Where—"

She cut herself off as he tapped in a second code and the green-tinted stars began to move slowly.

For more than thirty seconds, they continued to move, drifting slowly in every direction until, finally, the two patterns matched.

Ansfield swore under her breath. "How long ago?" she asked, almost in a whisper.

Spock consulted a reading. "Approximately ninety thousand years," he said.

"If the two of you wouldn't mind letting us laymen in on the secret," Kirk said, "I would appreciate it."

"Sorry, Kirk," Ansfield said. "I thought you were following along. That second pattern Spock put up, those were the stars surrounding the gate *now*. As I'm sure you know, a starship's automatic mapping function requires its computers to automatically record the proper motions of all stars within several parsecs whenever they emerge from warp drive in previously unexplored territory. All Spock had to do was tell the computer to project those motions backward in time until the patterns matched."

"Precisely, Commander," Spock said in answer to Kirk's brief, questioning glance. "The patterns matched at eighty-nine point three thousand years in the past."

"Which means," Kirk said, "that the gate system— this part of it, at least—has been abandoned for almost ninety thousand years."

"Or that that's the last time they bothered to update their maps," Ansfield said. "If whoever runs these gates is anything like Starfleet, they just may not have been keeping up with their paperwork."

Kirk started to smile, thinking once again how Commander Ansfield reminded him of McCoy, but then, suddenly, the chill that had been sporadically brushing at his spine gripped it solidly, sending a shudder through his entire body. Automatically, his eyes darted about the bridge.

"Spock," he said sharply. "It feels as if your friend is back."

"I know, Captain. I feel it as well."

Bracing himself for an assault like the one he had experienced before, Kirk tensed, his fingers gripping the edges of the arms of the command chair. Ansfield, he saw, was watching him worriedly, and he could feel the eyes of everyone on the bridge.

But then, as abruptly as it had come, the chill was gone.

But not completely.

"All decks," he snapped, activating the shipwide intercom. "The entity has returned. Everyone on full alert. Phasers—"

"Captain!" Sulu, stiffening and jerking his hands back from the helm controls, almost screamed. "It's me! It's got *me!*"

Chapter Twelve

THE SECURITY TEAM flanking the turbolift doors stepped forward, phasers drawn and leveled.

"Don't fire—yet!" Kirk said quickly. "Mr. Sulu, can you hold on? Can you keep control?"

"I *think* so, Captain," Sulu grated between clenched teeth.

"Good." Kirk activated the intercom to McCoy's office. "Bones, get up here. It's got Sulu."

"On my way, for all the good it'll do," McCoy said, irritation as well as concern evident in the sharpness of his voice.

"Mr. Spock, take the helm."

Sulu, struggling to stand up and pull away from the helm controls, suddenly went limp, hitting the deck with a thud. Kirk was on his feet instantly, then kneeling next to the helmsman, but before he could say anything, Spock, in the midst of stepping down from the science station to the helm, stiffened abruptly.

"Captain," he said, his voice unnaturally stiff,

almost mechanical. "I believe it is now making an attempt on me."

"If anyone can hold out—"

Chekov, at the navigator's station, gasped and almost screamed, his hands darting sideways toward the helm controls before they stopped, trembling.

Spock, apparently released after only a few seconds, staggered as if, like Sulu moments before, his muscles were betraying him. Sulu himself, pale and breathing heavily, was already struggling to his feet.

Chekov, grimacing, working his mouth as if trying to speak, began to reach for the helm controls again, but before he could touch them, before the recovering Spock or Sulu could reach him, one of the security guards fired.

But Chekov didn't fall.

Instead, he lurched violently sideways toward the helm, crashing into the helmsman's chair and sprawling over it facedown.

For a moment he lay there, motionless. Spock, apparently fully recovered from his own brief contact, reached down to lift him from the chair.

But as his fingers neared Chekov's arms, Chekov began to move again, and Spock pulled back, watching.

Slowly, Chekov got his arms under himself and, pressing against the seat of the helmsman's chair, pushed himself up.

"Mr. Chekov," Kirk began, but he cut himself off as Chekov raised himself enough to allow his face to be seen.

The eyes were closed, the mouth hanging partially

open, as if all the facial muscles were relaxed. Slowly, he turned to face the helm controls.

The turbolift doors hissed open, and McCoy burst through, followed by the same orderly who had accompanied him earlier. The security team turned toward them sharply, phasers still drawn, but almost immediately they turned back to Chekov and the others near the helm.

"Get your tricorder on Mr. Chekov, Dr. McCoy," Kirk said sharply.

"What the blazes—" McCoy began, but then he, too, saw Chekov's face. Frowning, he hurried forward, unsheathing the tricorder's scanner as he went. "What happened to him?"

"He was struck by a phaser on medium stun a few seconds ago," Kirk said.

"Then what the devil's he doing moving around?" McCoy snapped. "He'd be out cold if he'd been—"

Simultaneously, Chekov's eyes opened and McCoy brought the tricorder scanner within range of Chekov.

McCoy's jaw dropped as he looked at the tricorder screen. "He *is* out cold—according to this. Then what—"

"I suspect, Doctor," Spock said, "that the entity that earlier attached itself to Captain Kirk has now attached itself to Mr. Chekov. It had, only moments earlier, attempted to attach itself first to Mr. Sulu and then to myself. Now, because Mr. Chekov himself was presumably rendered unconscious by the phaser, the entity is temporarily without opposition and is in control of Mr. Chekov's body."

As if to confirm Spock's words, Chekov turned to

face the helm, lowering his now open, unblinking eyes to the controls.

"And you're all just standin' around *watching?*" McCoy turned abruptly to the orderly who had followed him onto the bridge. "Here, give me a hand, and we'll get him down to sickbay where he belongs!"

As McCoy was speaking, one of Chekov's hands raised itself, slowly and uncertainly, toward the control board. Spock, still standing next to Chekov, watched until he saw which control the hand was reaching for, then reached out himself and grasped Chekov's wrist.

At the touch, Chekov's entire body stiffened spasmodically, and Spock himself felt some of the same irrational fear that had surged through him minutes before when the entity had tried to attach itself to him. Obviously, though the entity remained confined in Chekov's body, it could still have a powerful effect on anyone who came close enough.

"Spock, what the blazes are you doing *now?*" McCoy rasped as he reached for Chekov's other arm in an automatic comforting move.

But instead of being comforted, Chekov—the entity that was controlling Chekov's body—jerked violently, trying to pull away from McCoy's touch and tear himself out of Spock's relentless grip. No longer was he trying to reach the helm controls. He was simply trying to escape, thrashing violently in all directions. Spock, now gripping both of Chekov's arms as much in an attempt to keep him from damaging himself as to keep him from accidentally striking the helm controls, began to pull Chekov away.

"Security, give Mr. Spock a hand!" Kirk snapped.

Phasers still in hand, they hesitated a moment but then hurriedly put them away and moved forward, past McCoy.

As they touched Chekov, trying to grasp his legs and waist, they froze momentarily, their eyes widening, but they didn't pull back.

An instant later, after one final spasmodic outburst, Chekov collapsed.

For a long moment, there was only silence as a dozen pairs of eyes darted in all directions, looking for the next victim.

Then Spock, lowering Chekov gently to the deck, said, "The entity has withdrawn."

"But for how long?" Kirk asked. "And what was it trying to accomplish?"

"To return to the gate, I suspect, Captain," Spock said. "At the moment I attempted to restrain Mr. Chekov, he was reaching for the control that would have reversed our course."

"And you still sensed no hostility? No menace? Even before, when it was attempting to take you over?"

"None, Captain. I felt only the irrational fear generated in my own mind and in that of Mr. Chekov."

"Thank you, Mr. Spock," Kirk said, and then, after a moment's silence, he turned and stepped from the command chair toward the communications station. "Lieutenant Uhura, open a channel to Starfleet Headquarters again. Perhaps this latest development will change their minds."

By the time another orderly and a stretcher had

arrived to help McCoy transport Chekov to sickbay, Admiral Wellons of Starfleet Headquarters was on a voice link with the *Enterprise*.

"Admiral Noguchi is not available, Captain," Wellons said stiffly. *"But I see no reason to countermand his orders. That map you say you have may be invaluable."*

"Agreed, Admiral, but it won't be of any use to anyone at Starfleet Headquarters. The map tells nothing of how the gate operates, only where it goes. The only chance we have to learn something useful, something that can help us put a stop to this outbreak of new gates, something that can help us find a way to fight whatever it is that's coming *through* those gates, is to reenter the gate. In addition, the danger of infecting the Federation with this entity which has apparently attached itself to the *Enterprise* is greater than ever."

Irritably, Kirk began to outline what had happened in the last few minutes, but before he had more than begun, Admiral Wellons cut him off.

"Kirk!" Wellons snapped. *"I have had just about enough arguments for one day! Your reputation as a loose cannon on Starfleet's deck is well known to me. Out of respect for your family, Admiral Noguchi has often been more than lenient with you, but I will tolerate no more of it! No more! If you are incapable of obeying a simple command without wasting valuable time debating it like a rebellious Academy freshman, I will relieve you and turn the* Enterprise *over to someone who can! Is that understood?"*

"Understood," Kirk said, his voice brittle.

"Very well. Now, if there is no more—"

"I beg your pardon, Admiral," Spock broke in. "This is Lieutenant Commander Spock, and I must agree with the captain. Our own computer has already completed an analysis of the map which I am confident is as thorough as anything Starfleet computers could accomplish. Unless you possess information you are deliberately withholding from us, I would submit that our making systematic use of that map is the only logical course open to us. And finally, the captain has not exaggerated the danger of infection."

"You are both inviting court-martial! Are you planning to force me to have the Devlin escort you back to Starfleet headquarters? I will if you make it necessary."

"We understand, Admiral," Spock said, his voice as level as always. "We would, however, like to speak with Admiral Noguchi."

"The orders will be the same, no matter who you speak to! Others, however, may not be as tolerant as I have been!"

"Nonetheless—"

"You will return! Under arrest, the lot of you, if that is the only way!"

Spock did not respond for several seconds. Instead, he stood silently, as if listening to the subspace hiss that was all that came from the speakers. Kirk frowned but remained silent, knowing that Spock never acted irrationally, never acted without a reason. And to act—to interfere—as he had in the last two minutes, he must have a very powerful reason indeed.

"Do you hear me?" Wellons demanded, now sounding not only angry but distracted as well.

"We do hear you, Admiral," Spock said, a slight shift in tone apparently indicating capitulation. "We

122

are currently under way to Starfleet Headquarters at warp factor six. If we maintain that speed, we will arrive in approximately eleven point three nine standard days. Will that be satisfactory, sir?"

Another pause, and then, *"Yes, that will be satisfactory. Captain Kirk, does your first officer speak for you as well?"*

"Of course, Admiral," Kirk said quickly.

"Very well, Captain. You seem to have come to your senses. We will, however, alert the Devlin *to your misgivings."*

And the link was broken.

"Mr. Spock," Kirk said. "You have a reason—a logical reason—for everything you do, so I can only assume you have one for what you did just now. Including the way you worded your supposed compliance with Wellons's orders. *'If* we maintain that speed,' I believe you said."

"Yes, Captain, those were my words."

"All right. Why? Are you suggesting that, logically, we could ignore a direct order from Starfleet Headquarters?"

"I am, Captain. It is, I believe, our responsibility—our duty—under the circumstances."

"Circumstances? What circumstances?"

"It is my opinion, Captain, that our investigation of the gate is more vital than ever. Indeed, it could conceivably hold the only chance the Federation has for survival. Starfleet Headquarters, I fear, has already been infected."

Chapter Thirteen

SPOCK'S ANNOUNCEMENT BROUGHT total silence to the bridge.

"Very well, Mr. Spock," Kirk said finally. "Convince me."

"Lieutenant Uhura," Spock said, turning to the communications officer. "I assume you have a complete record of the exchange with Starfleet."

"Of course, Mr. Spock."

"Please play back the twelve point five seconds between Admiral Wellons's threat to have us arrested and his asking if we had heard him."

"But there was nothing said during that time."

"Nonetheless, Lieutenant, play it back."

With a puzzled glance toward Kirk, she complied. Spock, as he had before, listened silently. Then he tapped a code into the computer.

"I will now have the computer produce an enhanced version of that same period. The background of subspace noise will be suppressed, and all other sounds will be increased in volume and clarity."

"Your Vulcan hearing picked up something we humans missed, Mr. Spock?" Kirk asked.

"I believe it did, Captain. Listen."

Again, silence fell on the bridge.

And there was a voice. Even with computer enhancement, it was so faint as to be barely audible above the remaining background sounds—Wellons's rapid breathing, the rustle of his clothes as he moved restlessly, muffled footsteps on the plush carpets of a Starfleet office.

But the voice was there, and after a few moments a second voice and possibly a third broke in, all speaking at once. No words could be made out in the jumble, but the emotions were plain—a mixture of anger and fear.

And then, even fainter, the distinctive whine of a phaser and the sound of something striking the floor. An instant later, Wellons's voice, amplified to deafening proportions, returned and drowned out everything else.

"It is possible that further processing could bring out some of the words, Captain," Spock said. "But I believe this is enough to support my supposition. Though I cannot be positive, I believe that one of the voices in the background belonged to Admiral Noguchi."

"He's right, Kirk," Ansfield said. "My memory for voices is almost as good as my memory for star patterns. That was Noguchi all right."

"Let's hear it again," Kirk said quietly.

Wordlessly, Spock obeyed.

When the dozen seconds had passed again, Kirk was silent for another dozen.

"And the source of this infection?" he asked finally. "The massive gate that Admiral Noguchi said had appeared within a parsec of Starfleet Headquarters?"

"That is my assumption, Captain, although it is possible that other gates, even closer to Starfleet Headquarters, have appeared but have gone undetected."

"And the entity that you say has attached itself to us, Mr. Spock—considering everything that's happened, considering your belief that Starfleet Headquarters itself has been infected by something very much like it—doesn't it strike you as suspicious that it seems to want us to return to the gate? Perhaps it wants to keep us away from the Federation, so that the other infection will have sufficient time to spread"

"Even if we increased our speed to warp eight, Captain, it would take us six standard days to reach Starfleet Headquarters. If the infection is indeed going to spread, that would give it more than sufficient time. Also, it must be taken into account that, as of this moment, we possess no knowledge or weapons with which to combat that spread."

"You're saying, then, that we should accede to its desire to return to the gate?"

Spock nodded. "I believe we should—though it would be more accurate to say that what we tentatively perceive as its desire coincides, for the moment, with what we tentatively perceive as our own best interests and those of the Federation."

"And the likelihood that we will find something in the gate system that will allow us to fight the infection?"

"I cannot say—but I estimate the odds for success

to be significantly greater than those that would prevail if we were to return to Starfleet Headquarters at this time. I strongly suspect that there is little new knowledge to be gained there, whether the infection has spread drastically or not. Within the system of gates, however, from which this entity presumably has sprung, there is the potential for great gains in knowledge. And knowledge, not force, is obviously the Federation's only hope in the present circumstances."

Kirk pulled in a deep breath. Disobeying a Starfleet command, no matter what the reason, was not easy, would *never* be easy.

But Spock was right. Against whatever had come through those gates, force was obviously worse than useless. As it had been for the Aragos, and who knew how many others in how many other distant parts of the universe in the past ninety thousand years, force was literally suicidal.

"Very well, Mr. Spock," Kirk said. "The logic of the situation is inescapable. Mr. Sulu, reverse course. We're going back."

Captain Sherbourne, darker than Uhura, taller than Spock, glowered at Kirk from the *Enterprise* main viewscreen, his deep-set eyes pointedly avoiding Dr. McCoy's disgusted scowl. Around him, a small section of the bridge of the *Devlin* mirrored that of the *Enterprise*.

"*I repeat, Captain Kirk, lower your deflectors!*" his bass voice rumbled. "*I have my orders, directly from Starfleet Headquarters. You are hereby relieved of command. My first officer, Commander Bontreger, will beam over and take command of the* Enterprise *for the purpose of returning it to Federation territory. You, Captain Kirk, will surrender and be confined to quarters."*

"I'm sorry, Captain Sherbourne, but that's out of the question," Kirk reiterated, keeping his voice as level as he could. "We have explained our position. We have given you the evidence. You have heard the tape of what was going on in the background during our exchange with Admiral Wellons."

"Which you could have faked with ease, I'm sure. And even if it's genuine, it proves nothing."

Kirk sighed angrily, giving up the pretense of calmness, and continued. "We have even offered to transmit the map to your own computer so that you can analyze it and take it back to Starfleet yourself."

"At this point, getting the map to Starfleet Headquarters is of secondary importance! Of primary importance is your obeying orders and not reentering that gate!"

"Blast it, Sherbourne." McCoy, who had been grimacing silently throughout the exchange, broke in. "Can't you see what's at stake here?"

"Better than you, apparently, Dr. McCoy," Sherbourne said stiffly.

"Bones—" Kirk started to caution McCoy, but the doctor wasn't in the mood for caution.

"Your own ship's sensors showed you what happened on the Aragos planet!" he grated. "That whole civilization was literally wiped out! Ninety percent of its people were slaughtered! And it's already starting to happen to the Federation! You're just too blind to see it! Or too stubborn to accept it!"

"Dr. McCoy," Sherbourne said coldly. *"You have a reputation for rampant emotionalism. At the present time, however, you would be well advised to restrain yourself—before you find yourself sharing the precarious position in which your captain has unwisely placed himself."*

"I'm *already* sharing it! If you think—"

"Captain Sherbourne," Kirk broke in sharply. "Arguing is pointless. As my officers and I see the situation, I have no choice in this matter."

"As I see it, Captain Kirk," Sherbourne said stiffly, *"the streak of rashness you displayed during your Academy days has obviously become more pronounced over the years, until it has overwhelmed your rationality and your sense of duty. Whether you are simply misguided in this particular instance or were affected by whatever happened inside that gate, I have no way of knowing. All I know is, I did not come here at maximum warp just to disobey Starfleet orders myself and let you pass. You are not reentering the gate. Now, I order you for the last time, lower your deflectors."*

"Unless you plan to fire on another Federation ship—"

"If you force the decision upon me, I will, Captain Kirk, believe me. Unlike you, I truly have no choice in this situation."

Glancing at the chronometer, out of Sherbourne's view, Kirk saw that less than three minutes remained until they reached the point in the gate's cycle that they had selected. If they didn't enter the gate then, it would be more than four hours until the next destination for which the map listed a series of secondary destinations would come around, and by then a second ship would have arrived to back up the *Devlin*.

Kirk had risked warp eight in an effort to reach the gate before the *Devlin,* but Sherbourne, after an emergency call from Starfleet, had done the same. Sherbourne had also risked approaching the gate to within less than twenty million kilometers, and there he had waited, certain that the *Enterprise* couldn't slip by undetected.

And it hadn't.

The *Devlin,* all deflectors up, had put itself directly in the *Enterprise*'s path, and there it had remained while Sherbourne obstinately refused to budge despite the evidence Kirk and the others had presented.

"Captain Sherbourne," Kirk said. "For the sake of the Federation, I must take this chance. I would prefer entering the gate with my ship in peak operating condition, but entering it in any condition is preferable to remaining here or returning to Starfleet at this point, with nothing gained, with no hope to offer the Federation."

Sherbourne set his jaw firmly. *"That doesn't alter what I have to do, Captain."*

Kirk glanced again at the chronometer. "Mr. Sulu," he said. "No sudden moves, but take us ahead, impulse power. Scotty, put everything you can spare into the deflectors."

"Aye, Captain." Scott's voice came from the engineering deck.

"Damn it, Kirk!" Sherbourne half shouted over Scott's reply. *"I don't want to fire on you, but I will! Believe me, I will!"*

"I believe you, Captain Sherbourne. That's one reason we're maintaining our deflectors at maximum strength."

"Mr. Spock!" Sherbourne called. *"I haven't heard from you yet. Certainly you can't be going along with this insanity! It just isn't logical to risk everything—"*

"But it is quite logical, Captain Sherbourne," Spock said. "Based on what we have experienced—what the captain has told and shown you—it would be *illogical* for us to do otherwise."

"The way things are going," Ansfield added from her offscreen position next to Spock, "we're probably the only chance the Federation has!"

"I'm warning you," Sherbourne said, raising his voice and shaking his head angrily. *"I'm warning everyone who can hear me on the* Enterprise. *You will be fired upon! Even with full power to your deflectors, phasers and photon torpedoes can—"*

Sherbourne broke off as the *Devlin* helmsman spoke. *"All systems locked on, Captain. Ready to fire at your command."*

"You heard that, Kirk! Spock! Ansfield! All of you!"

"We heard, Captain Sherbourne," Kirk acknowledged tersely. "Mr. Sulu, ready for evasive maneuvers."

"Aye-aye, Captain. Ready."

"Captain Sherbourne," Kirk said. "We will not return fire, but—"

"Mr. Sulu," Spock said abruptly. "All stop."

"Spock!" Kirk turned toward the science station with a scowl. "What the devil—"

On the *Devlin,* Captain Sherbourne breathed a huge

sigh of relief. *"I knew a Vulcan couldn't be a part of this insanity, Spock,"* he said.

Ignoring Sherbourne, Spock stiffened, his eyes half closing for a moment. Kirk, his own eyes darting from Spock to Sherbourne and back, signaled to Sulu to follow Spock's lead. McCoy scowled at Spock but held his silence.

The *Enterprise* hung motionless less than a thousand kilometers from the *Devlin*.

"Be ready, Mr. Sulu," Spock said, his voice filled with the same stiffness it had displayed when the entity had attempted to take him over earlier. "Something is about to happen."

"Now what the blazes—" McCoy began, but he was cut off by a scream.

A scream from the *Devlin*.

"Full impulse power, Mr. Sulu. Now," Spock ordered, "while the *Devlin's* bridge is distracted."

As Sulu's fingers touched the controls, the *Enterprise* surged ahead. On the screen, Sherbourne was leaping from the command chair toward the helm. Just visible at the bottom of the screen, the helmsman's face appeared, twisted in a mask of terror as he leaped up from his station into range of the viewscreen.

In that moment, the *Enterprise* shot past the *Devlin*.

Ahead, the gate loomed large to the special sensors.

On the screen, the bridge of the *Devlin* was chaos. The helmsman had already collapsed, and the navigator started to scream. An instant later, the navigator fell, and then Sherbourne himself, now reaching past the fallen helmsman for the controls, stiffened as if paralyzed.

Just as Kirk himself had stiffened when the entity had descended on him.

"Spock!" Kirk snapped. "You knew this was going to happen!"

"I knew only that *something* was going to happen, Captain."

"But what's that thing *doing?*"

"Apparently, much the same as it was doing on the *Enterprise* bridge earlier, Captain."

"But why—"

"Captain," Sulu broke in sharply. "Entering gate in twenty seconds."

On the screen, still linked to that of the *Devlin*, Captain Sherbourne lurched forward, staggering, as if suddenly released from a set of invisible chains. An instant later, the helmsman and the navigator were struggling to their feet. For a moment, Sherbourne's deep-set eyes were blank, but then they focused abruptly on the screen.

Continuing his interrupted lunge toward the helm, Sherbourne slammed past the helmsman. *"Damn you, Kirk!"* he shouted as his fingers punched at the controls, bringing the *Devlin* around at a dangerous rate. *"I* knew *you'd made a deal with that—that* thing!"

"I'm sorry, Sherbourne," Kirk said, fighting down a sudden fear that the *Devlin*'s captain was right. "Tell Starfleet that if—*when*—we find an answer to the problem, we'll be back."

In a flare of color, the bridge of the *Devlin* vanished from the screen, replaced by the visual hiss of subspace static.

Simultaneously, the thousands of stars of the Sagittarius arm vanished, replaced by an emptiness that could only be that of intergalactic space.

"All stop, Mr. Sulu," Kirk snapped. "Mr. Spock, get that gate on the screen. We don't want to lose *this* one."

"Aye-aye, sir," Sulu responded, while Spock worked silently and efficiently with the sensor controls.

Within seconds, the main viewscreen was filled with the multicolored computer-generated image of the gate they had just emerged from. Like the one they had entered earlier, it was a massive, chaotic kaleidoscope, the colors and size shifting continuously. On an auxiliary screen over the science station, a visible-light image showed only the blackness of space, except for a cluster of minuscule specks of light in one corner.

"Lieutenant Uhura?"

"Nothing, Captain, on any frequency."

"Mr. Spock, is your friend still with us?"

"The entity is still present, Captain."

Involuntarily, Kirk shivered as the combination of the emptiness of space and the unseen presence that still lurked among them bore down on him, sending a chill rippling up and down his spine.

"And doing what?" he asked, pulling in a breath and tightly hunching his shoulders in a momentary effort to banish the chill.

"Unknown, Captain," Spock said. "It is simply present."

"Waiting to see what *we* do, I suppose."

"That is possible, Captain."

For a moment, Kirk looked at the auxiliary screen and the specks in one corner. They could be the Milky

Way galaxy and its satellites, or the Andromeda galaxy, or any of the millions of others that had been charted in the last three hundred years—or of the millions or billions still uncharted even now.

But the identity of those distant specks made no difference.

Whether the *Enterprise* was a million parsecs from the Federation, or a billion, or *ten* billion, was of no importance.

Resolutely, Kirk turned back to the main view-screen. This was what was important now, this thing that flashed and flickered and danced madly with some form of energy that only the Aragos sensors could detect. This constantly shifting opening in space itself that swallowed starships whole and spit them across the universe. This door to what was—perhaps—the home of a being that had annihilated countless civilizations over thousands of centuries and now threatened to annihilate the Federation.

Unless they could learn its secrets.

He punched a button on the command chair.

"Mr. Scott, any ill effects from our latest trip?"

"None that ye can notice, Captain," Scott's voice came back from the engineering intercom.

"Thank you, Mr. Scott." Kirk broke the connection. "We're going back in and hope that there's a different and more informative map associated with *this* gate. Mr. Sulu, take us to one kilometer. From that point, the computer will have the helm."

"Aye-aye, sir."

As before, the closer they approached, the more chaotic the sensors showed the gate to be. In visible light, it remained undetectable, no matter how close they came. There was, in fact, no way to tell it from the gate in the Sagittarius arm.

At one kilometer, Spock briefly studied the computer readouts, currently displaying the highlighted series of navigational commands that would guide them past the limbo lurking within the gate and into the bubble of "real space" hidden at its center. The second series, to guide them back to normal space, was displayed separately, not yet highlighted.

Kirk leaned forward in his chair. "All right, Mr. Spock," he said. "Whenever you're ready."

Coming as close as a Vulcan ever could to mentally crossing his fingers, Spock keyed in the code that sent the map's navigational commands to the helm.

The *Enterprise* aligned itself at a forty-five-degree angle to the gate and moved ahead.

After more than a minute, the forward edge of the saucer touched the surface of the gate and slowed. The sensors, almost a hundred meters back, on the front of the secondary hull, showed the surface of the gate, still swirling and flickering chaotically, begin to stretch and bend, as if it were an elastic membrane onto which the chaos was being projected.

Spock—and the rest of the bridge crew—watched the viewscreen intently. For five seconds, then ten, then fifteen, the apparent stretching continued, with the main hull of the *Enterprise* virtually surrounded by the crackling energies of the gate, even though, in visible light, nothing could be seen.

Then, in an instant, just as it had before, the universe vanished, and Spock found himself—his mind—floating free.

And listening.

Unlike the first time, he wasted no time with the chimera of false freedom that once again assaulted him. Knowing what to expect, he had prepared himself. It had been in this state when his sense of the entity that had attached itself to the *Enterprise* had been the strongest. This time, with that preparation, perhaps he could establish a stronger link, perhaps even gain some useful information.

But before he could more than form the thoughts in his mind, the same sense of dizzying, bodiless motion that had marked the beginning of the end of his stay in limbo that first time gripped him again.

And he was once again on the bridge of the *Enterprise*. Once again, all viewscreens operating on visible light showed only featureless grayness, a never-ending fog, while those fed by the Aragos-modified sensors showed patternless chaos.

According to the chronometer, less than a second had passed.

"Captain," Uhura called almost instantly. "A signal is coming in. It appears virtually identical to the one that gave us the map."

As before, the incoming signal was piped directly into the computer's memory banks.

"Dr. McCoy," Kirk said into the intercom once the data were flowing smoothly. "How is Mr. Chekov doing?"

"As well as can be expected." McCoy's harassed-sounding voice came back after a brief delay.

"And the physicals you were going to run—"

"Blast it, Jim, things haven't settled down long enough for me to do anything!"

"I know, Bones. But even if you can't do it yourself, get someone on it. We're flying blind in here, and I need all the information I can get—on everything."

McCoy was silent a moment before letting his breath out in an acquiescent sigh. *"I know, Jim. Chapel has three of the orderlies on the tables now, running all the checks. I suppose you want to interrupt her to see how she's doing."*

"Since you suggest it, yes."

"Yes, Captain?" Nurse Chapel's voice came a moment later. She had obviously been listening to the exchange.

"Any results yet?"

"Nothing that appears significant, Captain. All diagnostic readings and all tricorder readings are well within normal ranges. So far, there is no reading that appears to bear any correlation to the subjective time each felt he or she spent in 'limbo,' as you referred to it."

"Keep at it, Nurse. And notify me immediately if you *do* find anything—anything that looks even the least bit peculiar. Understood?"

"Of course, Captain."

As he switched from sickbay to engineering, he was certain he heard McCoy snort in the background.

"Mr. Scott?" he said a moment later. "All ship's systems still functioning properly?"

"Aye, Captain, no' so much as a bellyache," Scott answered. Then he added in a faintly accusing tone, *"Not even in the warp-drive engines, despite the strain ye put them under."*

"I'll try not to overwork your engines in the future, but try to keep them ready just in case."

Silently, then, Kirk settled back in the command chair, his eyes on the featureless grayness of the main viewscreen. His mind, however, roamed uneasily among the dozens of unanswerable questions that confronted him, until, finally, it came to an uncomfortable rest on the one that was both the most disturbing and, for now, the most unanswerable: could there be a degree of truth in the accusation Sherbourne had shouted after him?

Was he, no matter how unknowingly, doing precisely what the entity wanted?

The data transmission rate was no faster than before, but this time the signal cut off after less than half an hour.

"Take us back out," Kirk said abruptly once they were sure no more information was coming. "And we'll see what we were given *this* time."

Again, Spock keyed in the code that sent the navigational commands to the ship's computer. The ship oriented itself according to the map's commands, although the featureless gray that surrounded them still gave no indication of motion.

Impulse power came on.

Suddenly, the entire ship shuddered violently.

And vanished.

But this time, it wasn't a bodiless, sensationless limbo that everyone on the *Enterprise* was plunged into.

Instead, they were submerged in an ocean of pain, as intense and real as a thousand knives slicing through their flesh.

Chapter Fourteen

AUTOMATICALLY, SPOCK'S MIND retreated into the disciplines that allowed Vulcans to virtually isolate their conscious minds from their bodies whenever unbearable pains—or pleasures—descended on them.

But this time there was no body to retreat *from!*

There was only the same nothingness he had experienced before, but now it was filled with pain, more excruciating than any he had ever experienced, as if each and every nerve in his otherwise nonexistent body were being held to its own individual, searing flame. And it was heightened by his frustrating helplessness, by his inability to either pull away or strike back.

Finally, out of the ocean of pain, a logical thought emerged. *In this state,* his mind told him firmly, *my body does not exist; therefore, it is suffering no real physical damage. The pain is, in that sense, only an illusion, and illusions are of no importance.*

Suddenly, it was tolerable. Once the logic of the situation became clear to him, his mind could once more function almost normally.

And a thought came to him. *What of the others, the humans, with their almost nonexistent tolerance for pain and their totally inadequate mental discipline?*

Through the pain, he reached out to them, as he had before.

And, as he had before, he sensed their presence.

And touched them, feeling their own pain combine with his into one all-enveloping, molten nightmare, but a nightmare that was somehow easier to bear because of the sharing.

And the entity was there as well, still distant and withdrawn but experiencing the same agony. Not drinking it in or reveling in it, not even sharing it, but still experiencing it, even more intensely, Spock was certain, than himself or any of the others.

For the moment, the fear that had, until then, been the signature of its presence was gone, swallowed up by this new and different torment.

But the entity, Spock realized, was suffering yet another form of anguish. Before, in his first virtually timeless sojourn in limbo, he had sensed a need in the entity, a wordless, desperate need that had existed seemingly forever. And now, despite the pain the entity was suffering—or perhaps because of it—the need was even more intense.

And there was a form to that need.

A need to—absorb? To *be* absorbed? As Spock and the others, only moments before, had seemed to absorb each other, making the pain somehow more bearable for them all?

But there was more than a simple desire for the pain to fade.

It was a yearning, and for an instant it was as real as

141

if it were his own, and the suppressed yearnings of his own childhood, the unacceptable yearning for love and closeness with his parents, suddenly gripped him and twisted at him with an emotional ache that was almost the equal of the seemingly physical agony that still ripped at his phantom body.

But then, in a fraction of a second, all the torments were gone.

And the universe returned.

Spock's mind, though relieved of the emotional anguish and the illusory pain, was once more weighted down by his physical body.

Around him, the bridge sprang into existence. The others—

Instinctively, he caught Commander Ansfield as, ashen-faced, she lurched, half falling.

The others, seated, did not fall, but neither, in those first split seconds, were they entirely aware of their surroundings.

Spock's eyes went instantly to the main viewscreen. For a moment, it was blank, showing only total darkness. Then, as if a shrouded light had been turned on, a dozen massive ships of alien design, their images dark and fuzzily indistinct, appeared and began to expand dizzyingly as the *Enterprise* careened toward them on a collision course.

Releasing Ansfield, leaving her to lean heavily against the science station console, Spock vaulted the handrail and lunged for the helm, where Sulu was only then showing signs of regaining control of his body. In the command chair, Kirk was lurching to his feet in his own rubber-kneed effort to reach the helm. Behind him, at the communications station, Lieutenant Uhura was grimacing as she tried to straighten in her chair.

Spock's fingers stabbed at the helm controls, bringing the impulse engines to surging life and surrounding the *Enterprise* with the invisible shield of the deflectors.

For an instant, the ghostly images continued to grow alarmingly, but then, as the impulse engines reversed and took hold, the images stabilized.

"Good work, Mr. Spock." Kirk's voice, beginning to steady, came from just behind the first officer. On his feet now, the captain was leaning against the handrail. "But what the devil happened? And where did those ships come from?"

Abruptly, as if the indistinct images were only now fully registering, Kirk shook his head sharply, frowning. "And what wavelength is the computer using for its images? And the stars—"

There were, Kirk realized even as he spoke, no stars on the screen. Only the ships, massive and darkly indistinct. Beyond them was only empty space.

"Full sensor scan, Mr. Spock," Kirk snapped. "Mr. Sulu, override the computer and go to visible-light images."

"Aye-aye, sir," Sulu said as Spock stepped wordlessly from the helm and returned to the science station.

The viewscreen went blank.

"Mr. Sulu—" Kirk began, but Sulu was already speaking.

"There *is* no visible light, Captain," he said, his voice hushed in surprise.

143

"No visible light? That's impossible, Mr. Sulu!"

"I know, sir, but—" Sulu broke off, rechecking his controls. "But that's what I'm getting, sir. There is no visible light."

"No *stars?*"

"None, sir. The images of the ships previously on the screen were being produced by wavelengths far beyond infrared."

Kirk frowned. "Mr. Spock, what do the sensors show?"

"Only one ship registers on the sensors, Captain."

"Only one? There were at least eight or ten, and they were far from small!"

"I am aware of that, Captain. Nonetheless, the sensors show only one ship other than our own, and it is indeed quite large. Its mass, in fact, is approximately twice that of the *Enterprise*. In addition, its temperature is a uniform nineteen point six degrees Kelvin. That, of course, explains the extreme wavelengths the computer was forced to utilize to produce an image. The spectrum of black-body radiation at temperatures that close to absolute zero—"

"I remember my basic Academy physics, Mr. Spock," Kirk interrupted. "What else do the sensors show?"

"There are no indications of life or of functioning energy sources, Captain," Spock resumed, unperturbed, "although a mass of antimatter consistent with a warp-drive engine is present."

"And the other ships?"

Spock hesitated, his eyes flickering across the readouts, double-checking before replying. "As I have already stated, Captain, the sensors indicate the other ships do not exist."

Kirk shook his head disbelievingly. "Return control of the imaging to the computer, Mr. Sulu," he snapped. "Get those ships back on the screen. Lieutenant Uhura, are you picking up anything on any frequency, either subspace or standard?"

"Nothing, Captain, not even background static."

On the screen, a half-dozen ships appeared, and for a moment the images seemed to waver, as if they were reflections on the surface of a sea in whose hidden depths something silently patrolled.

"Which one registers on the sensors, Mr. Spock?"

Spock glanced at the screen, then returned to his instruments. "The largest, Captain, and presumably the nearest. It is the one in the upper left of the screen."

Kirk studied it briefly, intensely, then scanned the others. The ship in question was a massive pyramid, bulky and plodding-looking, probably a freighter of some kind. Of those the sensors insisted didn't exist, one had convoluted, menacing contours that reminded him of a Klingon scout ship magnified hundreds of times. Another resembled nothing he had ever seen before, lumpy and irregular, as if it had been grown rather than built from some purposeful design. Yet another was comparatively small and extremely sleek, its almost needlelike structure apparent even in the fuzzy long-wavelength image.

And one, almost as massive and blocky as the first, was dominated by a jagged hole over what may once have been a crew compartment.

Shaking his head again, Kirk turned from the main viewscreen toward the auxiliary screen that monitored the modified sensors.

Abruptly, a leaden tightness clutched at his stomach. The auxiliary screen, like the main screen moments before, was blank.

The kaleidoscopic energies of the gate should have filled half the sky—*had* filled it when the *Enterprise* had first emerged into this space, Kirk was positive— but now there was nothing.

The gate had vanished.

For a long moment, Kirk scowled at the blank screen, as if by concentration he could cause the gate to reappear. "Spock," he began, but before he could say more, the intercom from sickbay crackled on.

"What the blazes did we get into now?" McCoy's irritated voice filled the bridge.

"I have no idea, Bones, but—"

"Whatever it was, it knocked half a dozen people down here completely off their feet, including myself! They don't appear to have any permanent damage, but I'd just as soon we didn't have to go through it again, at least without warning!"

"I'll do my best, Doctor," Kirk said, irritation beginning to show in his own voice. "But since I haven't the faintest idea what happened, I can't give you any guarantees."

Swearing under his breath, McCoy broke the connection as Kirk punched up engineering. "Scotty, are we still in operation? The sensors—"

"I'll let ye know, Captain." The reply came sharply. *"As soon as I find out myself. For a minute there, I was no' sure I was still in operation. What did ye—"*

"If I find out what happened, I'll let you know. All I know now is that we're back in what may be normal space, but it's obviously not the normal space we left a half-hour ago. We need everything in top working order, Scotty. We may be stuck here for a while," he finished, glancing again at the blank auxiliary screen that, by all rights, should have been displaying an image of the gate they had just come out of.

Another momentary silence, then an indrawn, slightly ragged breath. *"Aye, Captain, I'll get back to ye."*

Kirk swiveled in his chair. "Any evidence of the gate, Mr. Spock?"

"None, Captain," Spock said.

"Could it be the sensors?" Kirk asked into the silence that followed Spock's words. "Could that shakeup have knocked the sensors out?"

"Their circuits are still performing precisely as they were before," Spock said, his matter-of-fact tone fully restored. "However, because we do not yet fully understand the functions of the Aragos modifications, we cannot be positive that the diagnostic programs are monitoring all the essential parameters."

"Which means what? That the gate really *is* gone but that you can't be sure?"

"That is essentially what I said, Captain. However, sensor readings immediately after our emergence from the gate indicated it *was* present—until approximately the moment impulse power was reversed and the *Enterprise* began to decelerate."

"So it *was* there. I wasn't imagining things when I thought I saw it on the screen, at least those first few seconds." Kirk shook his head. "If it hadn't been, we couldn't have come here in the first place! Without a gate to come through—"

Kirk stopped abruptly as a possible—and decidedly unwelcome—thought popped into his mind.

"We obviously didn't come back out through the same gate we entered," he said. "Is it possible that we came out through a gate like those others? Like the ones that have been appearing—and disappearing—in the Federation? Could we have come out through one of those and had it simply vanish behind us?"

"That is a possibility, Captain," Spock admitted. "The record of sensor readings simply indicates that the gate was present those first few seconds. There is no indication of its shape. But if your hypothesis is true, it would tend to confirm our original theory that those unstable gates are indeed connected to the system as a whole."

Kirk nodded grimly. "Not the pleasantest method of confirmation, however. But considering the way those gates looked—jagged and uneven, like 'rips in space,' someone said. Perhaps they're rips in the gate system itself. The system may simply be breaking down, which wouldn't be that surprising after more than ninety thousand years. It's springing leaks, and we just now slipped out through one of those leaks."

"It is a logical possibility, Captain, but by itself it would not account for the pain we experienced."

"It might. If we made our exit through a leak in the system, not through a gate, it could be the equivalent of being dragged out of a house through a broken window instead of walking out through an open door."

"An intriguing analogy, Captain," Spock said thoughtfully.

"Or it could have been caused by this friend of yours, couldn't it?" Kirk resumed. "This entity? If it can stir up raw emotions just by its presence, who's to say it can't do the same with physical sensation—or, rather, with a mental version of a physical sensation?"

"That, too, is possible, Captain, but I would tend to think it unlikely."

"Unlikely? Why?"

"Primarily because, while I sensed the entity's presence, I also sensed that it was experiencing pain similar to our own, perhaps even more intense. In addition, during my last encounter with it, I sensed what I can only describe as an exceedingly powerful desire to join with, perhaps even be absorbed by, some other sentient creature or creatures."

"You're saying it's *lonely?*" Uhura asked.

"That particular term is highly inadequate to describe the feelings that I sensed, but there is a grain of truth in it."

"If you're through shooting all this theoretical breeze," Commander Ansfield's impatient voice broke in, "maybe we can start thinking about more practical matters, like, for instance, where we are and what we're going to *do.*"

Kirk laughed sharply, as much a release of tension as anything else. "You're quite right, Commander," he said, turning toward the helm. "Mr. Sulu, give us a view in some other directions."

"Aye-aye, sir."

Sulu's fingers touched the controls, and the indistinct images began to shift across the screen as the field of view moved.

More ships appeared.

In every direction, there were ships, dozens of them, then hundreds, of all shapes, all sizes, even one that looked very much like a Federation cruiser, except that the lettering across the top of the primary hull bore not the least resemblance to any symbols stored in the library computer.

Roughly one in ten showed signs of massive damage, as if something had exploded inside the ships.

Not one registered on the sensors.

And not one showed any sign of activity, any lights, any life.

"It's like a graveyard, sir," Lieutenant Woida, Chekov's massive, blond replacement, said, unsuccessfully attempting to suppress a shudder as he watched the ships move somberly across the screen.

Kirk frowned but did not respond. "Mr. Sulu, find a spot that's clear of ships and use maximum magnification. Even if we're in intergalactic space, there has to be *something* out there."

But they found nothing on the first try.

Or the second.

On the seventh try, an almost invisible string of faint specks appeared.

Patches of similar specks were soon found in a dozen other directions.

Kirk was the first to find his voice. "How far?" he asked.

"Without a detailed spectral analysis, Captain, it would be impossible to make an accurate determination," Spock said.

"Never mind accurate, just give me a rough idea. A million parsecs? Ten million?"

"Fifty million would be more likely, sir," Sulu said. "If those are galaxies, not stars, maximum magnification would give us definite shapes at anything under ten million parsecs. These are simply points of light."

"He is correct, Captain," Spock said. "It would appear that we are in the approximate center of a void at least a hundred million parsecs in diameter."

The leaden feeling returned to Kirk's stomach and intensified as the extent of their isolation suddenly became clear. The existence of such voids had been known for more than two hundred years, since the late twentieth century, when astronomers had begun their first serious attempts at mapping the known universe. As a Starfleet Academy cadet, Kirk had been required to familiarize himself with holographic maps of the clusters and superclusters of galaxies that stretched out nearly ten billion parsecs in all directions from the Milky Way galaxy and the voids that existed among those galaxies—bubbles of sheer emptiness hundreds of millions of light-years in diameter, where no galaxies, no stars, no matter of any kind existed.

But knowing of them, even striding through the holographic projections themselves with million-parsec steps, could not prepare a cadet—or the captain that he became—for the reality of suddenly finding himself more than a hundred million light-years from the nearest star.

However, he told himself abruptly, prepared or not, that was where he was. That was where the *Enterprise* and all aboard it were.

And that was where they would stay, the way all

these hundreds of other dead hulks had stayed, unless he did something about it.

"Mr. Woida," Kirk said sharply to the navigator. "Lay in a course that retraces the path we've followed since we emerged into this space. Even if we can't see the gate on the Aragos detectors, there's at least a chance that it's still right where we left it."

For a moment, there was only silence, but then Woida pulled his eyes from the viewscreen with a visible effort. "Right away, sir," he said briskly, his massive fingers darting across the controls. "Course laid in."

"Execute, Mr. Sulu. Impulse power and caution."

"Impulse power, sir."

Slowly, the *Enterprise* turned, reorienting itself for the attempt. When it had achieved the proper heading, a dozen ships of a dozen radically different designs were scattered across the viewscreen.

The *Enterprise* moved forward toward them.

"The one ship no longer registers on the sensors, Captain," Spock announced a moment later.

Kirk's eyes darted toward the science officer but then returned to the viewscreen and the eerily indistinct images of the ships that lay ahead. "Continue scanning, Mr. Spock. Mr. Sulu, continue on the laid-in course."

After a minute, one of the ships, an almost perfect sphere with no visible means of propulsion, began to drift ever more rapidly off the screen, its apparent motion indicating that it was the closest. Though Spock had not seen it on the screen when they had first emerged from the gate, it must have been within a few dozen kilometers of their flight path. On the return path, the *Enterprise* would pass directly beneath it at the same distance. The other ships on the screen, hundreds or perhaps thousands of kilometers distant, were in all likelihood beyond the gate. Or beyond where the gate had been.

Suddenly, new readings appeared on Spock's instruments.

"Captain," he reported instantly, "the sensors have picked up the spherical ship at a distance of eight hundred seventy-three kilometers. Mass, two hundred eighteen thousand tons, no indication of any functioning power source. No life readings. No—"

"What was the distance of the first ship when the sensors lost it?" Kirk interrupted.

"Eight hundred seventy-four kilometers, Captain," Spock said, not needing to check the readings.

"Coincidence, Mr. Spock?"

"Not likely, Captain. For whatever reason, it would appear that the range of our sensors—"

Suddenly, the auxiliary screen flared into kaleidoscopic life.

The gate was back.

"All stop, Mr. Sulu," Kirk snapped, relief flooding through him.

"All stop, sir," Sulu acknowledged.

"Distance at which the gate reappeared, Mr. Spock?"

"Eight hundred seventy-three kilometers, Captain."

"Which means," Kirk said, "it's been there all the time. But our sensors, including the ones the Aragos modified, now have a very limited range and couldn't detect it, any more than they could detect any of those derelicts out there."

"That would appear to be the case, Captain," Spock agreed.

For a moment, Kirk's eyes returned to the main screen and the dozen ships that hung there in the darkness, some little more than fuzzy outlines. Curiosity and apprehension gripped him. Curiosity about what incredible secrets, what knowledge, could be gained from an exploration of those hundreds of hulks. And apprehension, even fear, about why these ships were still here, thousands of years dead, drifting within a few thousand kilometers of the gate, within easy reach of any ship with even the most primitive of impulse drives.

Why had *they* not returned through the gate?

The entity? he wondered abruptly. Had it—or something like it—infected all these ships and maneuvered them here, as the *Enterprise* had been infected and maneuvered? And had it then kept them from returning through the gate? Had the ships' crews simply killed themselves, as that of the *Cochise* had almost done? As so many other crews—and civilizations—had done in the past?

It was time to find out.

"Ahead minimum impulse power, Mr. Sulu. Mr. Spock, get what information you can from the sensors as we proceed."

"Of course, Captain."

Ahead, the gate swirled and flickered with its unknown energies.

Two hundred kilometers from the gate, the sensors

picked up another ship, this one not visible on the main viewscreen. "Temperature less than five degrees Kelvin, Captain," Spock said. "Too low for even the wavelengths the computer is currently utilizing in imaging the other ships. Primitive atomic drive, totally nonfunctional. No indication of life. Readings indicate an age of approximately twenty-nine thousand years."

Kirk shivered. "And your insubstantial friend—is it still around?"

"To the best of my knowledge, Captain, it is."

"And it's not trying to prevent us from returning to the gate," Kirk said thoughtfully. "Put the gate on the main screen."

A moment later, the ghostly images of the dead ships were replaced by the vivid, kaleidoscopic colors of the gate as seen by the Aragos-modified sensors. Punching up the shipwide intercom, Kirk told the crew briefly what had happened. "We will be attempting to reenter the gate within the minute. There are no guarantees, however, so be ready for anything— particularly for the reappearance of the entity."

Without cutting off the intercom, he pulled in a breath and fastened his eyes on the swirling crazy quilt on the screen. "Take us in, Mr. Sulu," he said.

"Aye-aye, sir."

Tensely, Kirk waited as Spock counted down the distance to the gate. If the entity was going to act, if it was going to try to force them to stay, it would have to act now. It would have to attempt once again to enter Kirk's mind and control it. Or perhaps Sulu's.

But whoever it tried to attach itself to—

Suddenly, everything vanished.

They had entered the gate.

They were going to make it!

No matter what the reasons those hundreds of other ships had been trapped or abandoned, the *Enterprise* was going to make it!

But then, just as the exultation was racing through Kirk's bodiless mind, every nerve in his imagined body once again erupted in agony.

Chapter Fifteen

THIS TIME the pain was, if anything, more intense, but it was also much more brief. To Kirk, it felt like little more than a second before it vanished.

Almost simultaneously, the bridge reappeared around him. Once more, the *Enterprise* was hurtling out of the gate, directly toward the cluster of ships it had so narrowly avoided the first time.

But this time, perhaps because they had suffered through the experience before, perhaps because of the briefer duration, recovery was quicker.

Sulu, after only a single shuddering gasp, reversed impulse power and brought the *Enterprise* to a halt well before the ships ahead of them presented any danger.

Three more times, they reentered the gate. Once, they maneuvered around it and approached from the opposite direction. The final time, they entered it under full computer control at near warp speed.

The results were virtually identical each time: a moment of nothingness followed by a moment of intense pain followed by forced ejection into the lightless heart of the same intergalactic graveyard.

Following the fourth attempt, Spock leaned more closely over his instruments.

"Captain," he said as the bridge returned to normal around him. "During our last approach, the sensors detected a phenomenon I had not noted during our lower-velocity approaches. The *Enterprise* appears to be enclosed in—in something."

"'Something,' Mr. Spock?" Kirk asked, frowning. "That's a bit imprecise. What is it, a force field of some kind?"

"Negative, Captain. This is something I have never encountered before. It appears to be totally immaterial, totally without energy, and yet it reflects a minuscule percentage of the sensor beams' energy. The phenomenon was much more pronounced during our last, more rapid approach to the gate, but it is still detectable." He looked up at Kirk. "It surrounds us at a distance of approximately eight hundred seventy-three point one kilometers—the same distance at which the sensors apparently cease to function."

"Spock, could this 'something' be what's limiting the range of our sensors?"

"It would appear likely, Captain."

"But you say the sensors don't tell us anything about whatever it is that surrounds us?"

"No, sir. They indicate its existence and its distance, but that is all."

"And it moves with us? Keeps us as its center?"

"As far as I have been able to determine, Captain."

Kirk grimaced, looking again at the screen and the ghostly hulks that floated there. "Whatever it is, it has to have a source. One of these ships? One that isn't as dead as the others? One that doesn't want us to find it?"

"That is, of course, a possibility, Captain," Spock said as Lieutenant Woida, still at the navigator's station, unsuccessfully tried to suppress a shiver.

"A possibility that we can at least check out," Kirk said briskly. "Mr. Sulu, take us on a tour, impulse power. Take us within sensor range—which is apparently now approximately eight hundred seventy kilometers—of every ship out there, one at a time if necessary. And keep the deflectors up."

Sulu acknowledged, and a moment later the *Enterprise* surged ahead, the first cluster of ships beginning instantly to grow larger.

"Mr. Spock, the instant you detect any life-form or any functioning power source—"

"Of course, Captain."

One hour and one hundred thirty-five lifeless hulks later, Spock announced that the sphere surrounding the *Enterprise* had begun to shrink.

"You're positive?" Ansfield asked, still hovering near Spock, reading most of the displays over his shoulder.

"Quite positive now, Commander. Its radius is approximately eight hundred seventy-two point two kilometers, a decrease of—"

"Then we had better get a move on before we lose the use of the sensors entirely," Kirk said. "Mr. Sulu, all deliberate speed."

"Aye-aye, sir."

Another hour, and another two hundred forty-one ships later, Spock looked up from his readouts.

"Functioning antimatter power source and a form of deflector screen and primitive sensor probe, Captain," he announced. "And a life-form reading."

Kirk, his attention wandering after nearly four hundred negative announcements from his first officer, was instantly alert, his eyes snapping to the viewscreen. "Which ship?"

"The ship at the lower right of the screen is the probable source, Captain."

The image Spock indicated was even fuzzier than the others, literally a three-hundred-meter-diameter blur. No features other than its irregular spherical shape were distinguishable.

"Keep moving, Mr. Sulu," Kirk snapped. "Continue the search pattern for the moment, but don't lose sight of that ship. Mr. Spock, have we found the source of whatever's affecting the sensors?"

"Unknown, Captain. However, all sensor readings pertaining to the alien ship appear decidedly erratic. In addition, the radius of the sphere surrounding the *Enterprise* decreased rapidly during the eleven point two seconds the ship in question was within sensor range. And the image on the viewscreen is not of the ship itself but of its deflector screens. Those screens are apparently designed not only to protect the ship but to modify its radiation pattern in such a way that its true surface temperature is not readily apparent through observations made in the standard electromagnetic spectrum."

"In other words, Mr. Spock, it's lying in the weeds."

"If I correctly perceive the meaning of that peculiar figure of speech, Captain—"

"It's been trying to hide from us. Or from someone."

"Almost certainly, Captain."

"And based on the way the field that's affecting our sensors suddenly shrank the moment that ship came within range, it's obvious there's a relationship of some kind between the ship and the field, whether or not the ship is actually the source."

"That would also seem likely, Captain."

"And the life-form readings?"

"One life-form aboard, Captain, but the readings regarding its nature are ambiguous. It is carbon-based, but there are contradictory indications regarding its physical form. Certain metabolic peculiarities point toward humanoid, but others are incompatible with that form."

"Drive?"

"Functional impulse power, Captain. Indications of nonfunctional warp drive."

"Weapons?"

"Nothing that could be identified as such by our sensors, Captain." Spock studied his console closely. "However, the sensors modified by the Aragos indicated a device capable of omnidirectional projection of massive amounts of energy that appear to be similar to that generated by the gates themselves."

A sudden hope stabbed through Kirk. Could this be someone who knew the secrets of the gates? One of the race that constructed them, even? But if so, what was it doing here? And could it—or would it—help them?

Or was it here only to destroy them, to add them to the already well-populated cosmic graveyard?

The image of a spider hovering hungrily in its web forced itself into Kirk's mind. There were dozens of shipboard theories regarding the gates, but the one that had generated the most discussion and spawned the most variations was that the entire gate system was a massive trap. The entities themselves, in that theory, were not the creators of the gate system but a form of poison that adhered to anyone passing through.

But perhaps the entities were more than a simple poison. Perhaps they were some form of artificial predator, programmed to capture those beings they failed to kill, programmed to capture them and bring them back into the limbo between the gates, to where those survivors could be hooked and dragged, like struggling fish, to where, on the end of a billion-parsec fishing line, the fisherman—the exterminator?—lay waiting.

Remembering the agony they had all experienced each time they had been spit out here, he realized uneasily that the hook analogy was certainly apt enough. And of the hundreds—thousands?—of ships that had been deposited in this intergalactic graveyard over the millennia, this one they had just discovered was the only one that showed any signs of life.

"What about that alien ship itself, Spock? What does it look like behind the camouflage its screens are putting out?"

"Like this, Captain," Spock said, tapping a code into the science station controls and indicating one of the auxiliary screens.

Kirk frowned. Small and utilitarian, vaguely resembling two shuttlecraft welded together side by side, the

162

ship Spock had put on the auxiliary screen looked more like a personal craft than anything military. There were no markings of any kind visible. Nor were there any immediately obvious openings. The only breaks in the regularity of the surface were an antennalike device that could have been a sensor array and, next to it, a solid oval-shaped ring mounted on four stubby legs.

"Lieutenant Uhura?" he said, still watching the tiny ship, puzzled. "Any activity on any frequency?"

"None, sir."

"And the range of our sensors, Mr. Spock?"

"Decreasing at approximately ninety-two point three kilometers per hour, Captain."

"How much time do we have?"

"At the current rate, approximately three hours and seventeen minutes, Captain."

Frowning, Kirk glanced around the bridge. "I'm open for comments. Anybody?"

"Now that we've found something alive," Ansfield said quickly, "I recommend we take a shot at communicating. Before whatever it is out there decides to take a more lethal kind of shot at *us*. And before the sensors quit working altogether."

"Opinion, Mr. Spock?"

"It is impossible to calculate the odds for or against the advisability of such a move, Captain. It is, therefore, a decision that must be made by human intuition rather than by logic."

"But you see no logical reason not to follow Commander Ansfield's suggestion?"

"On the contrary, Captain, there are a number of logical reasons to attempt to avoid all contact with the alien ship. However, there are equally as many logical reasons to do precisely as she suggests. The validity of those mutually contradictory reasons depends entirely on the intentions of the alien and the power of its ship, and we currently have no reliable information regarding either. It is, therefore, impossible to determine an optimum course of action by the use of logic alone."

"In other words," Ansfield interjected impatiently, "flip a coin. I can supply one if it will help get this show on the road."

Spock arched one eyebrow a fraction as he looked toward Ansfield. "Is it your belief, then, Commander, that the results of decisions made on the basis of intuition are no better than the results of those made by pure chance? I have often been given to understand, particularly by the captain and Dr. McCoy, that human intuition—"

"Mr. Sulu," Kirk interrupted, speaking rapidly and not waiting for individual acknowledgments, "return us to within sensor range. Lieutenant Uhura, transmit our peaceful intentions, all frequencies, all languages. Mr. Spock, monitor that ship with everything that's working, no matter how erratic the readings. Pay particular attention to the device that's putting out energy similar to that emitted by the gate."

Ansfield nodded her approval as she renewed her scrutiny of Spock's readouts.

But there was no response from the tiny ship, other than a marked increase in the metabolic rate of the seemingly paradoxical life-form aboard it.

And another quantum decrease in the range of the

sensors, down to less than seven hundred kilometers in less than a second.

Kirk's frown deepened at Spock's announcement of the newly shortened sensor range, and he turned to Uhura. "Any indication that our transmissions are being received, Lieutenant?"

"Indications, yes, Captain. There is increased absorption at certain standard frequencies, but it is impossible to be certain without—"

Suddenly, an urgent voice erupted from the speakers.

"I must speak with the leader of this ship!" the computer translated immediately.

It was not the translation, however, that sent a shock through everyone on the bridge and sent Spock's fingers darting across the science station controls to confirm the life-form readings he had scanned only minutes before.

It was the voice itself, audible beneath the computer's translation. Despite a singsong intonation and a heavy but identifiable accent, it spoke in what they all recognized as a Klingon dialect.

Chapter Sixteen

KIRK TOOK A deep breath. "I am James T. Kirk, captain of the U.S.S. *Enterprise,*" he said warily. "Who are you? What do you want?"

"I am Kremastor," the voice said. *"You must return with me to the nexus!"*

"Nexus?"

"The phenomenon that brought you here. You must return with me, now!"

"Can you help us get through it?"

"It is possible we can both reenter safely—if we waste no more time!"

"Our instruments tell us that you have a device on your ship that is capable of generating a form of energy similar to that generated by the gate—the nexus, as you call it. Is that—"

"It is something I must use later! There is another device which will allow you—us—to reenter the nexus unharmed."

"If you have such a device, why haven't you already used it? Why do you need our help?"

"It is too complicated to explain! There is no time! We must act now, while we have the chance!"

"The language you speak—"

"It is not my language!" the voice, verging on panic, broke in. *"It was one of many contained in the computer of another ship that came through the nexus earlier. It is the only one that was also among those languages that your own ship was transmitting."*

"The life-form readings are definitely not Klingon, Captain," Spock said quietly.

"In that case, Kirk," Ansfield snapped, "I respectfully suggest we do as the gentleman asks. I don't see that we have a lot to lose."

Kirk hesitated a moment, glancing at Spock and then at the image of the tiny ship on the viewscreen, then nodded abruptly.

"Agreed, Commander. Kremastor, how do we proceed?"

"I will bring my ship alongside yours. Together we will approach the nexus."

"And then?"

"When we are close enough, I will activate the device that will allow us to reenter the nexus. Once we have reentered safely, you may do as you wish."

"And if you and your device separate from us, will we be thrown back out here? I assume you've seen—"

"There is no time for this! The dead space around your ship has maintained itself longer than any I have ever seen, but it is still shrinking at an increasing rate!"

"What is—" Kirk shook his head. "Bring your ship alongside, but keep talking! What is this 'dead space'?"

Immediately, the tiny ship began to draw closer. *"I do not know what the dead space is,"* Kremastor said, sounding almost plaintive now. *"I only know that it surrounds each vessel as it emerges from the nexus, and that it normally blocks my own ship's instruments. But the dead space that surrounds your ship for some reason behaves differently. It helps the device that will allow us to reenter the nexus."*

"And what device *is* that?"

"It is a device that nullifies the Trap—the thing that brought you—that brought us both here."

"And all these other ships?"

"Those, too, but it is too late to help any of them."

"How is it that you alone of all these hundreds survived?"

"Because I am *alone! And because I have not been allowed to die!"* Kremastor almost shouted, and then, as if struggling to regain control: *"We must proceed to the nexus. There is no time—"*

"Kirk," Ansfield broke in. "I think Spock's little friend is coming back."

"I was beginning to feel it myself," Kirk said with a grimace. "I was hoping it was my imagination. Kremastor, do you—"

But the connection had been broken.

"Lieutenant Uhura, what happened?"

"I don't know, sir. The signal was simply cut off."

"Get it back! Kremastor, whoever or whatever it is, may be our only chance to get out of here!"

"Trying, sir, but—"

"We're being scanned again, Captain," Spock broke in. "Additionally, there is evidence of some form of transporter activity originating in Kremastor's ship. It appears to be—"

Suddenly, Spock's voice was drowned out by a deafening mixture of hissing and crackling. For an instant, everyone looked around urgently, trying to find the source of the sound, wondering which piece of equipment had suddenly started to fry itself.

But then they realized it was not coming from any piece of equipment.

It was coming from the air all around them.

A moment later, a tingling numbness filled everyone's body, as if an electrical charge were being induced into every inch of flesh, inside and out.

Then it was gone, and in the instant the feeling vanished, the bridge was filled—literally filled—with a fog of pulsing light.

Squinting against the blinding brilliance, everyone on the *Enterprise* bridge looked dartingly for the source, but, as with the noise that still crackled around them, there was no single source. The light, too, was coming from everywhere, from the very air around them.

Slowly, the light began to coalesce, swirling like fog being drawn into a bottle, until it was a single column, less brilliant now, running from deck to ceiling directly in front of Kirk's command chair. At the same time, the crackling faded to a tolerable level.

But as the sound faded, the column of light began to sculpt itself into a surrealistic version of a humanoid body, swirled for a moment, then moved toward Kirk, extending an arm of light as it moved.

In the split second that the pulsing light reached out

toward Kirk, Commander Ansfield made her decision. Three thoughts flashed through her mind virtually simultaneously, spurring her into immediate action.

Kremastor had spoken in a Klingon dialect.

Typically impatient, she herself had urged Kirk to go along with Kremastor's wishes.

And, finally and most importantly, Kirk was needed on the *Enterprise*. She was not.

Indeed, at times, Kirk seemed to virtually *be* the *Enterprise*. Around him, the crew functioned as smoothly as she had ever seen a starship crew function. Even McCoy, with his continual grousing, and Spock, with his encyclopedic knowledge and unsurpassed logic, respected Kirk and his odd mixture of intuition and courage. And it was not the empty, grudging respect that many captains received simply because they were captains. She had heard stories, often envious, of the remarkable rapport between captain and crew, but now, after her few days on the *Enterprise*, they were no longer stories. As far as she was concerned, they were fact.

Without hesitation, she darted down the steps from the science station.

Apparently aware of her sudden motion, the extended arm of light shifted toward her.

She collided with it, finding it not a solid object but a kind of resistance, like a force field.

"Ansfield!" Kirk yelled, reaching toward her.

Abruptly, a tingling numbness gripped her entire body, and an instant later the bridge vanished behind a fog of light.

Then the light intensified, forcing her to clamp her

eyes tightly shut. The deck vanished from beneath her feet.

The column of light that had absorbed Commander Ansfield amid an even louder, harsher outburst of crackling flared out until all definition was lost, and then, for a moment, the entire bridge was once again filled with blinding light.

And then nothing.

Except for some faint static on the radio, the light and sound were gone, Commander Ansfield with them.

"Captain, the screen!"

It was Sulu's voice, and for the first time since the light had appeared on the bridge, everyone looked toward the main viewscreen, where the alien ship now stood out like a nova among the other ships. During the moments of chaos on the bridge, it had pulled back, almost to the limit of the still-shrinking sensor range, but it had also had to lower its deflectors to allow its transporter to operate.

"Don't lose it, Mr. Sulu," Kirk snapped, hoping against hope that the alien's transporter operation had been less deadly than the noise and the pyrotechnics accompanying it had indicated.

But even before the words were out, the glow of the alien ship vanished from the screen.

An instant later, the sensors lost it as well.

Chapter Seventeen

DISORIENTED AND HELPLESS, Commander Ansfield floated in the midst of the light and noise, her eyes clamped tightly shut against the blinding glare. Obviously, unless the artificial gravity had given out entirely, she was no longer on the *Enterprise*. The light had almost certainly been the result of the transporter energy that Spock had detected, but the transporter must have been either a very primitive one or one that was on the verge of breaking down.

But at least it hadn't killed her. Yet. It had taken her somewhere.

But where? To Kremastor's ship? Unless there was another operational ship out there, one that had successfully eluded their search, it *had* to be.

Slowly, the intensity of light bombarding her closed eyelids began to ease, but abruptly, long before she dared open her eyes, gravity returned, sending her thudding onto a hard, concavely curved surface.

An instant later, the light, a dull glare even through her closed lids, faded almost as abruptly as gravity had returned. At the same time, the crackling noises faded, leaving only a soft mixture of a hiss and a rumble.

Cautiously, she risked lifting her lids a fraction. When she was not blinded by a resurgence of the light, she opened her eyes the rest of the way.

For an instant, a new wave of vertigo swept over her as she found herself lying in a featureless gray sphere about three meters in diameter. Muted, shadowless light seemed to come from nowhere and everywhere simultaneously, just as the blinding glow of the transporter had done on the *Enterprise* bridge. But whatever the source of the light, it was obviously not intended for human eyes. Under it, her skin was sallow, almost jaundiced, the blue of her uniform contrastingly darker.

"Who are you?" It was Kremastor, his words filled with a mixture of anger and terror. "Why did you interfere?"

Masking her unsteadiness, Ansfield got to her feet. The very featurelessness of the spherical room was disorienting. Despite near-normal gravity, it was an effort to keep from swaying.

"Why did *you* try to kidnap the captain?" she asked, scowling as she looked around. "Send me back before you make an even bigger fool of yourself than you already have!"

"I cannot send you back! I can have no further contact—"

"I thought you needed our help, Kremastor—or whatever your real name is! Was that all a lie? Just so you could get close enough to use that broken-down transporter of yours?"

"No! I *do* need your help! Everything I said was true, but—"

"Then why did you pull an idiotic stunt like this?"

There was a shuddering silence, and then: "The creature that accompanied you through the nexus—are you its allies?"

"You know of it, then?"

"Of course I know of it! *Are* you in league with it?"

"With *that* thing? Of course not! Why—"

"If that is true, why were you not fighting among yourselves? Why have you not destroyed each other, as all the others have done?"

"Because we've got better things to do!"

"That is not an answer!"

"It's all you're going to get until you send me back! It's all you'll get from *anybody*, so there's no point in trying to snatch someone else in my place!" Clamping her lips closed, she folded her arms in rigid defiance.

"But you must answer! I must understand what is happening! I must be *certain* that you are not in league with that creature! No one in the last twenty thousand years has been able to withstand its influence, but you—"

"Twenty thousand *years?*" Ansfield looked around her, searching for Kremastor. "What *are* you? A computer?"

"It doesn't matter what I am. All that matters—"

"If you want any answers, it matters! Now, *what are you?*"

Suddenly, the ship shuddered around her.

"What is it?" Ansfield asked sharply. "What's happening?"

But there was no answer, only the continued shuddering, growing increasingly violent until it seemed about to rip the ship apart.

But then, as quickly as it had begun, it stopped.

And from somewhere came a moan, wordless and agonized.

"Kremastor? Was that you? What happened?"

But there was no answer, no sound of any kind, for at least a minute.

Then the air started to glow and crackle again. Was she being sent back? she wondered abruptly. Were they going to try for Kirk again?

"It won't do you any good to send me back and kidnap someone else!" she shouted. *No one on that ship will give you any more than I have!*

The glow intensified and began to pulse. The crackling grew louder.

And from somewhere came, not Klingon words, but words from a language apparently beyond the capability of her universal translator. But to her own ear, no matter what the language, there was shrill desperation in the high-pitched voice.

Closing her eyes to a slit against the increasing intensity of the pulsing light, she waited.

The instant the alien ship raised its shields and vanished from the screen and from the sensors, Sulu hit impulse power, aiming the *Enterprise* directly toward the ship's last known position.

But it was too late. The ship did not reappear on the sensors, and by the time the computer reverted to the far-infrared imaging necessary to pick up the bulk of the derelicts, the fuzzy, irregular sphere was nowhere to be seen.

"What happened?" Kirk snapped. "Where is it?"

"It ran, Captain," Spock said, studying the record of sensor readings. "While we were distracted by the display its transporter made, the ship moved to within ten kilometers of the limits of our sensor range. The last sensor readings, taken virtually the instant the transport of Commander Ansfield was completed, indicate a maximum application of impulse power. In addition, our own sensor range took another quantum leap downward as the ship departed. It dropped to six hundred fifty-seven kilometers and is now shrinking at an increasing rate."

"How long until the range is zero?"

"At the present rate, Captain, approximately sixty-eight point three minutes."

"Mr. Sulu, initiate search pattern at maximum warp factor consistent with this—this junkyard we're in. Deflectors on full."

"Aye-aye, sir."

"Mr. Scott, have a tractor beam ready to lock onto the alien ship the instant the sensors pick it up."

"Aye, Captain."

And the derelicts vanished from the screen, replaced by an eerie blur as the computer drove the *Enterprise* outward in a mad spiral. Only the computer's virtually instantaneous reactions kept them from colliding with the hundreds of derelicts scattered randomly for at least a million kilometers in every direction.

Suddenly, less than two minutes into the search, the

Enterprise dropped out of warp drive and doubled back on full impulse power.

"Visual contact," Sulu announced seconds later. "We overshot, but the computer is bringing us back to within sensor range."

On the viewscreen, the fuzzy, irregular sphere had reappeared among the derelicts. It was growing rapidly.

"Within sensor range, Captain," Spock said seconds later. "Impulse engines driving ship on heading zero five one mark zero zero eight."

"Match velocity, Mr. Sulu."

"Matching, sir," Sulu said a moment later, and the fuzzy sphere was centered on the screen, motionless while the other derelicts flashed by.

"Tractor beam, Mr. Scott, but gently. We want to hold it, not destroy it."

"Aye, Captain, making contact—now."

"Impulse engines increasing power, Captain," Spock said. "It is trying to pull away."

"Keep with it, Mr. Sulu, but no sudden moves. If—"

"Sensor range decreased to four hundred seventeen kilometers, Captain. It is possible that the range of the tractor beam—"

"Closer, Mr. Sulu! Keep us within sensor range."

On the screen, the fuzzy sphere ballooned. "Fifty kilometers, sir."

"Life-form readings, Mr. Spock."

"Two, Captain—the alien life-form and a human, presumably Commander Ansfield."

"She's alive, then?"

"Alive and conscious, Captain."

Some small part of the tension eased, and Kirk returned his attention to the screen. "Lieutenant Uhura, resume transmitting our friendly intentions on all frequencies, but use only the Klingon dialect the alien itself used. But add that though we still mean Kremastor no harm, we will be forced to take action unless Commander Ansfield is returned—immediately and unharmed."

"All frequencies, sir."

For nearly a minute, there was no response.

Then, without warning, the alien's shields vanished, leaving the tiny ship glowing brilliantly in the center of the viewscreen. Instantly, the computer adjusted the image, and the other derelicts vanished, leaving the alien ship alone in the surrounding blackness.

An instant later, the bridge was filled once again with a pulsing, sourceless light and a deafening mixture of hiss and crackle.

"A similar form of transporter energy, Captain," Spock said, raising his voice above the din. "But it is even more unfocused than before."

"From the alien ship, I assume," Kirk shouted back, and Spock only nodded his reply as the crackling continued to grow even louder and the light began to coalesce once again into a column.

But before the form was complete, while independent fragments and streaks of light still pulsed everywhere on the bridge, the hissing and crackling was joined by a piercing whine, like a high-speed motor suddenly gone out of control.

And the embryonic column flared outward.

And vanished.

The fragments remained a moment longer, but then they, too, flared and vanished.

The whine peaked, sending hands to cover painfully assaulted ears, and then it, too, was gone.

And finally, the hissing and crackling changed momentarily to a rasping buzz and then cut off abruptly.

"Transporter energies no longer present, Captain," Spock said into the sudden silence. "But the sensor scan has returned. And both life-forms are still present in the alien ship."

"Response from alien ship, sir," Uhura broke in, and an instant later the stiffly accented Klingon dialect filled the bridge.

"I tried to return the one you call Commander Ansfield," it said, *"but my transporter has failed."*

"Then you will have no objections if we use our own transporters to bring her back," Kirk said flatly.

"You have trapped me." Kremastor's voice was resigned, empty of all urgency. *"I can do nothing to prevent you from doing whatever you wish."*

"Very well. Once she is safely on board the *Enterprise,* we can discuss your request that we accompany you to the vicinity of the nexus."

"There is no longer any need."

"What? Why not?"

"The dead space surrounding your ship no longer has the effect it did earlier. It is impossible now for either of us to reenter the nexus."

Or you want us to think *it's impossible,* Kirk thought silently. "Nonetheless, we will discuss it," he said. "In the meantime, we will transport over to your ship and bring Commander Ansfield back with us."

Signaling for Uhura to cut off the transmission, he punched the button that connected him to engineering. "Mr. Scott, do all systems check out?"

"Aye, Captain, so far as I can tell," Scotty's voice came back a moment later. *"Whatever brought us here, it does no' seem to have had any effect on the equipment."*

"Very well, Mr. Scott," Kirk said, and he went on to outline the events of the last few minutes. "Kremastor's shields are down," he finished, "but Commander Ansfield doesn't have a communicator to lock onto."

"We could bring her back wi'out one, if the coordinates were precise enough and the other ship does no' so much as twitch."

"I know, Mr. Scott, but considering Kremastor's behavior so far, I wouldn't count on it. But I assume there would be no problem in transporting someone *to* his ship."

"None, Captain. The remote materialization circuits—"

"To the bridge, then, Mr. Scott. You have the conn. Mr. Spock and I will beam over with an extra communicator. Bring Commander Ansfield back immediately, then, but don't bring Spock and me back until one of us gives you the word."

"Aye, Captain, but—"

"I'm not convinced Kremastor was telling the truth when he said it was no longer possible for us to reenter the gate," Kirk explained, "so Spock and I will try to find the device he told us about originally. If we do find it and can get it operating, you be ready to head back through the gate. I hope there's time for you to bring one or both of us back after we've activated the device, but if there isn't, don't jeopardize your chances of getting out of this graveyard."

Cutting off the intercom before Scott could reply, Kirk turned to Spock. "How much time to zero sensor range?"

"Approximately sixty-two point five minutes, Captain, if the shrinkage continues to accelerate at the present rate and if there are no more quantum changes."

"Then we had better get a move on," Kirk said briskly, standing up and heading for the turbolift. "We have to assume that the range of the transporters is no greater than that of the sensors. Kremastor himself stayed within sensor range while kidnapping Commander Ansfield."

Gesturing to Lieutenant Denslow to take over the science station, Spock joined Kirk at the turbolift. "Good luck, Captain, Mr. Spock," Uhura said as the doors hissed open, and before they closed, her words had been echoed by everyone on the bridge.

In the transporter room, they stepped into the transporter circles. Kirk's eyes met those of Lieutenant Crider at the transporter controls.

"Energize," Kirk said.

"Energizing," Crider acknowledged as he began to slide the transporter controls down.

A moment later, as the warble of the transporter built in his ears, Kirk felt the distinctive tingle of the transporter energies as they gripped him and held him motionless for scanning.

Quickly, the tingle reached its peak, indicating that the scanning was complete, and the transporter room began to fade from view.

But even as it did, he realized that something was wrong.

Chapter Eighteen

AT THE TRANSPORTER CONTROLS, Lieutenant Crider frowned. The readings weren't right. Dematerialization had gone normally, but *rematerialization* at the destination, in the alien ship—

The energies of the transporter beam were being scattered somewhere between the *Enterprise* and the other ship! Rematerialization had not yet begun, but if it did, if those unfocused, incoherent energies *were* converted back into matter, there was no way of even guessing at the results!

Controlling his panic, Crider sharply reversed the controls, trying to draw the scattered energies back into the transporter matrix.

"Mr. Scott!" he called into the intercom over the repeated warble of the transporter controls. "Something's interfering with the transporter!"

"What's happening, lad?" Commander Scott's voice crackled back.

"I don't know, sir. I'm trying to get them back, but—"

"On m' way!" Scott snapped.

His heart still pounding, Crider moved the main controls slowly, carefully, in the reverse direction, watching the readouts, ready to instantly adjust any of the dials if he saw the slightest sign that the energies he was trying to retrieve were again being scattered or in any way interfered with.

But whatever had happened during the attempted transmission was not repeating its interference, at least not yet. Even so, retrieving objects or people from an aborted transmission was tricky at best. Slowly, the energies flowed back into the matrix, and the readings all inched toward stabilization, until—

The transporter-room door hissed open, and Commander Scott burst through. Glancing at the still vacant transporter platform, wondering if he had overlooked something during the checks he had completed only minutes before, he raced across the room to the controls. In the moment before Crider stepped aside, Scott took in the readings and their significance almost instinctively. He nodded as his own hands touched the controls, and he forced himself to be calm.

"Looks like ye've done everything humanly possible, lad," he said, continuing to ease the controls back even more slowly, more cautiously, than Crider had done. "It's like reelin' in a trout in a highland stream," he breathed, tight-lipped, half to himself. His eyes flickered back and forth between the readouts and the transporter platform. "Ye don't dare let them slip the hook. If ye do . . ."

His voice trailed off into silence as the warble of the

transporter grew louder until, finally, the air above the transporter circles began to shimmer and then grow brighter with agonizing slowness.

For a moment, the glittering snowflake glow started to fade. Scott, his face grim, eased off entirely on the controls for an instant, then darted one hand to the side to make a minute adjustment to one of the dials. After another moment of wavering, the glow stabilized and then resumed its progress toward solidity.

Like ghosts, the forms of the captain and Spock gradually came into view, transparent at first, then translucent and shot through with the same glittering snowflakes he had seen a thousand times before. But now there were specks of multicolored light interspersed, as if some other form of energy were interfering with that of the transporter beam.

Scott's eyes widened momentarily. He felt the tension knot his stomach, but there was nothing he could do that he and Lieutenant Crider hadn't already done. The captain and Mr. Spock were coming back, or they weren't.

They had slipped the hook, or they hadn't.

With a touch that bordered on tenderness, he slid the controls the last few centimeters.

As the tingle faded and the transporter room vanished from around him, Kirk's first startled thought was that he must have somehow been transported into the limbo that existed within the gates.

But this was different, vastly different.

Instead of sheer nothingness, an overwhelming dizziness gripped him, as if his body still existed and was being whirled madly about, spinning helplessly in free fall with nothing to hold on to, nothing to even provide a visual reference.

But wherever he was, whatever was happening to him, he realized with a sudden stab of fear, it must be the doing of the entity. It had to be.

In the moments before Kremastor had snatched Commander Ansfield from the bridge, the entity had been returning, reexerting its power.

And, despite what Spock contended, Kirk was rapidly becoming certain that the entity, whatever its nature, whatever its motives, was behind everything that had happened to them since they had first encountered it.

One of the entities had boarded the *Enterprise* and had at first tried its conventional tactics, attempting to possess Kirk and a number of others, but that hadn't worked. They had been able to resist it, had been able to control the fear and paranoia that had destroyed countless other ships, countless other civilizations. As a result of the crew's successful resistance, the entity had been forced to adopt new tactics. It had attempted to lull them into a false sense of security by withdrawing, but it of course had not withdrawn entirely. It had remained attached to them somehow, attached to the *Enterprise,* but distantly, cautiously, its presence detectable by no one but Spock.

But it had obviously continued to influence them the whole time. It had even come out in the open and stirred up the temporary chaos on the bridge of the *Devlin,* the chaos that had allowed—forced?—the *Enterprise* to slip through the gate.

And into the trap toward which the entity had been leading them all along.

And now?

Now that it apparently had them where it wanted them, what would it do?

And where *was* this place it had brought them? What was this alien ship that had apparently been lying in wait for them? This field that was inexorably closing in on them? Was the entity in control of it all? Or was the entity a pawn in the hands of those who had built the gate system, those who had perhaps built the entity itself? Was it—

Suddenly, the dizziness began to fade, the sense of spinning to slow, and Kirk wondered if some answers were about to be revealed.

Or if the entity, with or without malice, was about to do whatever it had drawn him here to do.

Tensely, he waited to see where, if anywhere, he would materialize.

The two figures lurched dizzily on the transporter platform, then regained their balance.

"Captain! What happened?" Scott was hurrying from the controls to the platform.

Steadying himself, Kirk pulled in a relieved breath.

"I was hoping you could tell me, Mr. Scott." He stepped down from the platform and moved with Spock toward the corridor and the nearest turbolift. "The last I remember, Lieutenant Crider was beaming us to the alien ship."

"Aye, Captain," Scott said, and he went on to quickly outline what had happened. By the time he had finished, they were back on the bridge.

"It's my fault, sir," Lieutenant Denslow, Spock's replacement at the science station, said agitatedly the moment they emerged from the turbolift. "I'm sorry. I just didn't see it in time!"

"See what, Lieutenant?" Kirk asked, going with Spock to the science station as Denslow stepped back nervously. "Did the field take another jump?"

"No, nothing like *that,* sir. The shrinkage is still accelerating steadily. What happened is that the alien ship developed a field of its own. It doesn't block the sensors entirely, just changes the readings, and it obviously doesn't block the tractor beam. I—I didn't realize what was happening until Lieutenant Crider called from the transporter room, and then it was too late!"

Spock glanced at the readouts and quickly called back a series of earlier readings. "We must share what blame there is, Lieutenant," he said after a moment's study. "The field began developing when we overtook Kremastor's ship, long before I turned the station over to you. That is when the readings pertaining to Kremastor himself first began to change, and I should have noticed. It was only moments after you took the station that the readings pertaining to Commander Ansfield were affected."

"Affected how?" Kirk asked sharply. "Is she still all right?"

"She appears to be, Captain. The changes are not indicative of a change in her condition or, indeed, indicative of any changes in the alien ship."

"Then what—"

"It is the definition that has changed, Captain. The

sensor readings are, in effect, being blurred, much as your own vision might be blurred by an intervening substance that is not totally transparent. This field could, in fact, be similar to the one that is closing in on us. The difference could be only a matter of degree."

"Like the difference between something that's translucent and something that's totally opaque," Kirk suggested.

"The analogy is not without merit, Captain."

"But whatever the field is, it blocks the transporters even though it only slightly hinders the sensors," Kirk said. Then he added, frowning, "Could this new field have caused Kremastor's equipment to malfunction? He said it was no longer possible for him to get us back into the nexus, but after the way he tried to run from us, I just assumed he'd changed his mind and was lying."

"Without further information, Captain, both possibilities appear equally likely."

"And there's still no indication where the fields are coming from or what's causing them?"

"None beyond what we have already discussed, Captain."

Kirk shook his head in frustration. "If I didn't know better, I'd say *we* were the source of the field. The *Enterprise* is at its center, and no matter how we move, we remain at the center, just the way we remain at the center of our deflector shields when they're on. And now that Ansfield is on Kremastor's ship, *it* has a similar, weaker field."

"That is true, Captain. Remember, however, that

the smaller field is centered on Kremastor, not on Commander Ansfield."

"You're saying Kremastor himself is creating the fields? Or at least the smaller field?"

"No, Captain. I am only saying that the field surrounding Kremastor's ship originated at precisely the point Kremastor occupied at the time of the field's inception. Whether there is a causal relationship—"

"I take the distinction." Scowling at the screen, Kirk turned abruptly toward the communications station. "Lieutenant Uhura, anything from the alien ship?"

"Nothing, sir."

"Mr. Spock, are its impulse engines still functional?"

"Still functional, Captain, but shut down."

"And our tractor beam?"

"Still holding. It is apparently affected less by the field around Kremastor's ship than are our sensors and transporters."

Turning back to the viewscreen and the image of the tiny ship, Kirk was silent for a moment, then drew in his breath.

"Mr. Scott, are you back on the tractor beam?" he asked abruptly.

"Aye, Captain."

"Then bring that thing in. I want a closer look at it. *And* at that field around it, before the big one closes in on us all. Get a crew down there to give it a thorough examination, immediately."

"Aye, Captain. I'll have it on board in five minutes at the most."

"Mr. Spock, keep a close watch on those life-form

190

readings. If either of them changes, particularly that of Commander Ansfield, let me know immediately."

"Of course, Captain."

"Mr. Sulu, is the helm still rigged as a remote control for the shuttlecraft we used earlier?"

"It is."

"Then send it out, now. Send it out beyond this field, and we'll see what happens to it."

"Aye-aye, sir."

With the hangar deck doors already opened for the entry of Kremastor's ship, it took barely a minute for a shuttlecraft to reach the still shrinking field and promptly disappear from the sensors.

Like a light winking out, all sensor readings from the shuttlecraft vanished. In the same instant, the subspace link with the shuttlecraft was cut off, and the signals it had been returning to the *Enterprise* ceased.

But on the viewscreens, the shuttlecraft remained plainly and solidly in sight, radiating brightly in infrared. Its impulse engines, still operating on the last order sent to them, continued to move the tiny vessel forward. The signals from the *Enterprise* helm, instructing the shuttlecraft to turn around and come back, were ignored, as if they hadn't been sent.

"Ship secured on hangar deck, Captain," Scott reported.

"Good timing, Mr. Scott. Mr. Sulu, overtake the shuttlecraft, and bring it back on board. Mr. Scott, be ready to give it as thorough a check as you're giving Kremastor's ship."

Within another minute, the shuttlecraft had been overtaken. The moment it was back inside the field, it reappeared on the sensors, and its controls once again responded to the helm. Thirty seconds later, it was back on the hangar deck, and Scott and his crew were swarming over both it and Kremastor's ship.

"Time, Mr. Spock."

"The shrinkage accelerated yet again, Captain, when the shuttlecraft reentered the field. The current projection is thirty-one point six minutes."

"Everything we do just speeds it up!" Kirk said, shaking his head sharply. "Mr. Scott, have you found any way into the alien ship? Any way to get at Commander Ansfield?"

"There are no breaks in the ship's surface, Captain."

"And the field around it, now that it's aboard the *Enterprise*, Mr. Spock?"

"Initially, it began to shrink, but it has now stabilized. It still encloses the ship and, I can only assume, would still block our transporters."

"If it begins to shrink again—"

"Of course, Captain."

"Mr. Scott, how did the shuttlecraft stand up to its trip?"

"A preliminary check shows all systems fully operational."

"And the records of what its sensors found outside the field?"

"No' a thing, Captain, no' even the other ships. Nor the Enterprise *itself. It's as if the sensors themselves did no' exist!"*

Kirk grimaced and turned abruptly toward Uhura and the communications station.

"Patch me through again, Lieutenant," he said grimly. "It's time we had another talk with

Kremastor. And let Commander Ansfield know what's been going on."

For what seemed like forever to Commander Ansfield, there was only silence. The glaring light and ear-punishing crackling had faded simultaneously, and when she had opened her eyes, she had found herself still in the same featureless sphere. At first she had shouted, but there was no response from Kremastor or anyone else, nor was there any reaction when she pounded on the sphere as hard as she could with her boot heel.

Finally, breathing heavily, she had fallen silent, and since that time she had listened.

But other than a faint humming and her own breathing, there had been nothing to hear.

But now, suddenly, the ship shuddered. Not as violently as the first time, almost gently, and again there was silence.

Until—

"Commander Ansfield, can you hear me?" The voice, like that of the alien, seemed to come from the air around her.

"Kirk, is that you?"

"Yes, Commander. Are you all right?"

"Except for being trapped in what looks like a goldfish bowl, I'm fine. What happened?"

"You were apparently transported into Kremastor's ship."

"I'd figured that much out for myself! I mean since then."

Hurriedly, he brought her up to date. *"You're in the*

hangar deck now," he finished. *"We'll see what we can do about getting you out. In the meantime—Kremastor! Can you still hear me?"*

"I can. What is it you wish?" the Klingon voice replied, sounding totally flat and resigned.

"You could start," Ansfield snapped, "by answering *my* last question. Are you a computer? You said you'd been watching ships arrive here for twenty thousand years, and no humanoid life-forms *I* know about live anywhere near that long."

"I am not a computer. For years I had a body not unlike your own, but for several lifetimes I have had only this ship."

"A cyborg, then?"

"Insofar as this ship is my only body, yes."

"If I could make a suggestion, Captain, Commander," Spock said, cutting off another question from Ansfield. *"It would be more logical and more efficient for Kremastor to explain who he is and what he is doing here rather than for us to attempt to question him on a series of specific points."*

"Just one more specific question," Ansfield said. "Kremastor, do you know of *any* way of getting me safely out of this ship of yours?"

"I do not, other than for your colleagues to disassemble my ship and, in all likelihood, myself. I would do nothing to hinder such action. After twenty thousand years of terror and futility, I would, in fact, welcome it."

There was a moment of silence, and then Kirk said, *"I have one more question, too. What happens when this so-called dead space disappears? Will all our equipment simply stop functioning?"*

"That is what has happened to many."

"But not to you? Your equipment has been functioning, you said, for twenty thousand years."

"Only in a very limited fashion. The warp drive is totally inoperable. My sensors show the nexus only as a faint ghost of what it really is. The nullifier—the device that would allow me to reenter the nexus—generates energy of some kind, but it no longer has any effect on the Trap."

"Twenty-six minutes to zero sensor range, Captain," Spock announced.

"And to massive equipment malfunction," Kirk breathed. *"All right, Kremastor, tell your story—fast. And hope it gives us some ideas."*

195

Chapter Nineteen

AT LEAST A THOUSAND generations ago, Kremastor began, shortly after his ancestors had discovered a form of warp drive, they stumbled across the nexus system, just as the *Enterprise* had. They also found the "maps" early on during their exploration of the system, but in their case it was apparently a complete set, not just the "local" ones that so far had been fed into the *Enterprise* computer. The maps showed that the system consisted of a series of approximately a hundred nexus, each of which was connected to every other nexus and to thousands of individual gates, one of which was the one Kremastor's ancestors had found approximately fifty light-years from their home world. The nexus themselves seemed to be intended primarily to serve as junction points for great numbers of individual gates, as the hub of a bicycle wheel serves as a junction for dozens of spokes. The nexus, however, were apparently accessible directly, and it was one of these, one of the most complex of the lot, into which the *Enterprise* had originally stumbled, only to pop out of another billions of light-years distant and almost equally complex.

Kremastor's maps were apparently more complete versions of those already in the *Enterprise* computer. Each nexus and each destination was identified by a code. Each nexus went through a continuous cycle, opening onto a different destination every few seconds. The times at which a nexus had to be entered in order to reach the various destinations were specified. No destination was more than a day distant, even if one had to pass through all hundred nexus to get there.

The set of maps Kremastor's ancestors were given told them how to reach any of more than a million individual destinations.

What the maps did *not* tell them was the location of any of those destinations with respect to any other destination.

As far as Kremastor's ancestors had been able to determine, not a single destination was anywhere within their own galaxy.

Nor could they discern the slightest pattern in the destinations. It was as if they had been picked at random from anywhere and everywhere in the universe. Of the destinations they explored, some were in the hearts of massive star clusters like the one the *Enterprise* had first been transported to. Some were in the deadly centers of galaxies that would have dwarfed the Milky Way. A very few were within light-hours of solar systems. Some were on the fringes of galaxies of all sizes. Many were deep in intergalactic space.

And a few—a very, very few—were like the one the *Enterprise* and all those other ships had found themselves ejected from. They opened on starless, lightless voids hundreds of millions of parsecs in diameter. A few opened on voids so huge that the entire universe seemed empty. No galaxies or stars were within range of the exploring ships' instruments.

For generations, Kremastor's ancestors had explored the nexus system. Just how many destinations they reached, he didn't know. The few surviving records didn't say, but it was obvious they could not have explored more than a few thousand of the more than a million destinations available.

Then, in a solar system only a few light-hours from a gate, they found the remnants of a civilization. It had destroyed itself in an atomic war thousands of years before.

Shortly after that discovery, ships began to disappear, to head out for new destinations and simply not return.

Finally, one of the missing ships did return, but all aboard it were dead. From what little Kremastor's ancestors could learn from the ship's fragmentary log, some form of insanity had come upon them as they emerged from the gate, and it had swept the ship.

Immediately, rigid quarantine procedures were set up. Because of the gate's distance from their home world, the quarantine worked, and when other infected ships returned, some with one or more crew members still alive, the home world remained safe.

Meanwhile, their scientists had been studying the gates, trying to measure and understand the forces that drove them. By the time the infected ships began to return, the scientists had succeeded to some extent in measuring those forces, even manipulating them, but they never came close to truly understanding them.

But manipulating them, it seemed, was enough, at least for the harsh but purely defensive measure Kremastor's ancestors devised. They were able to build the Trap and link it to more than half of the nexus. The Trap itself was a pure energy device that could reach into the limbo that surrounded the nexus, identify virtually any sentient being that had been infected, seize that being and all matter in its vicinity, including whatever ship it was traveling in, force it out through this or other equally isolated gates, and keep it from reentering. There, millions of parsecs from the nearest star, the ship would be in permanent quarantine. Even if the infected crews survived, they could not spread their infection.

Where the infection—the entities—came from, even what they were, Kremastor's ancestors had no way of knowing. Alone, they registered on no sensors, not even those of the Trap, just as they had registered on none of the *Enterprise* instruments, only on the minds of its crew. Only when one of the creatures attached itself to a living, sentient being could its presence be detected.

As a result, the Trap was far from perfect. As long as the creatures were not attached to sentient beings, they could roam the system freely, emerging whenever and wherever they pleased.

In the end, either the quarantine procedures that isolated the gate near Kremastor's home world, after generations of inactivity, grew lax, or one of the creatures emerged from the gate unattached and undetected.

Either way, the civilization of Kremastor's ancestors was infected and destroyed, just as that of the Aragos had been infected and destroyed thousands of years later.

But, like the Aragos, Kremastor's people had recovered. Over tens of thousands of years, they had made their way back to civilization, and they had found the records their ancestors had left behind, in permanent orbit around their home world.

And when they found those records, they had wondered: How many thousands of civilizations like their own had been destroyed by these creatures? How long would it be before, despite all their efforts, their own resurrected civilization would be destroyed once again?

So they decided: The only way to end the threat once and for all was to close down the system altogether. For another generation, then two, they studied the forces involved. Finally, though full understanding never came, they devised a way to shut the system down. They built a device that, once taken to the central nexus—the nexus the maps indicated was the source of the entire system—would be capable of destroying the system. When activated, it would literally turn the entire nexus system inside out, setting into self-destructive oscillation its still not fully understood energies. It was crude, the equivalent of Ensign Stepanovich's phaser blast in the *Cochise* engineering control room, but it was the best they could do.

And it would be effective.

But whoever undertook to use the device would, in effect, be going on a suicide mission. Even if he survived the action of the device itself—and he almost certainly would not—he would be trapped millions or billions of parsecs from home, with no nexus system to return through.

A dozen ships with the device were built and sent out, then a hundred. None returned, and the nexus system remained in operation.

Finally, one of the second hundred—a three-man ship, the minimum possible crew—managed to return. It was infected, with only one of the crew left alive.

All the other ships, they realized then, had also been infected. The crews had either destroyed themselves or had been caught in the Trap and forced out of the system into the permanent "quarantine" areas.

A series of cyborg ships was the solution Kremastor's contemporaries devised. Because the brain controlled the ship's functions directly through the computer, a single person—a single brain—could pilot the ship. Because the computer was programmed not to allow the pilot to shut himself down or damage himself in any way, he could not kill himself if—when —he became infected.

Because they expected the pilot to become infected and be forced out of the system by the Trap, they designed and built the nullifier, a device that could temporarily shut down the Trap. They could only hope that if he did indeed become infected, he would retain enough sanity to use the nullifier and complete his mission.

But Kremastor never got the chance, and he could only assume that those who had gone before had suffered similar fates.

He was infected virtually the instant he entered the system. Suddenly, he was terrified of everything, of the ship that was his own body, of the limbo that surrounded it, of his onetime friends and associates who had designed and built the ship and imprisoned him in it and sent him out, alone, to face an eternity of paralyzing terror.

And then the Trap reached out and grasped him and hurled him out of the system.

Despite the fact that his "body" was a mechanical and electronic thing, wired for neither pain nor pleasure, he experienced as much pain during the trapping as any fully organic victim ever had.

But the pain, he quickly realized, had been his salvation. In some way, it had overloaded the circuits of his brain so that when the pain stopped, the fear that remained was somehow tolerable. It still took a tremendous mental effort to overcome it, to work in spite of it, but after the sensory overload of the trapping, he was able to do it.

But he was not able to reenter the system. The nullifier, he discovered, would not work, nor would half the systems on his ship. His sensors and transporter worked only marginally, and no adjustment he was capable of making helped. If he had possessed a real body, he always thought, he might have been able to take the systems apart, find out why they didn't work, then rebuild and repair them. But working only from the inside, it was as impossible as a human performing open-heart surgery on himself.

So he had done what he could.

He had used his ailing sensors to learn what little he could from the hundreds of other ships that had apparently been trapped there before him. More than a hundred, he found, were those of either his contemporaries or his ancestors. Many of those who had gone ahead of him to attempt to shut down the system were here, all long dead, and now he had joined them.

Unable to shut himself down or even to sleep, he waited, hoping another ship, with a more effective nullifier, would come, not to save him but to complete the mission he himself had failed at.

But none came, and he soon began to wonder if, despite all the safeguards, his civilization had once again been destroyed by the creatures.

Finally, another ship had come through, but he did not recognize it. And when he tried to use his sensors on it, he discovered the dead space for the first time. It had blocked his sensors entirely, but it had shrunk and vanished in minutes, and when he was able to probe the ship, he found it crewed by aliens. Aliens who, not unexpectedly, had killed each other.

Over the millennia, then, more than a hundred additional alien ships had come. But all had been essentially the same.

Each one had only further confirmed his fears, reinforced his conviction that he was trapped here forever.

Until the *Enterprise*.

The moment the *Enterprise* dead space had touched him, the nullifier had revived. It had begun functioning, if not normally, close enough to normal to give him sudden hope that, after twenty thousand intolerable years, his mission might yet end in success.

But then, as they had been about to approach the nexus, the creature had begun to strengthen, and

Kremastor's fear, until then under control, had broken free.

And, belatedly, the significance of the fact that the *Enterprise* crew, though infected, were still capable of working together dawned on him: they must be allied with the creature.

Perhaps they were even its creators.

And if they learned the secret of the nullifier from him, they could destroy the Trap, and they would be able once again to roam freely through the entire nexus system, infecting and destroying.

"But I could not simply run," Kremastor finished. *"What if I were wrong? What if there were an innocent explanation for your survival? I tried to take your leader to question, but—"*

"Time, Mr. Spock."

"Fourteen point seven minutes, Captain."

"Mr. Scott, are you finding anything of significance, either on the shuttlecraft or on Kremastor's ship?"

"Just what looks like the shortest route to cut through to reach Commander Ansfield, if it comes ta that. A complete check o' the shuttlecraft shows no change whatsoever because o' its wee trip."

"All right, Scotty, leave some people there, but you get back up to the engineering deck. I want you there, where you can keep an eye on the situation firsthand, when—if—that dead space closes in."

"Aye, Captain."

Cutting off the intercom, Kirk turned to Spock. "I won't make it an order, Spock, but your Vulcan abilities may be the only chance we have to communicate with this entity. If you still feel it is not hostile—"

"Of course, Captain. If nothing else, I can perhaps persuade it to leave us. Lieutenant Denslow, take the science station."

Spock was silent then for a brief moment as he stepped back. His features were still impassive, but Kirk sensed unease behind the surface. Then Spock strode past Uhura and the turbolift to the unmanned environmental station. There he lowered himself onto that station's chair. Stiffly, he placed his hands on his knees, palms down.

"Captain," he said in a voice that was quiet even for him. "I strongly recommend that you keep a phaser, set to heavy stun, trained on me at all times." Without further comment, he extended his arms directly in front of himself, lifted his head slightly, and closed his eyes.

"Dr. McCoy," Kirk said into the intercom, "to the bridge. We're about to hold a seance, and I think we should have a doctor in attendance."

Chapter Twenty

EVEN UNDER THE best of circumstances, touching another mind was disturbing. Where strong emotions were involved, as they would be here, it was doubly disturbing, far more disturbing than mere physical pain.

But Spock obviously had no choice. Consideration of his own discomfort, no matter how acute, had to be put aside, as he had had to put it aside when he had melded with the Horta in the pergium mines of Janus 6. Her pain and anguish had flooded his mind, nearly overwhelming him, but with those emotions had come understanding.

And from that understanding had come an end to the killings on both sides.

Here the stakes were vastly higher. In only the last few days, this entity had been responsible for the deaths of Ensign Stepanovich and the entire crew of the scout ship whose distress call the *Eddington* had answered.

Fifteen thousand years ago, the Aragos civilization

had been virtually destroyed, and all evidence pointed to the involvement of a similar entity.

Even more millennia ago, other such entities had in all likelihood triggered that chain of wars in a distant galaxy, the chain of wars that had wiped out hundreds of civilizations and countless billions of lives before, finally, the captain had been able to break that chain.

And here, in this intergalactic graveyard millions of light-years from the nearest star, were nearly a thousand ships whose crews, if Kremastor was to be believed, had fallen victim to the same phenomenon.

And unless some link, some kind of understanding, could be established—and unless the *Enterprise* was allowed to reenter the nexus system and find its way home *with* that understanding—tens of billions of Federation lives were in jeopardy. The final communication with Admiral Wellons at Starfleet Headquarters had convinced Spock of the danger the Federation faced. New gates—new leaks in the gate system—had been appearing daily throughout the Federation, and at least one of the entities had apparently already found its way into Starfleet Headquarters.

Spock's own feelings, therefore, were of no consequence in the matter.

His *life* was of no consequence if, by its sacrifice, the odds in favor of the Federation's survival were increased by even the most minuscule percentage.

His eyes tightly shut, the physical universe as completely closed out as he could make it, Spock reached out with his mind.

The hundreds of minds of the *Enterprise* crew

surrounded him like a shimmering web, not seen but felt.

And everywhere around Spock, flowing around and through the web of minds on the *Enterprise,* permeating it and yet somehow holding itself aloof from it, was something that he recognized instantly as the entity.

But now he could sense that the entity was not alone.

Beyond the web, hovering like a threatening bank of dark and roiling clouds, were countless more entities, each separate yet all linked, tenuously but unbreakably, to each other and to the one that swirled so closely about him.

And in every one of the countless beings lurked the fear, the distinctive signature of fear Spock had recognized a half-dozen times before.

But it was the entity that concealed itself within that cloak of fear that he must touch, that he must contact.

Twice before, contact had been achieved, no matter how briefly, but each time it had been in the limbo that existed inside the nexus system.

Had those contacts been possible because it was only there that his mind was totally free of his physical body, able to dart and soar at will, like a bird suddenly released from the lifelong darkness of a shrouded cage? Even during those excruciating moments when the illusory pain of Kremastor's Trap had flooded his mind, there had been a feeling of lightness and freedom he had never experienced elsewhere.

With a massive, draining effort, he tried to recapture that feeling of utter freedom.

But here, now, in the few short minutes available to him, he doubted that such total mental freedom was possible. No matter how rigorously he isolated his mind, he knew that his body still existed. Its shadow still weighed him down, still blunted his mental abilities. He could feel his chest move as air flowed in and out. He could feel his heart as it beat out its ceaseless, complex rhythm, an unbreakable link to the objective time of the universe around him. He could physically feel the emotions with which the traitorous human half of that body threatened to overwhelm him.

And yet, despite it all, he once again felt the beginnings of contact.

Before, during those brief, abortive contacts in limbo, he had suddenly realized, without benefit of words or images, that the entity not only existed and feared but that it needed—desperately yearned for—something. That knowledge—the entity's own emotions?—had simply appeared in his mind, and, logic to the contrary, he had accepted them.

Those same emotions now reappeared, intensified, and he once again accepted them as quickly and completely as if they had been backed up by volumes of precise mathematical logic.

But this time there was more.

Attached to the fear and the painful yearning was an overlay of desperation and frustration, numbing and endless, a desperation that had built up through eon after eon until it was at least as intolerable as Kremastor's twenty thousand years of helpless, terror-filled isolation.

Slowly, the contact deepened, and Spock felt the entity grow more powerful, more substantial, like a poisonous fog congealing about him, turning from a mist to something clammy and restricting. And the growing fears of the others, of the crew of the *Enterprise*, were like a thousand invisible needles pricking at his mind.

And the darkly boiling clouds that were the other entities began to draw closer, the tenuous links growing thicker and stronger.

And he was able to touch, fleetingly, those other entities.

And suddenly he knew. They were not *only* a thousand separate entities.

They were also *one* entity.

Like permanent participants in a Vulcan mind fusion, they were simultaneously one and many.

And yet they were still incomplete, painfully and terrifyingly incomplete.

And that incompleteness, he realized in a sudden rush of understanding, was the source of the yearning he had felt so strongly, the yearning to be joined, to be absorbed back into the completeness that had once existed.

And in that yearning, he saw the route he must take if he were ever to establish a truly meaningful contact. He must allow himself to be absorbed, to become one with them, to lose his own individuality as he—

Suddenly, something wrenched at Spock's mind, as if a massive electrical charge had jolted through his body, but even as it happened, Spock sensed the cause of the shock: the field was closing in, passing through the entities, and in another moment it would isolate them from him the same way the *Enterprise* sensors were isolated from the rest of the universe.

And contact was broken.

The fear and frustration and yearning that had been the entity's was gone, leaving only the remnants of Spock's own fear and that of the hundreds of crew members, and then even that was blocked out.

The entity was gone.

He was alone.

And falling.

As in his last moments in limbo, Spock was gripped by an overwhelming sense of chaotic, whirling motion, except that now it was a physical sensation as well as a mental one, and something close to nausea clutched at his stomach.

Instinctively, his eyes snapped open, and the bridge of the *Enterprise* appeared around him.

For an instant, muffled in silence, it wavered, as if he were looking upward through the rippling surface of a lake, and the nausea squeezed his gut more tightly.

Then his surroundings steadied, and sounds returned, but for another instant the entire bridge was an alien world, its sounds only gibberish.

As if, he thought abruptly, a tiny fragment of the entity had briefly survived within him and he was seeing the *Enterprise* through that fragment's fading senses!

But that instant passed as well, and he saw Dr. McCoy leaning over him, tricorder scanner in his hand. "Spock, are you all right?"

Behind McCoy, Kirk stood watching, worry evident in his frowning features.

Spock hesitated a moment before replying, waiting until he could force the lingering nausea to retreat. "I'm quite all right, Doctor," he said finally.

"I wouldn't want to bet the farm on that, Spock." McCoy gestured at the tricorder. "You looked like you were going into one of your trances, and then all your readings turned crazy, even for a Vulcan."

"But they are back to normal now, Doctor?"

"As normal as they ever get. I'd be a lot happier, though, if you'd check into sickbay for an hour or two. But I suppose that would be too much to expect."

"Under the circumstances, Doctor, it would." Standing, Spock looked past him to the captain. "At least until a moment ago, the entity was still present, Captain, but—"

"But it's not present now?"

"I cannot say, Captain. I can only say that something seemed to happen to the entity while I was in contact with it. I suspect that the field that has been closing in on us passed through the entity approximately then. Whether it was hurt or even killed as a result, or if it has simply withdrawn, I could not tell."

"But did you learn anything?"

"Nothing that has immediate practical application, Captain. However, I am now virtually certain that the entity—entities—bear us no malice." Briefly, he went on to describe what he had experienced.

"A form of hive mind?" Kirk asked when Spock concluded.

"Not precisely, but that is as accurate a description as is possible at the moment. But there is a strong impression that it is still incomplete, that it is, in effect, searching for the rest of itself."

"And the reason for the fear it causes?"

"Unknown, Captain. However, as I have already indicated, I am virtually certain that it experiences the same or even stronger fear itself, and not only when it is in contact with ourselves or some other life-form. This state of fear appears to have existed continuously, without interruption, for tens of thousands of years."

"But you learned nothing that would help us establish communications with this entity? Or get rid of it so we can reenter the nexus system?"

"I did not, Captain. However—"

"Captain!" Lieutenant Denslow, still monitoring the science station readouts, called. "Field radius less than one kilometer. First contact with *Enterprise* due in thirty seconds."

"Scotty—" Kirk began into the intercom, but Scott's voice came back instantly.

"I heard, Captain. I'm ready."

Spock, moving quickly to take Denslow's place at the science station, took in the sensor readings.

"The rate of field closure is slowing, Captain," he said. "Also, it is no longer a sphere. It is developing two lobes, the larger of which appears to be centered on the primary hull, the smaller on the engineering hull." He paused a moment, as if performing a mental calculation. "Mr. Scott, the areas of first contact will be the aft portions of the warp-drive nacelles. The field is already largely within the radius of the deflectors. Mr. Sulu, are the deflectors still operational?"

"According to my instruments, they are."

"And there was no indication when the field passed through them?"

"None that I could see, Mr. Spock."

"Contact with warp-drive nacelles now, Captain, Commander Scott."

"No' a thing showing on the instruments, Captain," Scott's voice came over the intercom. *"Matter-antimatter engines still functioning normally. Power output—"*

Scott's voice cut off abruptly, then came back. *"Power output up ten percent, Captain!"*

"Cut back, Scotty!" Kirk snapped.

"Already doin' it, sir."

"It may be significant, Captain," Spock interjected, "that the field passed through the matter-antimatter core within seconds of the power increase."

"Output stabilized, Captain," Scott announced. *"Some o' the readings are a wee bit off, but nothing that can't be adjusted."*

"What *is* this thing?" Kirk snapped in frustration. "Spock, do the sensors show *anything?*"

"Negative, Captain. Beyond the field, it is as if nothing exists. Most of the nacelles do not now register on any sensor. And from the rate of inward progress—" Spock paused, one eyebrow arching minutely.

"All sensors dead, Captain," he announced. "The sensor array itself is now presumably outside the field."

Chapter Twenty-one

KIRK GLANCED AT the viewscreens. Those connected to the sensors were blank. Those operating on any portion of the standard electromagnetic spectrum remained operational, but the images were blurred. A camera in the *Enterprise* hangar deck showed the shuttlecraft, Kremastor's ship, and the engineering crew around them seemingly unaffected except for the blurring.

For an instant, then, the bridge seemed to waver, as if a distorting lens had been passed before Kirk's eyes, and at the same moment a wave of disorientation swept over him, ending in a pulse of dizziness and nausea.

But almost before he could react, the dizziness was gone. The bridge was once again rock solid.

Except—

Kirk blinked, shaking his head as if to clear it.

Everything was precisely as it had been before, except for color. Every color—the people, the clothes, the consoles and their lights, everything—was changed.

Spock's blue science tunic was a deeper blue.

The red of Uhura's uniform was lighter, shading toward orange.

His own tunic was lighter, too, much closer to yellow than before.

And the flesh—

Like the uniforms, everyone's face and hands—including his own—were slightly "off." Spock's faint coppery tinge had edged from green toward blue. Uhura and one of the security officers still flanking the turbolift door were a shade darker brown than before. Kirk himself, along with McCoy, Woida, Sulu, and the other security officer, had taken on a slightly jaundiced look, as if their blood had been diluted with orange juice.

"Jim!" McCoy was looking around disbelievingly. "What the blazes is going on *now?*"

"I have no idea, Bones. Mr. Scott, how are things in engineering? Is anything working? The sensors—"

"I know, Captain," Scott replied, static half obscuring his words. *"They're dead. And the readings on half the other systems have gone daft. I'm tryin' ta get them settled down, but it's like workin' wi' your eyes shut!"*

"Are the deflectors still operational?"

"I wish I knew, Captain! They're still drawing power —more than they should—but I canna say what they're doin' wi' the power."

"Understood, Mr. Scott. Do your best. Mr. Sulu, test-fire the phasers, minimum power."

"Minimum power, sir," Sulu acknowledged, activating the phasers.

An instant later, the bridge lights dimmed slightly.

"Phaser banks drawing inordinate power, sir," Sulu said, "but no phaser beams are evident."

"Phasers off," Kirk snapped, and a moment later the bridge lighting returned to normal. "Mr. Scott, what happened?"

"I canna tell ye more than Mr. Sulu already has, Captain. The phasers were pullin' more power than they do on maximum, but no' a thing was comin' out!"

"Lieutenant Bailey," Kirk said, turning sharply toward the security team that was still on the bridge. "Try your phaser, carefully. Lowest stun setting."

Aiming at the deck by his feet, Bailey complied. A faint, purplish glow ringed the muzzle, but that was all.

Frowning, Bailey released the firing button, waited a moment, then pressed it again. Suddenly, he gasped and dropped the phaser.

"It's hot!" he said, shaking his hand and adding a belated "Sir."

"So," Kirk said, "our phasers obviously don't work any better than our sensors or transporters. I wonder what *does* work. Mr. Sulu, try the impulse engines, minimum power. Take us back toward the gate while you're at it. Now that this field has done whatever it's done, it might be worth trying to get through again, to see if there's been any change in the welcome it gives us."

"Aye-aye, sir," Sulu acknowledged as he tapped the commands into the helm.

Obediently, the *Enterprise* turned, pointing its bow in the direction of the invisible gate. "So far, so good, sir," Sulu said as the ship halted its rotation.

After a moment, the deck seemed to tilt very slightly, but the fuzzy image of the other ships on the viewscreen remained steady.

"Are we moving?" Kirk asked.

"Impulse power is being applied, sir, but without operational sensors, it's impossible to measure our speed, if any."

Kirk grimaced. "Scotty, how do the impulse engines look from down in engineering? They're not overloading, like the phasers?"

"There's nothing ta indicate it, Captain," Scott's voice came over the intercom. *"They seem ta be operating normally—as normally as* anything *is operating, that is."*

Kirk watched the seemingly motionless ships on the screen for another few seconds.

"All right," he said finally. "Mr. Sulu, bring the impulse engines up to quarter power."

"Quarter impulse power, sir."

A moment later, everything tilted.

Uhura almost slid off her chair into the communications station before she caught herself. The security team lurched backward, hitting the bulkhead on either side of the turbolift before they could regain their balance.

"Cut power!" Kirk snapped, but Sulu's fingers were reaching for the controls before the words were out.

The deck leveled itself, sending everyone lurching in the other direction.

"May I take it, Mr. Scott," Kirk said when stability had returned, "that the artificial gravity system was a partial casualty of the field? It can no longer fully compensate for impulse-power acceleration?"

"Aye, Captain, it seems that way," Scotty replied. *"But at least the impulse engines seem ta be working."*

"Is there anything you can do about the gravity? Or about anything else?"

"I canna say. If the readings can be stabilized, ta give me some idea o' what's really happening, then there's a chance. But, Captain, if ye're thinkin' o' testing the warp drive, I'd not be too hasty."

"Don't worry, Scotty, I'm not suicidal. Yet. Besides, even if the warp drive worked perfectly," he added, glancing at the viewscreen, "it would take us several thousand years to reach the nearest star. Either we find a way back through the gate, or—" Kirk pressed another button on the command chair. "Kremastor, now that our dead space is gone, what's the state of your nullifier? I don't suppose it's started working again."

"It has not."

"And after seeing this happen—how many times did you say? a hundred?—you still don't have any idea what this dead space is?"

"None."

"Is it always the same?"

"I have never before observed it from the inside, but it is always similar."

"Similar? But not the same? Tell us about the differences. Scotty, Spock, Ansfield, are you listening?"

"Of course I'm listening, Kirk!" Ansfield's voice erupted through the communication link. *"The only reason I haven't been asking a mountain of questions myself is that I figured you had enough to cope with without me getting in your hair."*

Kirk smiled. "Go ahead, Kremastor, tell us about the differences."

"Very few of the dead spaces have been precisely the same. My sensors function more efficiently in some than others. In some, they would not function at all."

"Have they all been the same size?"

"None has been as large as yours, nor has any lasted nearly as long."

"Is there any correlation between the size of the dead space and the size of the ship? Or the amount of time it takes it to close in?"

"I have never tried to analyze such things. I know only that none before has lasted more than a few minutes. And none of the beings in the ships has survived much longer. All, except you, have destroyed themselves within hours."

Kirk shook his head. "The more I hear, the more it sounds as if this dead space is something the ships themselves generate. But what about the color change? Does that always happen?"

"Color change?" Ansfield broke in. *"What color change?"*

"When the dead space vanished and everything stopped working, everything changed color. Didn't it happen to you in Kremastor's ship?"

"I didn't think— The colors looked different to me when he first kidnapped me, but I thought it was just the strange light in here. And there at the end, I was too busy listening to what was happening to you people to pay any attention to anything else. Besides, I was already so sickly looking—I'm looking at my uniform now, and at my hands—the uniform is a much deeper

blue, and my hands are sort of jaundiced-looking, even more than when Kremastor first snatched me. Is it the same with you?"

"It seems to be," Kirk said. "All the blues are deeper, almost violet in some cases. The greens are shading toward blue, reds are closer to orange, browns are—"

"Kirk! I've got it!" Ansfield's voice exploded from the intership link.

"Got it? Got what?"

"I see what's happened! Why nothing works the way it should, why everything's changed color! And I think I know how I can get out of here without having to perform major surgery on Kremastor!"

Suddenly, she laughed. *"Spock, can you get down to the physics lab?"*

"I assume, Commander," Kirk interrupted, "that you have a logical reason for this request."

"Darned right I do! If Spock can run a few simple experiments for me, then I can tell Commander Scott how to get the transporters working again. I think."

"And how might that be, lassie?" Scott broke in from the engineering deck, an unusual mix of annoyance and sarcasm in his tone.

"It should be just a matter of making a few basic adjustments, Mr. Scott, that's all."

"I've been makin' basic adjustments until I canna see straight!" Scott said. *"And a few adjustments not so basic! Unless ye know something that turns some o' the universal laws of physics upside down—"*

Ansfield laughed again but cut it off sharply. *"Actually, Mr. Scott,"* she said, *"I think I do. I'm betting that the universal laws you mentioned don't apply here! That's what Spock has to do in the physics lab, find out what—"*

"Don't be daft! They apply everywhere! That's why they call them universal laws."

"Everywhere in our own universe, Mr. Scott, our own universe. That's the catch. About a minute ago, when Kirk was telling me about the color changes, I suddenly realized something. We're not in our universe anymore!"

Chapter Twenty-two

THE GRIN WAS obvious in Commander Ansfield's voice as she acknowledged Spock's first finding in the lab: the speed of light, in this universe, was just under three hundred fifteen thousand kilometers per second, an increase of roughly five percent.

"This means," she said, *"that we're involved with at least three separate universes here! In Kremastor's, c is approximately three hundred eight thousand kilometers per second. Which explains why his sensors and transporters worked a little bit. The difference between his universe and this one is only half the difference between this one and our own, at least as far as the speed of light is concerned."*

Scotty spoke ruefully over the intercom from engineering. *"I should ha' seen it m'self, Captain. The ten-percent increase in engine output had ta come from somewhere."*

"We all should have seen more than we did," Kirk acknowledged from the bridge. *"The evidence is really pretty plain—in hindsight."*

Ansfield laughed aloud then, although her seeming high spirits were as much the result of anticipatory nervousness as genuine elation. After all, she was still locked away inside Kremastor's doorless ship, and until she stepped off the transporter platform on the *Enterprise*, she couldn't be positive that the necessarily jury-rigged modifications Commander Scott and his crew were making would do the trick.

"None of you had my advantages, that's all," she said with another laugh. *"In that musty collection in my cabin, there's a lot of nineteenth- and twentieth-century science fiction along with the romances and the rest, and those old-time writers, even if they weren't much good at 'predictions,' had wild ideas for practically all situations, including a few not all that different from the one we're in right now.*

"Anyway, it was the 'field' that fooled everyone, including me," she went on. *"But when Kirk was describing the color changes, I suddenly realized that every change was in the direction of a shorter wavelength, a higher frequency. And that's when the light finally came on. Once I realized we weren't just in a remote corner of our own universe but in another universe altogether, where the basic physical laws weren't quite the same, everything fit. First, there was the speed of light, which was obviously a little higher here. That's why all the colors were shifted toward the high-frequency end of the spectrum—red toward orange, green toward blue, and the like. And as you just now said, Mr. Scott, that's why the output of the anti-matter engines jumped ten percent, the old Mc^2 bit. With a higher c, there's got to be a higher power output. And the fact that nothing associated with*

224

subspace worked should've been a tipoff, too. Like warp drive, access to subspace depends on Cochrane's equations, and the speed of light is at the heart of every last one."

She paused, realizing abruptly that she was starting to sound as if she were back in her former career in the university, lecturing a class. But after a moment, when no other voice filled the tense silence, she went on, though perhaps a shade more softly. *"As I said, the basic problem was that we all insisted on thinking in terms of a 'field' surrounding the* Enterprise, *but it wasn't really a field at all. It was just a little 'bubble' of our own universe and its laws that we brought along with us. That's why everything seemed to work normally at first, at least inside the bubble—Kremastor's so-called dead space. And what we saw as the outer edge of the 'field' was just the surface of the bubble, the boundary layer between the two realities—a discontinuity, like the discontinuity at the boundary between air and water. And what Spock said about the 'field' around Kremastor's ship starting with Kremastor himself—his brain, actually, since that's all that's left of him—fit right in, too. And the way the bubble changed shape when it closed in on the* Enterprise, *developing two lobes, one centered on the main deck, where most of the crew—most of the minds—were, and a smaller one centered on the engineering deck, where fewer members of the crew were. It's our minds that were maintaining that bubble—and Kremastor said ours lasted longer than any other he'd seen,"* she finished, *"although I suppose that could be because there are so many of us instead of any inherent superiority."*

"I assume, Commander," Spock said, not looking up from his experiments in the physics lab, "that this is an example of the 'intuition' of which Dr. McCoy speaks so often and so highly."

"You're darned right, Spock!" McCoy, in the lab with Spock, chimed in before Ansfield could reply. "And it's the main reason people are still in control of computers instead of the other way around."

"In this case, Doctor," Spock said, "it would appear to involve a form of pattern recognition. Given more time and data, I would have recognized the emerging pattern—"

"Don't kid yourself, Spock! You wouldn't have spotted it any quicker than you do the 'patterns' that Jim uses to beat you in chess!"

"But the patterns the captain employs in chess are often simply not logical, Doctor, whereas the logic here is plain." Pausing, Spock looked up from the lab instruments. "Except for the Universal Gravitational Constant, Mr. Scott, all other fundamental values appear to be close enough to their values in our own universe that the differences will not affect transporter operations," he said. "As soon as you complete the modifications necessitated by the increase in c, you should be able to transport Commander Ansfield out of Kremastor's ship."

From the intership link came an audible sigh of relief.

Once the modifications were completed, Ansfield was quickly transported out of Kremastor's ship and returned to the bridge. Meanwhile, Kremastor's maps of the entire nexus system had been transferred to the

Enterprise computer for Spock to study. When the sensors came back on line, however, he abandoned the maps to run a complete recheck of Kremastor.

"His life-form readings are still decidedly odd, Captain," he announced after a minute. "They are, in fact, virtually identical to the readings obtained during the brief, earlier scan. However, I can now envision a possible explanation."

"I assume you plan to let us in on it, Spock," McCoy said when the Vulcan paused to consult the records of the earlier scan.

"Of course, Doctor. The seeming anomalies have to do with the biochemical reactions by which the life-form sustains itself."

"I don't suppose these anomalies could have anything to do with the fact that he's just a brain supported by a spaceship instead of a natural body," McCoy said when Spock paused again.

"That is part of it, of course, Doctor, but the chemical reactions, the basic metabolic readings themselves, are slightly askew. These data lead me to speculate that Kremastor is maintaining yet another bubble in which certain of the natural laws of his native universe continue to operate. I would also speculate that we ourselves are doing the same. If we were not, even the minor differences that exist between the natural laws of this universe and those of our own would have already proven fatal to us."

McCoy frowned. "You're saying that if we don't get the blazes out of here in short order, these secondary bubbles could disappear the same way the primary one did? And we'll end up dead in a few hours?"

"There are far too many unknowns in the equation

227

for me to make a reliable prediction concerning our own survival time. For example, the very fact that we are aware of the existence of these secondary bubbles may itself have an adverse effect on them."

"In other words, your guess is as good as mine," McCoy snorted. "And you *seem* to be suggesting that what we didn't know couldn't have hurt us. Did I hear right, Spock? Did you say we might have been better off ignorant?"

"In these peculiar circumstances, Doctor, that is unfortunately also a possibility. However, the overall knowledge we have just gained does give us a chance to save both ourselves and the Federation, whereas total ignorance would have gained us nothing—with the possible exception of a longer life here in exile."

Kirk, listening to the exchange, turned to Ansfield. "If we can believe Kremastor, our only chance of getting back into the gate system is to get his nullifier working again."

She nodded. "That or get rid of our invisible friend."

"At least we have a *chance* of repairing the nullifier," he said. "But the question is whether Kremastor is telling the truth about it. Or about his entire 'mission.' Your evaluation, Commander? You have been in closer, more prolonged contact with him than any of us."

Ansfield shrugged. *"I* believe him."

"Anyone else?" Kirk asked, glancing around the bridge.

"He did give us the map of the nexus system, Captain," Spock pointed out.

"Which could be incomplete or a total fake for all

228

we know," McCoy said, but then he grimaced. "But what other choice do we have, Jim? I don't relish making a career out of getting chewed up and spit out by that blasted gate. And I relish even less the idea of spending the rest of my days millions of parsecs from the nearest fishing hole."

But they did try the gate one more time without the nullifier and over Kremastor's objections. The results, however, were no different from the first four times.

Except that when they recovered this time, the strength of the entity's presence had increased dramatically. Now it could be felt by virtually everyone on board, not just Spock.

"The clan is gathering," Ansfield said with a shiver.

And when they spoke to Kremastor moments later, it was obvious that he, too, was feeling the entity's presence, perhaps even more intensely than anyone on the *Enterprise*.

Minutes later, with a modified tricorder, Scotty began locating the circuits that powered the nullifier ring, itself mounted next to the sensor array on the front of Kremastor's blocky, otherwise featureless ship. Locating the circuits took only minutes, but considerably more time was required to cut through the seamless, diamond-hard coating that covered every square centimeter of the ship. Either an excess of power, causing the torch to cut too deeply, or a deviation of more than a few millimeters from the prescribed cutting path could have disabled essential circuits.

Nor was modifying the alien circuits easy. Kremastor, his internal sensors monitoring the endangered circuits, provided Scotty with guidance that grew steadily more nervous, as if the effect the entity was having on Kremastor was growing stronger by the minute.

But in the end, despite moments when Kremastor seemed almost incoherent, the job was completed. According to Kremastor's readings, the modified nullifier circuits were operating nearly as well as when the ship had first been constructed around him.

Finally, the hull was resealed, and all was in readiness.

A mixture of elation and dread dominated Kremastor's thoughts as he maneuvered out of the huge ship's hangar deck.

Elation that the nullifier was once again in virtually perfect working order. After twenty thousand years of fear and frustration and isolation, the possibility of completing his mission had been revived and now hung before him like a tantalizing vision.

And dread because of the ever more threatening presence of the creature. For all of those twenty thousand years it had been his constant companion, a constant source of numbing fear, but never had it been as powerful, as terrifying, as now.

Was it gathering its strength to stop him from destroying the nexus system?

As soon as the Trap was nullified, would it simply take complete control and once again have the same freedom it had enjoyed before?

But he had no way of knowing if the creature was even *aware* of his mission.

Or of Kremastor himself.

The one called Spock seemed to be convinced that

the creature had a mind—several separate minds, even—that was capable of thought, but he offered no proof other than his own unverified and totally ambiguous mental contacts with the creature. Kremastor, on the other hand, had lived in terrifying proximity to the creature, virtually in symbiosis with it, for millennia, and he had yet to detect any indication of intelligence, any attempt at communication. There had never even been a true indication that it was alive, that it was not simply a mindless phenomenon of nature, a by-product of whatever forces allowed the nexus system itself to exist.

But regardless of its nature or its intelligence or its motives, if its power continued to grow as it had these last few hours, he would once again be totally incapacitated, as he had been when it had first attached itself to him, before the trauma of the Trap had overloaded his mind and given him the painful immunity that had allowed him to function at least minimally. Therefore, if he were going to complete his mission, it had to be done quickly. He had no time to waste.

Those on the *Enterprise,* particularly the one called Spock, wished to "investigate" whatever could be found at what, according to the maps, was the source of the system, the central nexus. In order to gain information that they hoped would help them in their own struggles against the creatures that had already invaded their home territory, they insisted on accompanying him on his mission.

And on delaying the final destruction of the system.

"Wait at least one cycle," the one called Kirk had said. *"You have already been forced to wait for thousands of years. A few more hours, in return for the*

possibility of saving tens of billions of lives in the Federation, doesn't seem a lot to ask."

And Kremastor had agreed.

He had even promised to do as they asked, but he was becoming increasingly certain that he could not keep that promise. Billions of his own ancestors had already been killed by this creature, and he could not bring himself to take even the slightest chance of allowing the killing to continue indefinitely into the future.

If, when he arrived at his destination, the creature's strength was still building, he would activate the device immediately. The hundreds of lives on that ship, even the billions at risk in their Federation, were as nothing compared to his millennia-delayed mission and the possibility of its failure. It was too late to save his own people, and it might be too late to save those who called themselves human, but it was not too late to save the countless other races that had not yet encountered the nexus system and its deadly inhabitant.

But first, before he could do anything, the Trap that had kept him here all those millennia had to be nullified.

Slowly, Kremastor approached the nexus, the *Enterprise* barely a kilometer behind. His own sensors had not been modified, so the image was the same phantom it had always been in this universe.

This universe . . .

For a moment, the recurring realization that he was separated not only from his home world but from his entire universe froze Kremastor's mind.

But at the same time, the even more chilling realization that he and his mission were responsible for not one universe but dozens or hundreds descended on him once again.

He forced himself toward calmness and continued his approach to the nexus, its image deceptively pale and fragile in his sensors.

Finally, he was within range.

Without hesitation, without announcing his action to the *Enterprise,* he activated the nullifier.

The ring on the blunt prow of his ship pulsed invisibly. Only in the circuits he monitored was there tangible evidence of its activity.

For a minute, then two, he continued. There was no indication of success, but he had known there would not be. The only indication would be when he once again attempted to enter the nexus system.

Finally, he shut the nullifier down.

And waited.

In twenty minutes and thirty-seven seconds, if he and his contemporaries, now twenty thousand years dead, had interpreted the maps correctly, he could enter the nexus and emerge, only seconds later, from the central nexus.

"Was it successful?" the one called Kirk asked when Kremastor had been silent for nearly five of the twenty minutes.

"We will know when we attempt to enter," he responded.

No one said more. For the remainder of the twenty minutes, there was silence between the ships.

"Begin the approach," Kremastor said.

As his last word died away, his ship surged forward. The *Enterprise* followed, now less than a half-kilometer behind. Within seconds, it was even with Kremastor, and there it stayed. The nexus filled his view. At these distances, even the phantom image his sensors produced began to show details, but swirls of ghostly smoke rather than the vivid, stormlike ragings the aliens had described.

Abruptly, the creature's presence seemed to grip Kremastor even more powerfully than before, almost drowning him in terror, and for a moment he was paralyzed with fear, certain he would lose control and be unable to act.

But he held on. The knowledge that completion of his mission, after all these millennia of tortured waiting, was once again within reach gave him a strength he had never known before.

And forced the decision on him.

He would not delay the destruction of the system a single second, let alone the hours the strangers requested.

He *dared* not delay, no matter how grateful he might be, no matter what he had promised them. Obviously, the creature was more powerful than ever. Given the slightest chance, it could paralyze him as it had before and prevent him from acting against it, prevent him from carrying out the destruction of the nexus system.

Or it could take control of the strangers—if it had not indeed been in control of them from the start!— and use their weapons to destroy him before he could act.

It would then be free to roam the nexus system from universe to universe, free to destroy civilization after civilization without the slightest hindrance!

He had no choice.

The instant he emerged from the central nexus, before the creature had the chance to paralyze or destroy him, *he* would destroy *it*. He would activate the device immediately, destroying the nexus system once and for all!

Chapter Twenty-three

KIRK WATCHED THE GATE as they waited. Unlike the nexus—the junctions that joined the individual gates —the gates maintained a constant size, this one approximately five hundred kilometers in diameter.

But the display of energies was no less spectacular, and the realization that a million such displays had been operating continuously for tens of thousands of years was almost impossible to conceive of. Whatever the source of those energies, it must be literally astronomical, as if someone had harnessed the Shapley center itself.

Despite the virtual certainty that the system was beginning to break down, to spring dangerous leaks, some of which threatened the very existence of the Federation, Kirk could not help but feel a gut-wrenching regret at the thought of destroying the entire system. Not just shutting it down, which would take far more knowledge than either Kremastor's people or Federation scientists yet possessed, but *destroying* it.

To shut it down, the energies involved would have

to be understood, and Kremastor's people, after generations of study, had not had that understanding, any more than Benjamin Franklin had had an understanding of the nature of electricity when, with more daring than sense, he had almost killed himself by pulling a bolt of lightning from the sky with a metal key on a kite string. They had learned to measure and manipulate the energies to a small extent, but primarily by trial and error. The basic nature and source of those energies were no less mysterious now than when Kremastor's ancestors had stumbled onto that first gate.

But perhaps the situation was different now, Kirk found himself rationalizing as he continued to watch the gate's almost hypnotic pyrotechnics. After all, none of Kremastor's people had realized that the gates were connected not just to different parts of their own universe but to totally different universes. With this new and critical information to work with, understanding might come more quickly than anyone could imagine.

Perhaps the differences between the energy levels of the different universes were themselves the source of the energy that drove the gates, just as the difference between the energy level of a thundercloud and the energy level of the ground below produced bolts of lightning. Perhaps, with this information, the Federation could learn to fully control the energy, not just manipulate it empirically—blindly—with no real understanding of what they were doing. Perhaps the system itself could be controlled, even temporarily shut down while a solution to the problem of the entity was sought. The thought of its total destruction and the resultant immeasurable loss ran counter to everything Kirk had ever felt.

Especially now that it was clear that not just one universe but several were involved. There was, in fact, no longer even a reason to assume that any two gates were in the same universe. Instead of a million gates spread throughout a dozen or a hundred universes, it could be that each and every gate opened into a different universe. The nexus in the Sagittarius arm might be the only opening in that entire universe.

Except for the leaks.

But wherever the gates led—could it be to different times as well as different universes?—was there no way to avoid destroying them? Now that the existence of the deadly creatures that roamed the system was known, now that the crew of the *Enterprise* had successfully coexisted with one of them for several days, wasn't it at least possible that, with this knowledge, the rest of the Federation could be taught to do the same?

Until real, full-scale communication with the creatures could be established?

Spock had already come close to communicating, particularly on his last attempt. And he insisted that he had detected no "hostility" during that or any other contact.

Was communication the answer? Kirk asked himself abruptly. It had proven to be the answer—the only possible answer—dozens of times before. Even in that chain of wars that had been raging for thousands of years before the *Enterprise* had become involved, the answer had been communication. Once the latest in the long line of combatants had begun to talk to each other, the destruction had, at least for the time being, stopped.

But in that instance, the warring factions had both been humanoid, not even all that different from each other physically or mentally.

Here, despite Spock's findings, Kirk couldn't even be positive he was dealing with a living being.

Shuddering inwardly at the memory of the paranoid fear the creature had generated during its brief attempt to control him, Kirk realized that there was really no decision to be made.

He had no choice.

For the sake of the Federation, for the sake of those other, unknown future civilizations, he dared take no chances.

If the maps Kremastor had given them were correct, the *Enterprise* would have just under three hours from the time it emerged from the central nexus to the time when the first window to the Sagittarius nexus opened.

They would spend those three hours gathering as much information as they could, but when the time was up, they would leave, no matter how little—or how much—they had learned. They would not try to convince Kremastor that he should postpone the completion of his millennia-spanning suicide mission for the sake of gaining more knowledge, not even for another single eight-hour cycle of the nexus.

But even as the determination firmed itself in Kirk's mind, Kremastor's voice forced itself through the static from the other ship: *"Begin the approach."*

Kirk braced himself as both ships surged forward. If the modifications to Kremastor's nullifier were as successful as the modifications to the *Enterprise*'s artificial gravity system had been—full impulse power now produced only the slightest hint of any imbalance—there would, at more than half of light speed, be only a flicker as they entered the gate and emerged from the central nexus milliseconds later.

If the modifications had not been successful, and the Trap had not been nullified—

Tensely, he waited as Spock counted down the seconds.

And suddenly, between the syllables of "zero," the gate and the millions of parsecs of emptiness that surrounded it were replaced by a field of stars that could have been those of the Federation.

Relief flooded through Kirk. They had made it!

An instant later, the relief was replaced by a sudden chill.

The entity, whose presence had been growing stronger virtually up to the moment of entry into the gate, was gone!

"Spock, can you detect the entity's presence?" he asked sharply.

"No, Captain. And Kremastor's ship," Spock added, indicating the viewscreen, "appears to be gone as well."

Abruptly, Kirk swung back to face the screen. Spock was right. During the approach to the gate, Kremastor's tiny ship had been only a few hundred meters distant, clearly visible, but now there was nothing, not even the nexus from which they had just emerged.

"The sensors, Spock," he snapped, but Spock had

already turned and was absorbing the multiplicity of readouts.

"Nothing registering, Captain," he said after a moment. "But the sensors now have a range of less than ten kilometers, and that range is already decreasing rapidly."

"Full stop, Mr. Sulu. I want us perfectly still before the local laws take over and ruin our artificial gravity again."

"Full stop, sir."

"Lieutenant Uhura, any signals?"

"Nothing but static, sir."

"Mr. Spock, how soon before the bubble—"

Abruptly, everything wavered, just as it had in that other universe.

And colors returned to normal.

"Does this mean," Ansfield said, looking at the restored science blue of McCoy's uniform, "that we're at least back in our own universe?"

"Perhaps, Commander," Spock said. "That could account for the speed with which the bubble shrank. In that other universe, our minds were opposing the changes, while here, if your hypothesis proves true, our minds would aid the—"

"*Mr. Spock!*" Lieutenant Crider's voice broke in from the physics lab, where he had been stationed, poised to perform as quickly as possible the same measurements Spock had done in the previous universe. "*Initial results indicate c and the gravitational constant are virtually identical to—to 'normal' values.*"

"That's good enough for me," Kirk said abruptly.

"Mr. Scott, get started putting things back the way they were, sensors top priority."

"Aye, Captain," Scott's voice came from engineering. *"It'll take a wee bit longer ta do the transporters and the artificial gravity anyway."*

Spock fed the necessary programming changes into the computer. In less than two minutes, Scott reported the sensor circuits were all returned to their original configurations. Moments later, as the sensors were reenergized, the nexus reappeared on the screen. It was the same kaleidoscopic maelstrom they had seen in the Sagittarius arm, flickering in and out of existence, expanding and contracting wildly.

"Full sensor capability, Captain," Spock announced, "but there is still no indication of Kremastor's ship or of any significant amount of matter closer than the nearest stellar system approximately half a light-year distant."

"Could he be out of range?"

"Only if he has gone into warp drive, Captain— which would be impossible for him in this universe without massive modifications to his warp engines."

"Then he either didn't enter the gate when we did or he somehow stayed inside."

"Or the Trap's still working after all," Ansfield added. "If the entity isn't with *us* anymore, maybe it attached itself entirely to Kremastor, and that's why we got through and he didn't."

"Or the two of them are in cahoots!" McCoy growled. "Maybe that whole show they put on for us back there was just a fake to get us here. Wherever the blazes 'here' is!"

Ansfield shook her head. "You're too suspicious,

McCoy. But there's only one way to find out: go back in and look for him. Besides," she added, turning to face Kirk, "we need him. Without Kremastor and his ship, there's not a whole hell of a lot we can do here."

"Unfortunately, Commander, you're right," Kirk agreed. "Mr. Spock, if we do go back into the nexus, can the computer, now that it has a complete set of maps, be trusted to get us back out of there, the way it got us out of the Sagittarius nexus?"

"The maps can be trusted only to the extent that anything connected with the nexus system and the entity can be trusted, Captain."

McCoy snorted. "If I didn't know you better, Spock, I'd say that sounded an awful lot like another 'Your guess is as good as mine.'"

"In this case, Doctor, it is. As I have often stated, logic cannot make reliable predictions without sufficient factual data on which to base those predictions. If you accept Kremastor's story as fact—"

"We can argue philosophy later, gentlemen," Kirk broke in. "Whether we can trust what Kremastor told us or not, we only have two choices. We can go into the nexus and search for Kremastor and the device he *said* is capable of permanently shutting down the system. Or we can learn as much as we can here and then return to the Sagittarius nexus and hope that what we've learned will be enough to keep the Federation from self-destructing. But unless one of the things we learn is a way of plugging the leaks in the system—"

"Captain!" Uhura interrupted. "Standard electromagnetic signal coming in on several frequencies!"

"Source?"

"One-seventeen, mark thirty-two."

"Spock, sensor scan."

An eyebrow arched minutely as he bent over the displays. "Nothing within range, Captain, but that heading coincides with the center of the nexus."

"And the signals are similar to those we received inside the nexus, sir," Uhura said, "the ones that gave us the first of the maps."

"Another map?" Kirk frowned. "A duplicate of what Kremastor has already given us?"

"I do not believe so, Captain," Spock said. "Although the computer cannot yet extract any intelligible information from the signals, it is able to compare the raw data it is receiving with the raw data it received before, and there are no matches. As yet, this is totally new information."

"Which is what we're here for," Kirk said abruptly. "It looks as if our search for Kremastor has been delayed."

Like the signals that had given them the maps, the new signals were designed for direct communication between relatively primitive computers. As a result, the data transfer rate was slow, almost as slow as the rate by which the data making up the original maps had been transferred. The window to the Sagittarius nexus was little more than an hour away when the flow of data finally stopped and the computer began its analysis.

Spock leaned closer, watching the computer readouts as the analysis progressed. After a minute, one eyebrow arched.

"Not just another map, Mr. Spock?" Kirk asked.

"No, Captain. The signals this time appear to have provided two things. First, an extensive language lesson so that what followed could be comprehended. And second, a warning."

"Warning?" Kirk said sharply. "Against what?"

"The use of the nexus, Captain. I can only assume that the warning was designed for those ships approaching the nexus from space, not those emerging from within the nexus. The warning directs us to keep a minimum distance of more than a billion kilometers."

"Nice of them. Could that be the range of the entity?"

"Such a range would not contradict our own experiences, Captain."

"And what else does this warning say? Even at a data transfer rate as slow as theirs, there had to be more than that."

"There is, Captain, a great deal more. Much is in the form of mathematical equations, presumably describing the nexus system itself, but there is what appears to be a lengthy verbal message as well."

Kirk glanced at the kaleidoscopic energies of the nexus. "Mr. Sulu," he said, "lay in a course to take the *Enterprise* through that window to the Sagittarius arm and back to Starfleet Headquarters. Set it to execute automatically if we ourselves are unable to do so. I want to be very sure that whatever is in our computer gets back to the Federation even if *we* don't."

"Aye-aye, sir."

"Now, Mr. Spock, let's hear that message."

"As you wish, Captain." Spock's fingers darted

across the science station controls, and a moment later a thin and reedy voice emerged from the computer.

"I am the last of the Risori," it began.

And as the words flowed, it slowly became clear what had happened, nearly a thousand centuries ago, to the people who called themselves the Risori.

More importantly, it became clear that this *was* the central nexus, the one from which the entire nexus system had sprung.

The warning, as most on the bridge already suspected, had been against the entity, the infection.

And, not surprisingly, the Risori were indeed the ones responsible for the nexus system.

What *was* surprising was that they were almost totally ignorant of its workings. They understood even less about the forces involved than had Kremastor's people. Their technological level, in fact, appeared to be well below that of the Federation. The method of data transmission employed in the warning was not, as Kirk and the others had assumed, a concession to the possibly less advanced races for whom the Risori had left the warning. Instead, it was, for them, state of the art.

In addition, the Risori hadn't even developed a rudimentary warp drive.

And the entity, the infection, was an even bigger mystery to the Risori than it was, now, to the crew of the *Enterprise*. The Risori who left the warning, the last of his race still alive at the time, knew only that it had suddenly appeared somewhere in the nexus system, that it had infected one or more of the exploratory ships, and that their own world and the half-dozen colony worlds that were all they had established during generations of nexus exploration were virtually wiped out by wars within a year.

The Risori, although "responsible" for the nexus system, had not "built" it, nor had they simply found it, as Kremastor's ancestors had done. What they *had* found was the equivalent of a single gate, apparently fixed in space as their solar system moved slowly past it. For several years, it was within easy reach of their impulse-power technology, and before long, a ship had entered the gate. And found itself—elsewhere.

For years, the Risori probed the gate with every instrument their scientists could devise. And eventually they discovered within the gate a new form of energy, the mathematical descriptions of which suggested to both Spock and Ansfield that it was closely related to the energies that were manipulated when a ship went into warp drive.

And they learned to harness that energy, first for their own ships, then for their world. Just as nineteenth- and early-twentieth-century humans had been able to use and mathematically describe electricity without ever understanding its true nature, the Risori used and mathematically described the energy they obtained from within the gates.

But then, purely by accident, they turned that energy back on the gate itself.

The gate had instantly expanded, and when a ship entered the enlarged gate, it found itself at a different "elsewhere."

By the same kind of trial-and-error methods that Kremastor's people had used millennia later, the Risori "developed" the nexus system for more than a generation then, feeding the energy back into it in a hundred different ways, opening a hundred different gates.

And with each new gate, the available energy increased.

And changed.

Then, without warning, the gate became a nexus.

A vortex, spinning madly through whatever dimensions it existed in, opening thousands of gates, one after the other.

Like a tornado born out of the complex, conflicting energies in a planetary atmosphere, a nexus was born out of the energies within the gates, the energies that had been blindly twisted and altered by the Risori.

And the nexus sustained itself on those same energies.

And spawned new vortices, new nexus. For Kirk, his midwestern childhood suddenly fresh in his memory, the description stirred vivid images of tornado after tornado growing out of the energies of a single violent thunderstorm. He even wondered if the tiny "pockets of reality" they had found in the very centers of the nexus were somehow analogous to the eye of a hurricane, a point that remained perfectly calm while destruction raged all about it.

And he marveled that the Risori, knowing they had virtually no control and little real understanding of this awesome process, had ever brought themselves to enter it, to even attempt to chart it.

But enter it they had, for a half-dozen generations.

Even so, there were so many destinations available that only a minute percentage were ever actively explored. The "maps," broadcast throughout the nexus system by transmitters safely hidden in the "reality bubbles" within the nexus themselves, were the equivalent of an astronomer's map of the sky, in which the only information for a vast majority of the stars is their locations, simply telling another astronomer where to point his telescope to look at specific stars. The nexus maps the Risori generated gave similar information, but the "location" corresponded to a specific time during the cycle of a nexus.

The only other information consisted of codes indicating which gates had been passed through and the conditions found on the other side. In those rare instances, such as the Sagittarius nexus, where the destinations were within galaxies or star clusters, maps of the stars surrounding those gates were made. In those even rarer instances, six in all, in which a habitable planet was found within impulse-drive range of a destination, the Risori established outposts, then colonies.

And because they put virtually all of their resources into exploring the nexus system, they never developed warp drive, which, ironically, could have given them ten or a hundred times the six habitable planets that the nexus system ever gave them.

And then the infection—the entity—came.

No one knew what gate or gates it had come through.

No one knew what it was or what it wanted, even if it was a living thing.

No one knew how to stop it.

They only knew, too late, that it was destroying them.

And then the Risori were gone, leaving behind only

the maps and the warning, which, powered by the same energies that had created and sustained the nexus, would continue as long as the nexus themselves remained in existence.

The Sagittarius arm window was less than five minutes away when Kirk gestured for the Risori voice to be silenced.

"*Is* the system controllable, Mr. Spock?" Kirk asked sharply.

"Based on the limited information so far obtained, Captain, I would say yes, but not for many years. Even the simplified mathematical descriptions included in this message indicate that a warping of space itself plays a major role, but the equations require at least six dimensions to be valid. As far back as the twentieth century, however, there have been theories requiring the universe to have as many as eleven dimensions, so this by itself is not—"

"We have only four minutes to make a decision, Mr. Spock. Your best guess as to how long it would take to turn mathematical theories into something that could shut down an existing nexus without destroying the entire system?"

"A basic understanding could conceivably be achieved within a decade, Captain, but to convert that understanding into physical equipment capable of manipulating those forces—"

"Commander Ansfield?" Kirk interrupted. "Do you agree?"

"I certainly can't see it being done any faster. That was not freshman calculus being tossed around there."

"Then we have no choice. Returning to the Federation with no more than we have now would be pointless. Our only chance is to find Kremastor and hope that he's able to complete his mission."

"And if we can't find him?" Ansfield asked.

Kirk turned abruptly to the helmsman. "Mr. Sulu, you have three minutes to get a shuttlecraft ready to enter the nexus. Spock, Uhura, transfer as much data as possible concerning the entities and the nexus system to the shuttlecraft's onboard computer."

Acknowledging, they began.

Sulu brought the *Enterprise* about and, on full impulse power, took it to within a dozen kilometers of the nexus, then hastily checked that the remote controls were still engaged and that the shuttlecraft answered the helm.

Spock, mentally calculating shuttlecraft computer capacity as he worked, selected blocks of data and routed them to the communications section, where Uhura fed them directly to the shuttlecraft computer. At the same time, she initiated a series of commands that would cause the shuttlecraft, once through the nexus and in the Sagittarius arm, to continuously broadcast the information on as many subspace channels as the shuttlecraft communications system could handle, including Starfleet Headquarters' top-priority emergency channel.

"Ready to launch, Captain," Sulu said as the hangar deck doors clamshelled open.

"Get it under way, Mr. Sulu. Thirty seconds to the Sagittarius window."

"Aye-aye, sir."

But even as Sulu reached for the controls, his fingers

251

barely an inch from the buttons that would send the shuttlecraft sweeping out through the hangar deck doors and into the nexus, he froze under a sudden avalanche of paralyzing terror.

The entity, wherever it had been the last three hours, had returned, with a vengeance.

Chapter Twenty-four

SEEING SULU GO RIGID, the tendons in his neck and hands suddenly standing out in sharp relief, Kirk started to lunge from the command chair toward the helmsman's station.

But the intent had barely formed in his mind, his upper body barely begun to lean forward, when his own body stiffened, his mind submerged in a sea of terror that made his earlier experience with the entity pale by comparison. Suddenly, everyone and everything was a source of deadly but unknown danger. Even his own body had become the stuff of nightmares, an alien physical shell holding him—his mind—a helpless prisoner!

Spock, hearing the involuntary gasps from both Sulu and the captain, turned abruptly, but before he could more than realize what must be happening, he, too, was immobilized by the same impossible, paralytic fear.

Moments later, Ansfield was cursing between clenched teeth at the irrationality of the fear that

253

suddenly gripped her, at the stubborn refusal of her muscles to respond to her commands.

Lieutenant Woida, still at the navigator's station, was caught as he made a desperate stab at the controls Sulu had not been able to reach.

An instant later, Uhura and McCoy and the security team by the turbolift joined the frozen tableau.

And the *Enterprise* impulse engines surged into life.

For an instant, Kirk's fear-clouded mind assumed with new panic that the entity had, in addition to paralyzing the entire bridge crew, taken over the helm.

But then the spark of rationality that even now remained in a corner of his mind reminded him: the automatic maneuver Sulu had laid in nearly an hour before, the maneuver that would take the *Enterprise* back through the nexus to the Sagittarius arm if it were not canceled.

"Computer!" he grated, his jaws aching from the effort. The maneuver had to be stopped. He dared not bring home to the Federation an entity that was, if the last few seconds were any indication, far more powerful than any either he or the Federation had yet encountered. "Abort instructions, code alpha three seven—"

But something stopped him.

And for the first time, he realized it was more than terror that was paralyzing his body.

Something—the entity!—was actually in his mind, controlling it, keeping him from acting, just as it was keeping Sulu's fingers from moving that last inch and a half to the controls that would have launched the shuttlecraft.

Terror, any terror, he could overcome, given time, but this he could not.

Not in time . . .

The gate loomed ahead, filling the screen with its chaotic energies.

The *Enterprise* plunged into them.

For an instant, there was the remembered freedom of limbo.

And then they were through.

The stars of the Sagittarius arm were spread out around them.

And, behind them, the swirling turbulence of the nexus.

But there was more.

Even through the irrational terror in which the entity was drowning him, Kirk saw that the Sagittarius nexus was no longer alone.

Like jagged wounds, a half-dozen of the leakage gates blotted out great swaths of stars.

And radiating out from the constantly expanding and contracting disk of the nexus itself were a dozen even more jagged, lightninglike rips in space, pulsing with an intensity that outshone the nexus itself.

Even more vividly than before, an image of tornadoes raging across midwestern plains filled Kirk's mind. But where planetbound tornadoes swallowed up trees and houses and cities, these storms, infinitely more far-reaching, more powerful, could—*would*—swallow up whole planets and suns.

If they weren't stopped.

If the *entity* wasn't stopped.

"Sulu!" He managed to force the word out against all the opposition the entity apparently could muster.

But then, as he began to form another word, the entity vanished.

As suddenly as it had returned, it vanished.

Within a split second, the fear and paralysis were gone, all muscles suddenly released from teeth-grinding tension.

"Get the shuttlecraft out, set it to broadcasting, now!" The words exploded from Kirk's throat, and only as they battered at his ears did he realize he was shouting.

Without acknowledging, Sulu managed to comply.

And Uhura to open an emergency channel to Starfleet Headquarters.

There was no response.

But as she scanned through the subspace spectrum, the speakers suddenly erupted with static.

And a voice, filled with hate and terror: *"Damn you, Kirk! You've destroyed the Federation!"*

And a face appeared on the screen.

It was Captain Sherbourne of the U.S.S. *Devlin,* his dark face haggard, his eyes glittering in the dim light of emergency backup power.

"Sherbourne!" Kirk half shouted, then forced himself to lower his voice. "What happened?"

"As if you didn't know, you and your gates to hell!"

"I *don't* know, Captain. We've tried the emergency channel to Starfleet Headquarters, but—"

"They can't hear you! They evacuated hours ago! It's probably gone by now, sucked up by these damned gates! They're everywhere!"

"In Federation space? The same as here?"

"Worse, damn it, worse!" Sherbourne's voice

256

choked. *"There was one spreading toward Earth, for God's sake! Earth!"*

Kirk turned abruptly from the screen, feeling more anger and helplessness than he had ever experienced. "Spock! Isn't there any way to get back to the central nexus? Without waiting for the next cycle? Even if we *can't* find Kremastor, we could do *something!"*

"I fear not, Captain," Spock replied, his voice efficient and unemotional even now. "I have already had the computer check Kremastor's maps for alternate routes through the system. If it were fully functional, such routes would exist, but even then the shortest would require five hours and forty-seven point five minutes. There is, however, another possibility, albeit only a theoretical one."

"At this point, any chance, no matter how slim, is better than none at all. Explain."

"Very well, Captain. From my preliminary analysis of the mathematical descriptions of the nexus forces, it is likely that what we call limbo is in reality the extradimensional space outside our own universe, the space in which both our universe and all those other universes are contained. An oversimplified but nonetheless appropriate way to visualize it in more comprehensible terms would be to think of each individual universe as a one-dimensional length of string, existing in three-dimensional space. These strings are apparently twisted in vastly complex patterns, doubling back on each other, touching each other, even knotted together in great tangles. Where the strings—the universes—touch, there is a gate or a potential for a gate. In a nexus, the energies the Risori inadvertently set in motion continually twist or warp one of the universes so that it sweeps through the surrounding extradimensional space, touching each of the hundreds or thousands of nearby universes—or distant points of the same universe—one at a time."

"Which means?" Kirk prompted urgently.

"It merely means, Captain, that in terms of the extradimensional space itself, all points connected by the nexus system are necessarily in close proximity. It is that very closeness that allows the gates—the contact points—to exist. Therefore, if we were able to enter that extradimensional space and navigate within it, we could in all likelihood locate and enter any of those other universes."

"Except," Kirk said grimly, "we *can't* navigate in it. We're blind and deaf in there."

"Precisely, Captain. Within that space, our own senses appear to be totally disconnected from our bodies, if our bodies, or anything physical, indeed do exist there. The Risori maps provide the computer with the commands that will return a ship through that space to the universe from which they entered, but that is all. The fact that such commands exist, however, does argue logically that physical objects such as the computer—and our bodies—do exist within—"

"What's the blasted point, Spock?" McCoy erupted. "Why the devil are you wasting time telling us about something that *can't* help us?"

"Aside from the fact that the captain requested an explanation, Doctor, the imparting of knowledge is *never* a waste of time. In addition, while it is true that I myself cannot logically envision a method whereby we could successfully navigate through the extradimensional space, is it not possible that, if you collectively applied your minds to the problem, the human intuition of which you so often speak might provide a solution?"

"And since when have you become a fan of intuition, Spock?" McCoy snapped. "In any event, it's not the sort of thing you can turn on or off just by snapping your blasted fingers! And if you think—"

On the *Devlin,* Sherbourne gasped loudly, and everyone on the *Enterprise* bridge spun toward the screen. Sherbourne's face was contorted, his lips pressed tightly together, his fingers gripping the arms of his command chair like a vise.

"Captain Sherbourne! What—"

"Haven't your creatures had enough fun, Kirk?" Sherbourne grated between clenched teeth. *"Do they want the rest of us this time? Is that why you came back, to help them finish us off?"*

"They're *not*—!" Kirk began, half shouting, but he broke off abruptly as Sherbourne's image vanished from the screen.

And then the nexus filled the screen, but it was no longer even circular. It seemed to have shattered, as if it were a plate that had been struck by a bullet. But even as they watched, the breaks healed. The multicolored chaos of energy arced across the gaps, welding the sections together into a misshapen whole.

But before the sealing was complete, a jagged lightning bolt of energy, several times as massive as the dozen that had existed before, erupted from one of the breaks.

And it was headed straight for the *Enterprise!*

Sulu, not waiting for orders, automatically started to take evasive action, but it was too late.

The runaway energy simply moved too rapidly, covering the distance between the nexus and the ship in fractions of a second.

Briefly, violently, the maelstrom of energies surrounded them, blotting out all the stars, all the other gates, everything.

Then the energies themselves vanished.

And with them, everything else.

Everything was gone—the *Enterprise,* the stars of the Sagittarius arm, their own bodies, everything.

Except their minds.

Once again, they were in the limbolike nothingness of extradimensional space.

Chapter Twenty-five

SPOCK WAS FREE.

His body did not exist.

Despite the catastrophic circumstances of an instant before, there was a moment when all the turmoil he had left behind was blotted out, when all that mattered to him was this sudden renewal of the freedom he had experienced twice before. There was even time enough for a strangely detached elation to fill his mind. *If this is what happens to all who are absorbed by the nexus system,* his thoughts told him, *perhaps it is for the best. Life-forms, particularly those that call themselves human, are forever being betrayed by their bodies. Here such betrayals would be impossible.*

But the elation fled, far more swiftly this time than during his first encounter with the bodiless temptations of limbo. Once again, he realized, though still with a touch of sadness, that he was simply rationalizing. His responsibilities had not vanished with the real world. They still existed, were still as powerful as they had been only moments before, and it would be both dishonorable and illogical to try to ignore them.

And then, as if let loose by a suddenly ruptured dam, the memories of the chaos and destruction that had been left behind in normal space flooded back. The unreal detachment vanished, and a sense of urgency gripped him once again. Starfleet Headquarters had been evacuated, perhaps already swallowed up by the catastrophically failing nexus system. Earth itself, according to Captain Sherbourne, was threatened, if not already absorbed.

And Kremastor, whose ship held the only known solution, was lost.

Or had fled.

By now he could be in any of an unknown number of universes.

Or in the limbo of extradimensional space, where he would be even more inaccessible.

But none of that mattered. He *had* to be found.

There was, therefore, only one logical course open to Spock: to search for Kremastor. To do otherwise, to not immediately undertake the one course of action that offered even a minuscule chance of success, would be both illogical and irresponsible.

Without hesitation, he reached out, opening his mind as he could never have opened it while burdened with the body that held him captive in normal space.

Though fully aware that the sensation could be mere illusion, Spock felt his mind spread outward like the expanding globe of the ship's sensors.

As he had done during his first experience in extradimensional space, he touched the others—

Commander Ansfield, Dr. McCoy, the captain, Uhura, Sulu, Woida, and the hundreds of others who had been on the *Enterprise*. But this time, instead of attempting any real contact, any communication or comfort, he only allowed their mental patterns to register and then let them slip away as his mind continued to flow outward.

Then another cluster of patterns—Sherbourne and the crew of the *Devlin?* Was that why the *Devlin*'s signal had vanished? Had they, too, been swallowed up by the chaos of the failing nexus system?

For an instant, Spock paused, knowing they were experiencing this for the first time, but after only the briefest of touches he pulled away and let their patterns fall behind. Even if he could communicate with them, what could he tell them that would help? And whatever time he spent in an attempt to communicate, whether he was successful or not, would only delay his search for Kremastor.

And he could afford no delays.

But would he recognize Kremastor even if he did find him? He had had no mental contact with him, so how could he recognize the pattern?

And what else would he find here? How many others had this limbo swallowed up over the millennia? Through how many millions or billions of mental patterns would he be forced to search?

And what if there were beings native to these dimensions? Could the entities themselves be such natives? Or had they—

Suddenly, without warning, there was contact.

But not with Kremastor.

In an instant, Spock's mind was inundated with blind, unreasoning terror.

In another instant, images from unremembered nightmares swarmed around him, summoned out of the nothingness to provide a reason for the otherwise inexplicable, illogical terror.

It was the entity, of course, perhaps the entire swarm of entities.

Logically, it could be nothing else.

And, knowing the terror's source, Spock also knew that he could control even this unprecedented assault. Particularly here, unburdened by an often treacherous body, he could overcome virtually anything.

Methodically, he began to blank out the hollow, nightmare images, the senseless, illogical images that the human half of his mind had always insisted on manufacturing but which his Vulcan discipline had, until now, been capable of suppressing before they reached his full consciousness.

Meticulously, he began to isolate the terror and lock it away from the logical, reasoning part of his mind, just as he had always isolated and locked his emotions away in a place where they could not affect his actions.

And as he slowly forced the terror to retreat, as he gradually regained full use of his mental capacities, another realization came to him.

He was not alone with the entities.

Another mind was there, another pattern—a pattern that had not been totally left behind with the others of the *Enterprise*.

Another mind, a human mind, that had almost certainly been savaged by the same irrational terror that had, in those first moments of contact, nearly destroyed even Spock's mind.

A mind that, based on all that he knew of the undisciplined nature of human thought processes, should have been reduced almost instantly to virtual catatonia. Even the captain, who had been able to withstand the lesser assaults when the *Enterprise* had first come within range of the Sagittarius nexus, could not have withstood this vastly more powerful assault.

But *this* mind was not paralyzed with fear.

From the moment it appeared, it had literally screamed out another, radically different emotion: *exultation!*

For an instant, the terror surged back into Spock's mind, and he found himself wondering wildly if the exultation he felt soaring about him could be coming not from the human mind he had sensed but from the entity itself. If, somehow, the entity had finally achieved some millennia-delayed objective and now saw its ultimate victory over all life within reach, *it* could be the source of the exultation.

But the instant passed, and the exultation remained.

Reaching out, he touched it.

And the mind behind it.

It was, he realized with only mild surprise, the mind of Commander Ansfield.

And in that instant of recognition, there was also a blending, sudden and chaotic, Ansfield's mind sweeping effervescently through his, its memories sparkling.

And he saw what had sparked the exultation, saw what had, suddenly and unexpectedly, flashed into her mind only moments before.

He saw the truth that she had discovered about the entity, and for one glittering moment he shared her exultation, shared her memory of that pulse of intuition. And he shared her even more exotic memory of how something in her mind had grasped the emotional energy previously bound up in terror and somehow turned it inside out, into the exultation that now dominated them both.

Only in humans would such an illogical transformation be possible, his Vulcan half thought with a mixture of envy and relief. Only in humans could love be turned to hate, joy to tears, terror to exultation, in an instant.

And only a human, certainly no Vulcan, could have had the flash of insight—inspired, he wondered, by yet another of her "musty volumes"?—that had revealed the truth to her.

A truth that he realized, now that he had shared her triumphant thoughts, was only logical.

And, more importantly, a truth that confirmed his own earlier convictions about the entity's lack of hostile intent.

For it was not malevolence that drove the entity's actions, only a constant, unending terror. For all the millennia it had roamed the nexus system, during all the times it had emerged into the alien universes it stumbled into, it had to have been at least as terrified as any of the life-forms it had encountered.

The entity was, her flash of intuition had told her, from a *truly* alien universe, a universe where the laws were not merely modified versions of those in a "normal" universe but truly and incomprehensibly different.

And, like all life-forms that cross into other universes, the entity had brought its own universe's natural laws with it. Otherwise, it could not have survived.

And it was the alienness of these physical laws that generated an instinctive terror in whatever life-forms the entity came near. As the alien, eight-legged form of a spider can generate an instinctive fear on a conscious level in humans, the fragments of the alien universe that the entity carried with it generated a much more powerful instinctive fear, a terror that reached into the deepest, most fundamental levels of the mind.

And those terrorized life-forms, unaware of the true source of the terror, reacted by dredging up imagined but familiar sources as rationalizations. Spock himself had reacted precisely that way only moments before he had become aware of Ansfield's presence. Like an imaginative human walking through a graveyard at midnight, he had conjured up a thousand imaginary horrors. To a sourceless fear, he had assigned a source, as had countless others before him.

And in real space, these encounters could only be worse. There the terror could be shunted onto real objects. A fellow crewman could be seen as a scheming enemy. An approaching ship could be seen as a deadly danger. Reflexively, the victims of such terror would strike out violently at whatever their emotion-drenched minds tricked them into believing was the source of that terror.

And the death and destruction would begin. And continue, often long after the entity perished or retreated into the nexus system.

But now, now that the truth was known—

With no reservations remaining, logical or otherwise, Spock threw himself fully into the amalgam that was himself and Ansfield.

Together, then, they reached out for that third, alien mind.

And touched it.

And allowed themselves, literally, to be absorbed, for, as Spock had realized during that brief, earlier contact, absorption by the entity was the only way that any real communication could ever be initiated.

The entity had no name, nor any need for a name.

It had never before conceived of the existence of any living thing separate from itself.

But slowly it began to understand, at least as much as such a being ever *could* understand when confronted with something as utterly alien as the concept of individual, separate beings.

Through the Spock-Ansfield amalgam of minds, it "saw" a universe where matter and energy existed, where intelligence was invariably imprisoned in some form of matter or dependent on some form of physical energy for its very existence.

Through the entity's mind, Spock and Ansfield "saw" a universe where neither matter nor energy existed, a universe where the only thing that existed was pure intelligence, an entire universe that *was* a form of intelligence.

They saw a gate to that universe ripped open, sucking a fragment of that universe through, into the extradimensional limbo where the nexuses whirled through their violent cycles. They saw the beginnings of its desperate search for its home universe, a search for what was, literally, the rest of itself.

They saw fragments of the entity split off and recombine and split off again as it continued its search. They saw it, after what must have been millennia, learn to maneuver through the twisting energies of the nexus and the limbo surrounding them.

And they saw it emerge, finally, into other universes.

And they felt the sudden terror caused by the alien laws of those universes, a terror that smothered it every single moment.

And they saw, filtered through their own distorting mental lenses, how those other universes had appeared to the entity: boundless wastelands, virtually empty of intelligence except for occasional, flickering firefly glows that either fled or were extinguished whenever it approached. Tiny, transient glows which the entity had never until now realized were anything other than detached fragments of itself. For, until now, in this amalgam with Spock and Ansfield, it had simply had no concept of individual, separate intelligences, just as it had had no concept of matter or energy.

Over the millennia, fragment after fragment had approached ship after ship, world after world, never able to make contact except for deluges of terror and utterly incomprehensible images and desires, but still it had not realized the truth. These things it encountered were simply fragments of itself, it thought, fragments that had lost the ability or the desire to recombine. Fragments that had, in effect, been driven insane by millennia of constant terror.

But then it became aware that certain of these aberrant fragments possessed a knowledge that allowed them not only to maneuver through the energies of the nexus system but to find specific universes, possibly even to find its own home universe. But it could not communicate with these fragments any more than it could with the others. It could only attach other, still-sane fragments of itself to any that might possess this knowledge and continue to try to communicate, to try to influence them to return to within the nexus system, where the terror was less, where the possibility of communication might be greater.

And then one of the fragments had encountered the fragments that were the crew of the *Enterprise.*

For the first time in millennia, it was able to establish at least the beginnings of contact with one of the aberrant fragments.

And it had done everything it could to draw those fragments into the nexus system and reestablish that contact without driving them away or extinguishing them, as it had done with so many before.

But then it had become aware that one of the other fragments—one with which it had coexisted for millennia but with which it had until that moment never been able to establish even the slightest contact—was about to destroy the nexus system. And it had gathered itself together and pursued that fragment into the nexus system, where it still remained, not extinguished but unable to function, unable to carry out its mission of destruction.

And it had returned to the fragments that were the *Enterprise.*

And, at last, there was communication.

But now, as virtually all the fragments were gathered together and recombined, as the entity's growing mind merged ever more completely with that of Spock and Ansfield, the entity finally realized that these countless glows were not simply aberrant fragments of itself, traumatized by prolonged exposure to the terrors of one alien universe after another.

Each one was a complete being like itself, but somehow indivisible and incredibly fragile!

They were beings that, it realized with horror, it had destroyed—by the billions!

And as the realization of the immensity of what it had done flooded the entity's mind, it drew back from the merging, not in terror but in overwhelming remorse and sadness.

And then it began to fade.

Like a human who is unable to face an intolerable burden of guilt will allow himself to die, the entity simply allowed its life force to drain away.

But the Spock-Ansfield amalgam would not let it go, for by then they had realized that this entity was their only hope for saving themselves and the *Enterprise*— even the Federation.

For what seemed like forever, somehow controlling their reaction to its alienness, they refused to release it, kept its life force from fading completely while they merged with it ever more completely.

Until, at last, it comprehended what they wanted, what they needed.

And it began to grow stronger. And sadly eager. It saw that, in what would undoubtedly be the last act of its existence, it had some small chance to make up for the millennia of death and destruction for which, all unknowing, it had been responsible.

It drew back from its own extinction.

Controlling its ever-present terror with a new, unbreakable determination, it detached fragments of itself to join these strange, delicate creatures and to guide them to their destinations. At the same time, other fragments returned to the paralyzed shell of that other creature, where, slowly and deliberately, they took control.

In an instant, Kremastor's world had turned inside out.

His hopes of finally completing his mission, so high one moment, had been totally crushed the next.

One second, he had been driving toward the gate, determined that the moment he emerged from the central nexus, he would initiate the destruction of the entire nexus system.

The next second, even as the ghostly energies of the gate enveloped him, the creature had struck.

And this time he had no chance to resist. The attack he had fended off only seconds before was feeble by comparison. This time, the moment the creature struck, Kremastor was lost, control of his ship gone.

And he was trapped.

In limbo.

With the creature.

It swarmed about him, violating his mind, driving him farther and farther toward the insanity that, he now feared, would provide his only relief.

Mentally, as long as he was able, he screamed for release, but it was as if the creature didn't hear.

Or simply enjoyed Kremastor's raging terror.

There was no response of any kind, only the continued, smothering presence.

But then, as abruptly as it had come, the creature was gone.

Once again, Kremastor was alone.

But even then, he could not act. He could only cringe in the nothingness, terrified that if he attempted the slightest action, the creature would return.

Forgotten was his mission.

Forgotten were the millennia he had waited.

Forgotten were his ancestors, the billions who had died.

Forgotten were his own people, who had sent him on this impossible task, hoping desperately that he could save the billions that remained.

Forgotten were the newcomers and their own tales of the creature's depradations.

Forgotten was everything but the literally paralyzing fear that the creature would return.

And then, after what seemed like an eternity of waiting, it did return.

But nothing changed for Kremastor.

Cowering in the nothingness of limbo, he could still do nothing but wait, hoping desperately that his renewed torture would soon end, that somehow he would be allowed to end his existence.

But then, although he hadn't believed it possible, the terror began to intensify.

Slowly, with great deliberation, the creature entered Kremastor. Now, apparently not satisfied with simply enveloping him, it merged with him.

His last sanctuary, his own mind, was lost to him.

And then, as the possession became complete, he felt the creature moving within him, altering his mind, devouring his consciousness, turning him into a hollow shell in which it would take up permanent residence.

And still he remained fully aware, unable to suppress even the tiniest fragment of the horror and revulsion that consumed him.

And his ship began to move.

The creature now had full control.

Kremastor could only observe, helpless, as the ship abruptly emerged from the nexus, its maelstrom of energies once again vivid and tumultuous in his sensors, not pale and ghostly as they had been in that other place.

Without hesitation, the ship turned.

And the device Kremastor had waited all these millennia to use suddenly came to life.

An irregular pulsing spread almost instantly across the nexus as the energies that drove it began to oscillate in the deadly feedback the device had initiated.

And as the pulsing grew stronger, Kremastor's mind finally was able to focus on something besides the paralyzing terror that still gripped him.

He could focus on the fact that, though he could not himself complete his mission, the creature was, impossibly, completing it for him.

And in the midst of the terror, a kernel of exultation began to grow as he saw the pulsing of the nexus continue to grow stronger, its energies being driven deeper and deeper into the oscillatory pattern that would soon destroy it.

And as the exultation grew, the nexus, like an increasingly variable star suddenly going nova, erupted outward in one final, all-consuming pulse.

And then he and the creature and the nexus were gone forever.

Chapter Twenty-six

ANSFIELD WAS GONE.

Spock was alone with the entity, and he was moving, streaking through a limbo that was no longer featureless but filled with shapes and colors, the shapes and colors that his mind produced as a feeble analogue for the chaotic nexus energies that the entity somehow perceived and navigated through.

And then, abruptly, the motion ceased.

And the shapes and colors twisted and faded and became a phantom image of the *Enterprise* helm controls.

And his own body, wispy and translucent, took shape as well, somehow sharing the space before the helm with an equally insubstantial Sulu.

And the amalgam that was Spock and the entity knew the course that had to be laid in.

His translucent fingers touched the controls.

And as the course was entered, his phantom body and the controls began to fade.

But barely were they gone when the bridge of the *Enterprise* leaped into existence around him, solid and real. The stars of the Sagittarius arm filled the viewscreen. Only inches in front of him, Sulu, precisely where his phantom image had been a moment before, lurched slightly as the material world made itself felt.

"Mr. Sulu," Spock said instantly. "Take us away from here, maximum impulse power, *now!* Ten million kilometers, minimum!"

"But warp drive—"

"Impulse power, Mr. Sulu. *Now!*" And then, as Sulu's fingers tapped in the commands, "The *Devlin*'s warp-drive engines, I suspect, are not currently functional, and I do not believe it wise to leave them behind. The nexus is about to be destroyed."

And they were moving.

And next to them was the *Devlin*. Ansfield and the fragments of the entity that had remained merged with her had guided it out of limbo just as the others had done with Spock and the *Enterprise*. Its impulse engines throbbing on emergency power, it kept pace.

Behind them, visible through the modified sensors, were the nexus and all the jagged leakage gates. Lightning bolts of energy radiated cancerously from virtually every one of them, as if space itself were on the verge of breaking up.

And the gates were pulsing now, all in unison, flaring into new brilliance, then fading.

Suddenly, the *Devlin* began to fall behind.

Spock, as if he had been expecting—or fearing—just such a development, spoke instantly. "Lieutenant Uhura, get Captain Sherbourne on the *Devlin*, now! On the screen!"

Hesitating only for a sideways glance toward Kirk, who sharply nodded assent, she complied.

An instant later, almost before Spock had finished transferring the pulsing images of the chaos behind them to a secondary screen, the *Devlin*'s bridge shimmered into view. Captain Sherbourne, his face even more haggard and intense than before, stood near the helm, using both hands to pull someone from the controls.

It was Commander Ansfield.

"Whatever you do, Captain Sherbourne," Spock's voice shot across to the *Devlin*, "don't stop your ship now! If you don't trust Commander Ansfield to work the controls, work them yourself, but *keep moving!* You must be at least ten million kilometers from the nexus or any of the related phenomena as soon as possible." And then, to Sulu: "Be ready with a tractor beam if it becomes necessary, Lieutenant."

Sherbourne, his grip on Ansfield only tightening, glared at the screen. *"Kirk! I don't know how you and that Vulcan managed to get this woman on board my ship, but—"*

"Do as he says, Sherbourne!" Kirk snapped. "I don't know how it was done, either, but I do know that if my first officer says that something needs to be done fast, it needs to be done—*fast!"*

"The nexus system is being shut down, Captain Sherbourne, permanently," Spock interposed, speaking rapidly but steadily. "It is not, however, an orderly shutdown, and damage to anything in the immediate vicinity is virtually inevitable. Simply look at the nexus yourself, and you will see the convulsions it is undergoing."

Abruptly, Sherbourne looked to one side, apparently toward an auxiliary screen, and snapped an order. His eyes widened, as if seeing the full magnitude of the chaos for the first time.

"What the devil—" he began, but he cut himself off almost immediately. For an instant, he returned his glare to the main screen and the *Enterprise* bridge that he saw there, but then, thrusting Ansfield to one side, he lunged to the unoccupied helm.

Once again, the *Devlin*'s impulse engines surged into life, dimming the bridge emergency lights with their power drain.

"Put the tractor beam on them, Mr. Sulu," Kirk said. "Just as a precaution, in case they start falling behind again."

"Aye-aye, sir."

But the *Devlin* kept pace.

At five million kilometers, one of the leakage gates exploded outward, drowning everything else in its momentary brilliance.

At eight million, the now jagged, misshapen nexus itself expanded in a single pulse to enclose all the other gates, not just obscuring them with its momentary brightness but enveloping them, like a gasoline-doused flame will flash out and engulf a hundred smoldering embers scattered around it.

At ten million, the screens were filled with undifferentiated brilliance.

At twelve million, as if the film of a nuclear explosion were being run in reverse, the brilliance began to shrink and fade simultaneously.

At fifteen million, it shrank to a single point and, with one last searing spark, vanished.

For another moment, the stars beyond wavered, as if distorted by waves of heat in an otherwise transparent atmosphere.

Then all was still, as if the nexus had never existed.

And the last fragments of the entity in this universe, the fragments that had guided Spock and Ansfield through limbo to the ships and had helped to guide the ships themselves out of limbo, withdrew and allowed themselves to fade from existence.

It took Scott and a half-dozen engineering officers from both ships nearly two days to get the *Devlin*'s warp drive back in working order.

Throughout the operation, on all watches, Uhura's communication equipment was set on automatic, trying to establish contact with Starfleet Headquarters. Periodically, despite the fact that, except under the most favorable and unusual subspace circumstances, only Starfleet Headquarters was capable of picking up a starship signal at these distances, she scanned through every starbase and starship channel.

Finally, at a sedate warp five, in deference to the jury-rigged nature of the *Devlin*'s repairs, both ships got under way, heading back for the Federation.

If the Federation still existed.

On the third day, Starfleet Headquarters responded.

It was Admiral Noguchi, voice only.

"Jim?"

There was a restrained cheer from both bridges at this evidence that at least part of the Federation had survived.

"Yes, Admiral. And Captain Sherbourne of the *Devlin*. We're on our way in."

"Sherbourne, Admiral. What happened? Earth was being threatened—"

"Earth is still here," he said. *"For reasons we can only assume had something to do with the activities of the two of you, the gate that was threatening Earth— and all the other gates, at least the ones we knew about—put on a fireworks display to end all fireworks displays and then vanished."*

Noguchi paused, drawing a breath. Then: *"Jim? Will they be back?"*

"They're not coming back, sir," Kirk said, and then added, glancing toward the science station, "thanks in large part to the actions of Commanders Ansfield and Spock."

There was a long silence, far longer than could be accounted for by subspace delay.

Then Noguchi's voice returned. *"Duly noted,"* he said quietly. *"I will notify Captain Chandler that his science officer distinguished herself under what I assume were difficult circumstances."*

"That's one way of describing them, sir."

"I am sure you will provide a more complete description, Captain. I will be expecting a complete and detailed report on the entire affair upon your return. From both of you."

"Of course, Admiral."

"And Captain Kirk, in consideration of those difficult circumstances, which I am sure affected everyone aboard both ships, I doubt that there will be any need to pursue the insubordination charges that Admiral Wellons instituted against you."

At the science station, Commander Ansfield turned sharply, frowning, but before she could speak, Spock put a lightly restraining hand on her shoulder.

Kirk only smiled. "Thank you, Admiral."

And the link was broken.

The Federation still existed.

And they were going home.